A WOMAN OF WORDS

JERUSALEM ROAD • BOOK THREE

A WOMAN OF WORDS

ANGELA HUNT

BETHANY HOUSE
a division of Baker Publishing Group
Minneapolis, Minnesota

Published by Bethany House Publishers
11400 Hampshire Avenue South
Bloomington, Minnesota 55438
www.bethanyhouse.com

Bethany House Publishers is a division of
Baker Publishing Group, Grand Rapids, Michigan

Printed in the United States of America

Library of Congress Cataloging-in-Publication Data
Names: Hunt, Angela Elwell, author.
Title: A woman of words / Angela Hunt.
Description: Minneapolis, Minnesota : Bethany House Publishers, [2021] | Series: Jerusalem road ; book 3 | Includes bibliographical references.
Identifiers: LCCN 2020050776 | ISBN 9780764233869 (trade paperback) | ISBN 9780764239267 (casebound) | ISBN 9781493431564 (ebook)
Subjects: GSAFD: Bible fiction.
Classification: LCC PS3558.U46747 W66 2021 | DDC 813/.54—dc23
LC record available at https://lccn.loc.gov/2020050776

Cover design by LOOK Design Studio
Cover photography by Aimee Christenson

Author is represented by Browne & Miller Literary Associates.

21 22 23 24 25 26 27 7 6 5 4 3 2 1

The Old and New Testaments are filled with stories of daring men and noticeably few courageous women. This is not surprising, for the inspired writers could not recount every story of each man, woman, and child who experienced God. But even though few women's stories are recorded, they are still worthy of consideration. The JERUSALEM ROAD *novels are fictional accounts of real women who met Jesus, were part of His family, or whose lives entwined with the men who followed Him.*

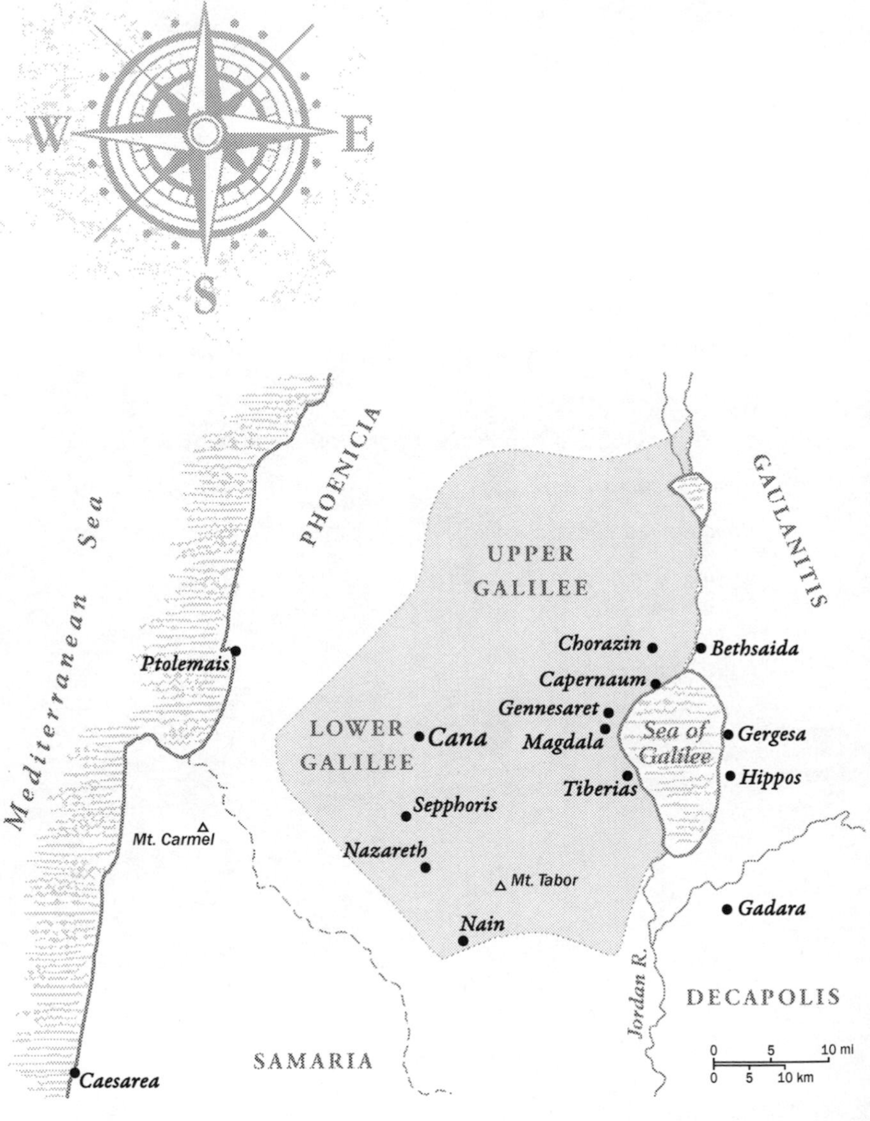
N
W
E
S
PHOENICIA
Mediterranean Sea
UPPER GALILEE
GAULANITIS
Ptolemais
Chorazin
Bethsaida
Capernaum
Gennesaret
LOWER GALILEE
Cana
Magdala
Sea of Galilee
Gergesa
Tiberias
Hippos
Sepphoris
Mt. Carmel
Nazareth
Mt. Tabor
Gadara
Nain
Jordan R.
DECAPOLIS
0 5 10 mi
0 5 10 km
SAMARIA
Caesarea

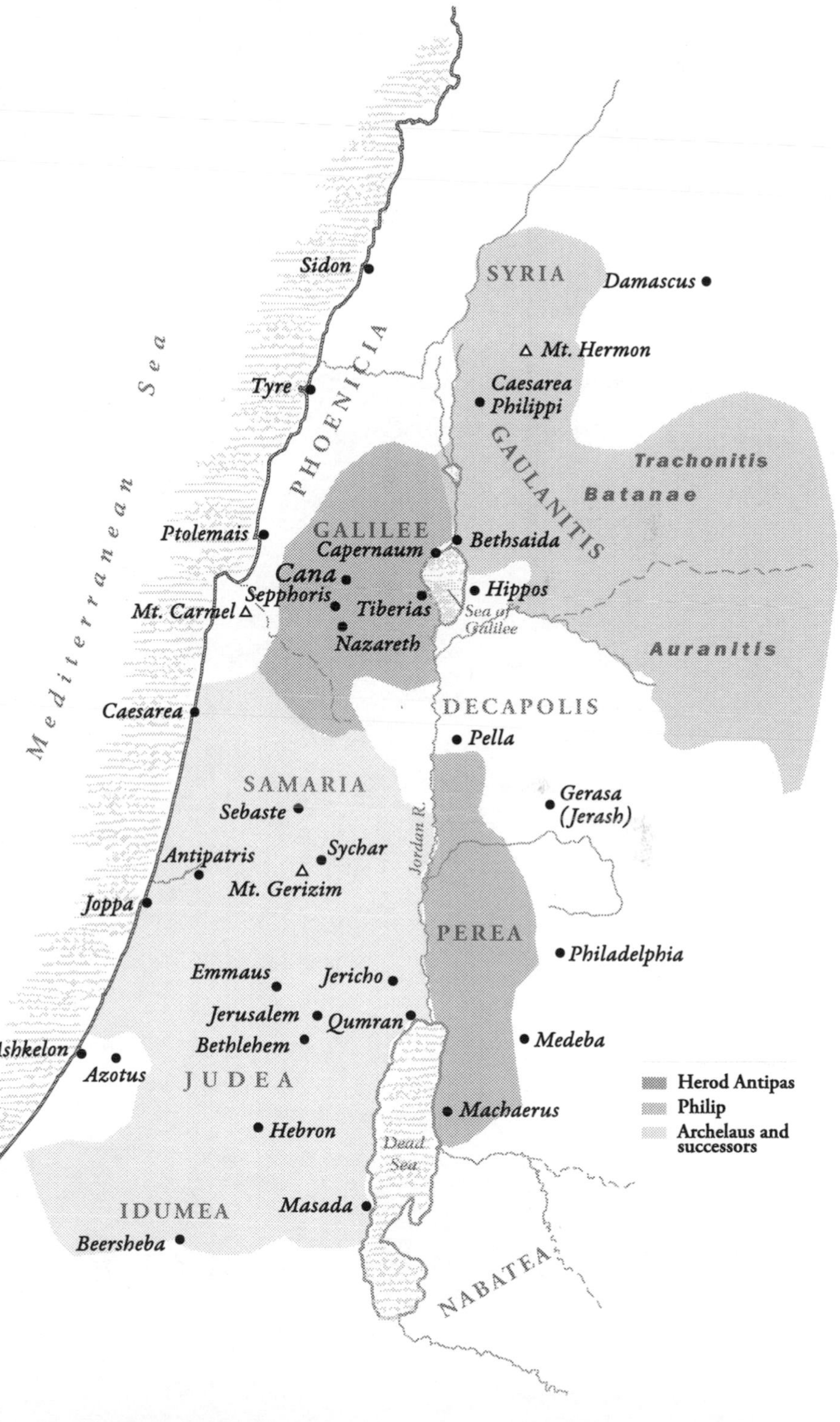

Mediterranean Sea
Sidon
Tyre
PHOENICIA
SYRIA
Damascus
Mt. Hermon
Caesarea Philippi
GAULANITIS
Trachonitis
Batanae
Ptolemais
GALILEE
Capernaum
Bethsaida
Cana
Sepphoris
Tiberias
Hippos
Mt. Carmel
Nazareth
Sea of Galilee
Auranitis
Caesarea
DECAPOLIS
Pella
SAMARIA
Sebaste
Gerasa (Jerash)
Jordan R.
Antipatris
Sychar
Mt. Gerizim
Joppa
PEREA
Philadelphia
Emmaus
Jericho
Jerusalem
Qumran
Medeba
Bethlehem
Ashkelon
Azotus
JUDEA
Herod Antipas
Philip
Archelaus and successors
Machaerus
Hebron
Dead Sea
Masada
IDUMEA
Beersheba
NABATEA

I praise You, for I am awesomely,
    wonderfully made!
Wonderful are Your works—
and my soul knows that very well.
My frame was not hidden from You
when I was made in the secret place,
when I was woven together in the depths
    of the earth.
Your eyes saw me when I was unformed,
and in Your book were written the days
    that were formed—
when not one of them had come to be.

Psalm 139:14–16

ONE

Matthew

Reuven ben Yusef, leader of the assembly of believers at Capernaum, wore a look of thinly disguised disdain as he stared at me. "What do you mean, you have to leave? You are supposed to stay here and work for us. Have we not given you a place to lay your head? Have you ever had to eat Shabbat dinner alone? Have you not been welcomed by everyone in the community?"

I lowered my head in what I hoped was an attitude of supplication. "Reuven, you and the others have been most kind. But my brothers Peter and John have asked me to come to Jerusalem, where I can assist them with leading the growing assembly of believers. The *ecclēsia* there is growing, with new believers being added every day—"

"But we *know* you, Matthew. We have known you for a long time."

"You can get to know someone else. I have found a replacement—"

"You are supposed to stay and marry my daughter!"

I blinked in honest astonishment. Reuven's only daughter was not yet thirteen, barely mature, and I was a man of thirty-three. I glanced around the circle to see if any of the other elders expected me to marry their daughters, but apparently Reuven had been the first to claim me as a son-in-law.

"Surely, my friend—" I looked back at him and smiled—"there are dozens of men who would make a better husband for your daughter. I am ill-suited for her and not yet ready to settle in one place. I cannot say where the Ruach HaKodesh will lead me, but at this moment I am confident He is directing me to Jerusalem."

Reuven narrowed his eyes as if weighing my sincerity, then he sighed. "I understand, Matthew, but you have broken my heart. My wife will never get over her disappointment. She has already embroidered linens for your bridal bed."

I coughed and lowered my voice. "Be fair, Reuven. Did I ever do or say anything to make you think I was interested in marriage? At present I have only one purpose: to serve our risen Lord Yeshua. I served Him here by teaching the new believers; I will serve him in Jerusalem by preaching. Peter, James, and John are working mighty miracles and sharing the good news. I long to follow in their footsteps and do mighty works in the name of our Lord . . ." My voice trailed away as I folded my hands in grateful humility.

I stood in silence until Reuven sighed. "Apparently we have no choice: we must let you go. But remember one thing—my wife and I will keep our guest chamber in a state of readiness should you wish to return to Capernaum. And if the Ruach HaKodesh says you should take a wife, remember my Leah. She is fond of you, I can tell. As am I."

I embraced the affable older man, kissed him on both

cheeks, and knelt when he gestured to the floor. As I balanced on my knees, Reuven and the other elders stepped forward and placed their hands on me—head, shoulders, and back—until I was covered by their flesh as well as their prayers.

"Send him, HaShem," Reuven prayed, "in the power of your Ruach HaKodesh. We willingly give our brother Matthew to the assembly in Jerusalem, to the community who needs every willing pair of hands. Strengthen his heart for the important work You will give him to do and strengthen his spirit to do Your will."

He closed with a traditional Hebrew blessing: "*Baruch Ata, Adonai Eloheinu, Melech haolam, shenatan li tikvah v'ko-ach v'he-vi oti l'avodah hadashah zo, kach ani yochal l'hitparnas." Blessed are you, Eternal our God, Ruler of time and space, who gives us hope and strength and has brought him to this new employment so he may make a living.*

When we had finished praying, I stood and smiled at the men who had become dear friends. "I am not leaving you without help," I said, walking around Reuven to place my hand on Yakov's shoulder. "Young Yakov is a good teacher, and I have already taught him everything I learned from Yeshua. He will pick up where I have left off, so you will not even notice I am gone. But know this—he, too, is unmarried."

A calculating look flashed in Reuven's eyes as he studied the younger man. "Yakov, what sort of wife should a young man seek?"

Yakov hesitated only a moment, then replied with confidence, "A virtuous woman who is understanding. But above all, she must love Adonai and follow Yeshua."

Reuven snorted in reluctant approval, then turned to me. "May Adonai keep watch between us while we are apart," he said, his voice trembling. "And may He soon bring you back to us."

I embraced Reuven again, then hugged the other men I had come to love and appreciate. When nothing remained to be said, I picked up the basket that held my few earthly possessions and walked through a group of older women who had gathered to bid me farewell.

I paused when one of them caught my sleeve. "In Jerusalem, you must find Mary of Nazareth," she said, her birdlike fingers tiptoeing over my arm. "You must pay her a visit and give her a message for me."

I smiled and bent lower. "What is the message?"

"Tell her—" she said, her voice cracking with age—"tell her the Ruach HaKodesh has impressed me to pray daily for her strength. She still has important work to do."

I patted the woman's hand and promised to honor her request. Then I stepped out into the night and breathed deeply of the cool evening air.

After two long years in Capernaum, I would soon be on my way to the Holy City. I would miss this Galilean town because it was home to so many memories—Yeshua called me here, along with Peter and Andrew, James and John. In the early months, Yeshua did many miracles here, and now the believers' assembly was thriving. I had been so busy working with the believers of Capernaum I had not even participated in the annual pilgrimage festivals that would have pulled me away from this city.

But now I would have an opportunity to make up for missing those glorious festivals. I would soon be working with men I loved dearly, friends who knew me better than anyone on earth. Peter, James, and John needed me, they said, and like a parched man I thirsted for the joy of their company.

The things we had shared together—adventures, lessons, laughter and tears—bound us closer than blood.

I hoisted my basket onto my shoulder and walked away from Reuven's house, whispering as I went, "I rejoiced when they said to me, 'Let us go to the House of Adonai . . .'"

The next morning, I joined a group of travelers moving south along the international highway. I would follow the road until I reached the Jezreel Valley, where I would doubtless bid farewell to most of my traveling companions as they took the longer route around Samaria. I would choose the most direct road because I was eager to get to Jerusalem as quickly as possible—and because Yeshua had taught me to love Samaritans.

Most of the travelers in my group were families who led pack animals or pushed small carts loaded with their provisions. Since we were several weeks beyond Passover, I assumed these people were not pilgrims but traveling south for other reasons. One family was clearly moving—the husband drove an ox-drawn wagon carrying several pieces of furniture. Two small children, a boy and a girl, rode atop the mound of furnishings, their bare legs dangling over a bench while the mother walked near them, an infant in the sling that crossed her body.

A pair of Pharisees walked at the head of the group, easily identifiable by their somber robes and the extravagant fringe on their prayer shawls. They did not attempt to mingle or converse with anyone else but kept their voices low and their eyes on the road.

I could not prevent a smile from twisting my lips. Yeshua had often scolded the Pharisees, for they were continually distorting the Torah's words and convoluting HaShem's intention. To the Pharisees, ordinary people were *am hararetz*, the unwashed and ignorant, hardly worth noticing. But Yeshua loved ordinary people and taught His followers to do the same. "Those who are healthy have no need for a doctor," He once said, "but those who are sick do."

If my fellow travelers were fortunate, the Pharisees would ignore them for the entire journey.

As time passed, however, I wondered if I should quicken my step and engage the dour pair—after all, a few Pharisees had come to believe in Yeshua. Yeshua's own brother-in-law was a believing Pharisee, as were the esteemed Nicodemus and Joseph of Arimathea. The latter had loaned the Lord a garden tomb, not that Yeshua needed it for more than three days. That crypt had since been walled up and declared off-limits by the Roman procurator, though I could not understand why anyone would want to visit it. The grave was not important, but the man who broke free of it had been changing lives for years.

I shifted my basket to my other shoulder and squinted at the road ahead. The day was warm, unseasonably so, and the Pharisees' sandals kicked up small puffs of dust that the trailing ox and wagon churned into a veritable cloud. By the time we stopped for water, we would all be covered in a layer of grime and sweat, just as we had been when we traveled with Yeshua.

A small, high voice jerked me from my thoughts. "Where are *you* going?"

I looked down to see a young boy walking by my side. The freckled lad looked up at me, his eyes alight with curiosity.

"I am going to Jerusalem. Where are you going?"

The boy grinned. "Bethany. My sister lives there."

"Bethany is a beautiful town."

"Have you been there?"

"I have."

"What did you do there?"

Ah. If ever there was a heaven-sent opportunity . . . "I went to Bethany to see a dead man come back to life."

The boy's mouth dropped open. "Truly?"

"Truly. His sisters had buried him, and he had been in the grave four days."

"And he came out alive?"

"He was called out. He was dead, but my master Yeshua said, 'Lazarus, come forth!' And so he did. He stumbled out, struggling against the gravecloths that bound him, and stood outside his tomb, as surprised as any of us."

The boy hesitated, blinking with bafflement, then looked at me again. "Are you a Torah teacher?"

"Yes," I answered. "I may not be the wisest teacher, but I am always learning."

"Abba says I should try to be a Torah teacher. He says it is the best thing to be."

I nodded. "It is an important job."

"Where did you study? In Jerusalem?"

Again, my lips smiled of their own volition. "I studied with Yeshua, who taught in Galilee, Nazareth, Judea, and even Samaria."

The boy's brown eyes widened with astonishment. "So many places! Did he have many students?"

"He had twelve. But sometimes He taught a group of seventy, and once He taught crowds of four and five thousand. He even gave them lunch."

"He must have been rich to feed so many."

"He was not rich with gold, but in wisdom. And whenever

He needed fish or food or the power to heal, He asked His Father, who supplied what He needed."

"Was his father a teacher, too?"

"His father was HaShem."

The boy's forehead knit with confusion. Then he glanced toward the cart, where a man was calling for Samuel. "Abba calls me."

"You are Samuel? Then you should go."

The boy took a step toward his father, then paused. "Can this Yeshua teach me, too?"

I stopped and knelt to look the boy in the eye. "Yeshua has gone to heaven to be with HaShem. But He left His students behind to teach others, and He has given them His Spirit to help them teach correctly. If you want to know more, ask anyone who follows the Way. They will explain everything to you."

"The Way?"

I nodded.

Samuel scampered toward the wagon. I waited until he had climbed up to his father before I resumed walking. Samuel might speak to me again or his father might forbid it. Either way, a seed had been planted, praise HaShem.

I inhaled a deep breath and smiled in anticipation of seeing my old friends. Perhaps HaShem would empower me to do the same kind of miracles Peter and John had wrought. Everyone, even in Capernaum, marveled at the miracle stories. Even those who spent their days on the Sea of Galilee had heard about Philip the Evangelist's preaching and the authoritative teaching of the Lord's own brother, now known as James the Just.

Perhaps the people in Capernaum would soon hear about me. Perhaps HaShem would enable me to give sight to a blind child or restore the use of a carpenter's wounded hand.

Perhaps I would speak a healing word to a fevered woman or bring a man back from the dead . . .

Nothing was impossible with God. To Him belonged the power and the glory, but oh, what joy we felt when the power of the Ruach HaKodesh flowed through us.

If James, Yeshua's skeptical brother, could become James the Just, I could become Matthew the Meek. For not out of pride did I yearn to hear my name spoken, but out of pleasure. I would be filled with the greatest joy imaginable if the Spirit of HaShem turned an ordinary man into an extraordinary instrument of God.

I lifted my head and continued walking, my heart brimming with confidence.

By the fifth day of my journey, my back ached between my shoulder blades and I felt limp with weariness. I had fallen in with a group of Samaritans who believed in Yeshua—probably friends of the woman Yeshua had met at Jacob's well—so the company was pleasant, though my legs and lungs were not used to so much walking. I was accustomed to sedentary work, not physical labor.

But the Ruach HaKodesh renewed my spirit as we approached the Holy City. My heart leapt within me when I glimpsed Jerusalem's outline in the distance, and soon I could see the four hills within the walls. Mount Zion rose above Mount Moriah and the Temple, the Akra, and the new development of Bezetha. Beyond the city walls, the verdant Mount of Olives, where we watched Yeshua ascend to His Father, towered above all.

"For Adonai has chosen Zion," I sang, knowing I would not sing alone for long.

"He has desired it for His dwelling."

"This is My resting place forever."

"Here I dwell, for I have desired it."

I was right—others joined in my song, and the singing did not end until we had passed through the city gate. I bade farewell to my traveling companions and joined the people mingling on the crowded streets.

I could not help but smile as I trod the slabs of white marble pavement. Only Jerusalem and Tiberias had such beautiful streets; most towns contented themselves with sunbaked bricks. But Jerusalem had always been a place of dignified beauty, a fitting setting for the home of our God.

In his last letter, Peter said I would doubtless find him at the Temple, so I walked toward the Temple Mount, my senses delighted by every sight that met my eyes. No wonder the Torah teachers said the world was like an eye—the ocean around the world was the white of the eye, the brown was the world itself, the pupil was Jerusalem, and the image within the pupil was HaShem's holy sanctuary. Jerusalem, city of peace, belonged to every descendant of Abraham and Sarah. No house here could be rented, for the buildings belonged to all and must be opened to guests during every pilgrimage feast. Never did the serpent or scorpion bite within Jerusalem's walls; never did fire desolate her streets. This city was more sacred than any other, since only within its gates could we eat the Passover lamb, the thank offerings, and the second tithes. We guarded the city against anything that might bring uncleanness—no dead body could remain in the city overnight, no grease fouled its soil, no vegetable gardens could be planted lest the smell of decaying vegetation defile the air. No furnaces could be built, for fear of polluting smoke. Never had an accident interrupted the services of the holy sanctuary or profaned the offerings. Never had rain extinguished the fire on the altar, nor had wind fanned back the smoke of the sacrifices. And despite the millions who visited during pilgrimage festivals, never had any man found the holy court too crowded for him to bow in worship before the God of Israel.

My thoughts shifted as I walked beneath the arch connecting the Temple Mount to Jerusalem's western hills. The air was cooler in the shade, so I drank it in, knowing I would soon be subjected again to the warmth of the sun.

A few more steps brought me to the Court of the Gentiles, still crowded with merchants selling doves, lambs, and bulls. The expansive court had not changed since the last time I visited Jerusalem, but now small groups of believers were scattered among the merchants and worshipers. Followers of the Way were easy to spot—they were openly affectionate, joyfully greeting each other with kisses on both cheeks, and occasionally standing with an arm loosely draped across a brother's shoulder.

The sight made my throat ache with nostalgia. How many times had I seen Yeshua stand with His arm around one of us? He was the Son of God, but He was also warmly human, as filled with life and humor as any man I had ever known.

After following Yeshua, I often thought it odd that while all Jews were children of Abraham, we did not behave as brothers or even cousins. Our evolving beliefs divided us over the years, yet Yeshua had taught us to put aside trivial disagreements as we clung to Truth. Those who would be leaders should be servants, He said, and those who wanted to be great should make themselves small. Not many people were eager to accept such role reversals, and fewer still adopted them.

I walked toward a group of believers by Solomon's Porch, a long shaded area supported by stately Roman columns. Here I saw believers scattered over benches—men in simple tunics sitting next to men in expensive garments, a woman with elaborate braided hair in conversation with a woman in a slave's tunic.

You were right, Yeshua. Look how they defer to one another. Surely the world will know us by our love for each other.

"Could it be Matthew?" I whirled at the sound of a familiar voice, and a lump rose in my throat when I recognized John, the disciple who had been closest to Yeshua. "Brother, it is good to see you!"

"And you!" I hurried over and threw my arms around John's lanky frame, then stepped back to take in his appearance. "You look well, though you are thinner than before. Are you fasting or has the work here worn you down?"

"Perhaps both." John grinned at my little joke. Yeshua always said we should wear our best when fasting, unlike the Pharisees who put on tattered clothing to advertise their pious suffering.

I glanced around. "Peter said I should meet him here. Is he away?"

"He has gone for food." John took my arm. "Let me take you to James."

"Which one? Your brother?"

"Yeshua's. James the Just has undertaken leadership of the assembly in Jerusalem, freeing us to preach the Gospel while he oversees the deacons who meet the needs of the sick, widows, and orphans. Many wealthy men live in Jerusalem, but the poor live among them as well."

"Yeshua said we would always have the poor."

"Indeed. Fortunately, the believers are generous. Come with me." John led the way as we left the Temple and wended our way over a narrow street. John knocked on the door of a small house and entered without waiting for a reply. I followed and spied the stubborn jut of a fisherman's chin. "Peter!"

He stood, a grin flashing in his beard. "Matthew! About time you reached us! How long as it been, a year?"

"Two, I think." I embraced him. "When you said you needed help, I felt the Spirit affirm your invitation. I am eager to assist however I can."

"Good." Peter released me, then propped his hands on his hips and looked at John. "Shall we explain what we need from Matthew, or should we wait for James?"

John shrugged and sat at a table spread with cheese, fruit, and pickled fish. "Why keep him waiting?"

Peter gestured for me to sit, then sat across from me and pushed a platter of fish in my direction. "Eat—it is not every day we get fish from Galilee."

I picked up a sardine and eyed it with suspicion. It had been so heavily salted and pressed it bore little resemblance to the fresh fish we enjoyed in Galilee. "Too bad the people of Jerusalem have no idea what sardines should taste like. If all their fish is pickled—"

"Less talking, more eating." Peter folded his arms. "While John and I explain why we asked you to join us."

I bit into the fish and put the taste out of my mind. I leaned forward, hoping to hear that they had been praying for another apostle to help them spread the Gospel in Judea. I would be willing to travel to Samaria, Syria, or sail with them to Greece—

"The assembly of believers here has grown," Peter began,

spreading his hands. "Now we care for not one assembly, but many. The groups meet at the Temple and in homes, wherever they can find a place to pray and worship. The Lord's people are generous, but the needs are also great. Though we have men who are willing to collect and distribute money to the various assemblies, they are laymen with businesses of their own to manage. We cannot expect them to devote much time to the work of keeping accounts—"

"So naturally we thought of you." John crossed his arms. "You are a talented scribe and highly skilled with numbers."

"You speak Greek and Hebrew," Peter added, stroking his beard. "So you would be able to correspond with the communities in Egypt and Greece."

"Have you learned Latin?" John's brows rose. "We have heard about communities of believers in Rome, and those brothers and sisters are not likely to speak Hebrew, either. A few of our men speak Latin, but not many—"

"You want me to keep records and write letters?" I could not keep a note of incredulity from my voice. "You want me to be an accountant and amanuensis?"

Peter beamed. "You always were quick."

"The Lord called you for a reason," John added. "When He saw you in the tax collector's booth, He knew one day we would need a bookkeeper."

I struggled to swallow the fish that had stuck in my throat and tried not to reveal my dismay. Had HaShem called me out of Capernaum to do what I'd been doing before I followed Yeshua? No one worked miracles behind a stack of correspondence. Numbers did not transform themselves by the power of the Ruach HaKodesh. Miracles should not occur with numbers—if they did, some bookkeeper needed to have his records examined.

Men who worked behind a desk were reliable, predictable, and dull. Was that how my brothers saw me?

"So," Peter said, still grinning, "will you help us sort through the mess of our records? I have no head for figures, and neither does John."

Of course they did not. They were anything *but* reliable, predictable, and dull.

I sighed and looked at the table.

"We are forgetting ourselves." John turned to Peter. "He has been traveling for days, so he has to be weary. We have burdened him with too much."

"No." I forced a smile, not wanting them to see how deeply I'd been disappointed. "I will serve in any way I can, but I was hoping to do the sort of work that you do. I have spent most of my life behind a desk, poring over papyri and numbers and scrolls—"

"You won't have to work on such things *all* the time," John said quickly. "I am sure you could finish the required record-keeping in a day or two each week. When you are not attending to the records, you can travel with us. Peter and I have been preaching at the Temple. Sometimes we preach at the Mount of Olives, where people gather at Gethsemane—"

The mention of that place had the power to send goose-flesh rippling up my arms even now. In an attempt to appear casual, I broke off a piece of bread. "I have been hoping for that sort of opportunity—I would like to teach and preach."

John and Peter looked at each other and shrugged. "Of course, if that is what the Lord leads you to do."

Satisfied, I lifted my hand. "That reminds me—one of the women in Capernaum wanted me to visit Yeshua's mother. Is Mary still in Jerusalem? Is she well?"

John and Peter burst out laughing. "Has that redoubtable

lady ever been less than well?" Peter said. "She is as strong as ever."

I looked at John, who had stepped forward to take care of Mary when Yeshua asked him to do so. "Does she still live with you?"

John shook his head. "She has taken a house with Miriam of Magdala. They live in the lower city, near the Pool of Siloam."

"Miriam takes care of her?"

Peter guffawed. "I would say they take care of each other. Remember how Mary directed the women when we traveled with Yeshua? And how Miriam took charge when Mary was away? How did James describe them? Rods of iron in velvet gloves. They have not changed. Those women may appear quiet and gentle, but no one is going to make them do anything they do not want to do."

I blew out a breath. "I am glad Mary is well."

"You must go see her." A spark of mischief glinted in Peter's eye. "She remembers each of the Twelve with great affection, so she will be happy to see you. You can't miss her house—it has a bright blue door. You can visit her tomorrow."

I wondered at the mirth behind Peter's expression, but his face revealed no clue as to the source of his humor.

"I will go." I picked up a piece of cheese and popped it into my mouth. "Sometime when we are not so busy, I will search for the house. But first I will need to look at your records, learn about the different communities, and talk to some of the men who collect the offerings. I will see Mary next week . . . if I can find the time."

Peter lifted a brow and smiled at John, and neither of them mentioned Mary again.

TWO

Mary

Our hostess, a new believer, welcomed us to her home, then sat on a floor cushion and motioned for Miriam and me to do the same. "I thought we could take a few minutes to talk before we pray," she said, her cheeks flushing. "I do not know you ladies as well as I would like, especially since we are now sisters, bound together by our love for Messiah Yeshua."

My heart warmed when she turned and gave me a nervous smile. I nodded slightly, assuring her that she had said exactly the right thing. Whenever I was introduced as Yeshua's mother, my presence had a somewhat stifling effect on people, so I always had to resist the urge to explain why I did not deserve special attention. I was a simple daughter of Israel, as amazed as anyone could be whenever I considered the great blessing HaShem had bestowed on me.

The woman next to me opened the conversation by telling us about the birth of her first great-grandchild, a truly blessed occasion. After concluding her story, she leaned forward and patted my knee. "You have several grandchildren, no? Does seeing them take you back to your own days of labor and travail? You bore six children, did you not?"

"Seven." I smiled. "And though I clearly remember the birth of my firstborn, the later memories are a blur of pain and confusion."

The other women laughed and began to speak of their own births, of babies who came quickly and others who took time to be born. As I listened, I struggled to remember my labor with James and Damaris. Though they were born in Egypt, we were fortunate enough to live in a Jewish community with a skilled midwife. I vaguely remembered her placing James in my arms and Joseph's beaming smile when he held our first daughter, but I could recall little else. That was the trouble with the past—a full life held far too much of it.

I was now a mature woman, full of memories. My husband had been gone for nearly twenty years, and Joseph had taken much of my past with him.

As another guest told of her travail in unwelcome detail, I lowered my voice and turned to the woman next to me. "Can you remember the births of all your children? Or do you sometimes struggle to recall them?"

She chuckled. "I count myself fortunate if I can remember what I served for supper last night. No one can remember everything, but I can recall the important events. You will, too."

"Will I?" I bit my lip. "We spent several years in Egypt, but I can't remember the house we rented. I can't remember much about the birth of my oldest daughter or my second-born son—"

The woman patted my hand. "Memories are like a linen

garment you wear and then put in a trunk. With each day that passes, you put more garments in the trunk. Later, when you are asked to recall an event, you have to open the trunk and shuffle through all that linen. But when you find the garment you are seeking, you lift it up, shake out the dust, and inhale its fragrance so the memory blooms again." Her smile broadened. "Your memories are still with you, Mary. They are only buried beneath others."

I nodded and resolved to think about what she had said when I had more time. Then our leader cleared her throat and waved for our attention. "One more task before we say our prayers," she said, unfurling a scroll. "I would like to share a letter written by James the Just. I believe we will all find something encouraging in his epistle."

She lifted the scroll and began to read:

> "'James, a slave of God and of the Lord Yeshua the Messiah,
> To the twelve tribes in the Diaspora:
> Shalom!
> Consider it all joy, my brethren, when you encounter various trials, knowing that the testing of your faith produces endurance. And let endurance have its perfect work, so you may be perfect and complete, lacking in nothing . . .'"

I closed my eyes, remembering the night James asked me to read his letter to check for errors. He had been nervous, afraid he would make a grammatical mistake, but I assured him he had done a good job.

I smiled, grateful that James's words, at least, remained fresh in my mind.

THREE

Matthew

John had invited me to stay at his house, but when I arrived, his guest chamber was occupied by a visitor who had come to learn about Yeshua so he could carry the story back to Rome.

Not wanting to disturb John's guest, Peter invited me to stay with his family. He led me to their house, reintroduced me to his wife, Anna, his mother-in-law, Mara, and his daughter, Dina. Anna and Mara had not changed much since our last meeting, but Dina certainly had. The girl had grown from a lanky child to a breathtaking young woman. The dark hair flowing down her back glistened like polished wood, and her face was well-modeled and feminine, with a rosy mouth and soft color in her cheeks. Long lashes covered her liquid brown eyes, and for a moment I could not look away.

Then, recovering my senses, I returned my gaze to her parents, resolving to keep Dina at a respectful distance from my thoughts and my person. I did not come to Jerusalem to be married.

Anna gave me a warm welcome, fed me a filling supper, and directed me to the guest chamber on the roof. Later that night I stretched out on the bed and heard the sounds of family life floating up from the open atrium—Anna reminding Dina to wash the dishes, Peter's mother-in-law asking about a missing necklace, the cat's yowling protest as Peter set it outside the door.

Of all of us who followed Yeshua, Peter might be the most changed. Courage had always been part of his character, but in the early days he had been more brash than brave. He had been a boastful fisherman, proud of his boat, his beautiful wife, his sweet little girl. But his betrayal of Yeshua had stripped away the arrogance, refining him the way heat refines gold and silver.

He still had a beautiful wife and a sweet daughter, but Dina was no longer a child. I closed my eyes to count the years—she had been a pretty girl of three when I first met Peter, so now she had to be fifteen or sixteen—the age when most young girls are betrothed. Peter had not mentioned a son-in-law, so perhaps he was waiting . . . but for whom? A beautiful and virtuous girl like Dina deserved a good husband, but Peter would have high standards for anyone who inquired about his only daughter.

I sighed and closed my heavy eyelids. As a younger man, I often wondered what sort of wife and children I would have, never imagining that my future family would be composed of a revolutionary Torah teacher, Galilean fishermen, a zealot, and a group of women who provided strong, often opinionated support . . .

I drifted on a tide of weariness and contentment until a

dream carried me to the sandy shores of the Galilee. The wind caressed my face as I turned my head and saw Yeshua sitting nearby on an overturned boat. A smile gleamed through His beard as He acknowledged me with a nod.

"Lord?" I approached Him, then halted, unsure of how to proceed. Did I approach him as a beloved friend or kneel before him as Yeshua ben Adonai?

"Matthew." My timidity vanished when He smiled and spoke my name. "The gift of Yahweh."

I managed a quick smile, then cleared my throat. "I have gone to Jerusalem to assist Peter and John. I'm sure you know this, but—"

"What do you want, Matthew?"

Guilt stabbed at my soul as a memory flooded my mind—the mother of James and John had dared to ask Yeshua if her sons could sit at His right and left hand in His coming kingdom. I was not asking for elevation, only for some different task.

"I want to serve you, Lord. Whatever you ask, I will do it."

Yeshua smiled.

"But would it be wrong for me—I mean, would it be possible for me to preach and teach as well as tend to the bookkeeping? Peter and John said I might do so, as long as you willed it."

Yeshua's smile deepened. "What father, if his son asks for a fish, will give him a snake instead? And if he asks for an egg, will he give him a scorpion? Trust the Father, Matthew. He will use you in ways you cannot imagine."

With that, Yeshua's image faded. When I blinked, I found myself lying on my bed in the moonlight, surrounded by the dimly lit furnishings of Peter's guest chamber.

It had been a vision. Only a dream. But one thing remained—HaShem would answer my prayer to be useful.

I rose after sunrise, dressed, and slipped out of Peter's house before my host could involve me in some other activity. I was eager to begin my ministry in Jerusalem and wanted to fulfill my promise to visit Yeshua's mother before other thoughts crowded my mind. This visit was a polite necessity, the least I could do to please the Lord. As soon as I left Mary's house, I would be free to embark on the task the Lord had prepared for me.

As I slipped through the narrow streets, dodging groups of women and men carrying produce to the market, I wondered how Mary filled her days now that her children were grown. Mary's son James lived in the Holy City, as did John, whom Yeshua had appointed to look after His mother. In addition, she was held in high esteem by all the members of the believing community. If ever a woman was loved and cared for, surely Mary was.

I locked my hands behind my back and trudged toward the lower city, sinking into memories of the days I traveled with Yeshua and Mary. Though I had respected Mary in those days, we did not become close. She spoke most often to Peter, James, and John. She also favored Andrew, another Galilean. But she never pulled me aside, nor did we ever fall into conversation as we walked the dusty roads. I never minded, because the women tended to travel in a group, and I did not know how I should address a woman who was neither my mother nor my sister. Yeshua spoke so easily to the women He met, but I could not look at a woman without hearing my father telling me to avert my eyes lest I see something indecent.

Yet I was not unaware of the women—how could I be?

From watching them, I realized that Mary and Miriam of Magdala were the unofficial leaders, often directing the other women as they served meals, sought lodging, and purchased supplies. I saw that Mary and Miriam led the others gently, without bawling orders or shouting commands. And often, whenever Mary or Miriam asked the others to do something, they began the task first, encouraging the others to join them.

I once wondered how our group managed to pay for food and lodging, so I asked Judas, the keeper of our communal purse. He lifted a brow at my question. "Why do you want to know? If you want to be responsible for our funds—"

"I do not want your job," I assured him. "I am only curious."

Judas laughed. "You need not wonder. Some of our food is donated by those who come to hear Yeshua. Much of it is purchased."

"But who has money enough to feed such a large group?"

He tilted his head toward the women toiling around the fire pit. "They do."

I stared at him, speechless. I had assumed some of the women were from wealthy families because Miriam, Susanna, and Joanna wore embroidered garments far beyond the means of a fisherman's wife. Joanna, I had heard, was married to Herod Antipas's steward, and Miriam wore a necklace of heavy gold links around her neck, rumored to be a gift from her husband.

"Their husbands send money to support them—to support *us*?"

Judas had glanced at the women, his mouth twisting in bitter amusement. "Miriam and Susanna are widows. They have estates and wealth of their own, and they give freely to support Yeshua's work."

Something told me Miriam had also managed to obtain a home for herself and Mary in Jerusalem.

I found the house with the blue door on Baker Street, only a short distance from the Pool of Siloam. The mud-brick house resembled dozens of others, but the colorful door set it apart. A low stone wall defined the courtyard, home to a handful of chickens and a solitary goat. The big-bellied goat, a female with long ears and pointed horns, chewed a mouthful of hay and stared at me with yellow eyes.

I glanced up to check the angle of the sun, determined not to disturb the home's occupants too soon. Seeing that the sun had reached an acceptable point, I stood outside the gate and shouted a greeting: "Shalom! I come seeking Mary of Nazareth!"

A moment later, the blue door opened and a woman peered out. Her eyes widened when she saw me, then she ran forward and wrapped me in an enthusiastic embrace. "Matthew! It is good to see you!"

I did not recognize Miriam of Magdala until she spoke. She had aged in the years since we parted. This Miriam was heavier, softer, and paler, but her smile shone with a maternal aspect she had lacked when I last saw her. Deep crevasses marked the corners of the brown eyes that rose to meet mine, and her lips had thinned. She still wore expensive embroidered garments, and the heavy gold necklace still gleamed at her neck. But her smile was genuine and her grasp warm as she took my hand and led me into the house.

"The others will be so happy to know you are here."

"Others? Who else lives here?"

"In this house? Mary, of course, and sometimes Mary's sister visits. Sometimes Mary's children stay with us when they come to Jerusalem, so the guest chamber serves us well.

Susanna visits during every festival, and we never know who else will come calling. Our house is often filled with people who want to hear stories about Yeshua."

She ushered me into a wide room furnished with couches, at least a dozen floor cushions, and two long benches, one against each wall. I could see that it would be a useful chamber for talking or dining with plenty of space for guests.

"Have you broken your fast?" Miriam asked. "I could bring fruit, almond cake, and lemon water, if you like. I love feeding our guests if—"

"I am not hungry," I told her. "I am here to see Mary . . . I have only just arrived in Jerusalem and wanted to pay my respects as soon as possible."

Miriam nodded and gestured to a bench. "Have a seat," she said. "I will see if Mary is ready to receive guests. She is doing well, but says it is a little harder to get out of bed every morning."

I sat, smoothed the wrinkles from my tunic, and hoped Yeshua's mother would recognize me. I had not seen her in years but did not think I had changed much. A few strands of silver peppered my hair, but otherwise—

"Matthew."

I stood at the sound of her voice and bowed my head out of respect. "Mary, it is good to see you."

"Call me Ima. Everyone does these days."

Mother? Calling her by that title felt overly familiar, but in many ways she had mothered all of us who followed Yeshua. And she *was* mother to Yeshua, who was now our brother through HaShem's merciful plan.

"All right. Ima." I smiled as she caught my hands and held them up, like a mother admiring her son in new garments.

"You look well, Matthew." A dimple winked in her cheek. "And you have not changed."

I wanted to reply that her appearance had not altered, either, but could not utter the words without bearing false witness. Her hair, which had been touched with gray when she traveled with Yeshua, had gone white, while deep lines bracketed her mouth and creased her forehead. She seemed shorter somehow, though my eyes might have been playing tricks on me.

"I bring you greetings from Abigail in Capernaum," I said, grateful I had something useful to say. "She said I should tell you that the Ruach HaKodesh has impressed her to pray for your strength, and that you still had important work to do."

Surprise blossomed on Mary's face, followed by a grateful smile. "How kind of her. And how good of the Ruach HaKodesh to remind others to pray for me." Mary dropped my hands and motioned to the seating area. "Please, sit wherever you are most comfortable. I am so glad you have come."

I chuckled. "Surely you knew I would visit soon after I arrived in Jerusalem."

She laughed softly and led me to a bench, where she sat and gestured for me to do the same. "I hoped you would, after Peter told me you had been invited to join the work here. But I know how easily you men are caught up in ministry. I know how you love each other, and how easy it is to forget the women who labored with you."

"We would never forget you, Ima."

"I am glad you did not." Her eyes, warm and gentle, moved into mine. "I have been invited to join you and a few others for dinner at Peter's house tonight. After the dinner, I would like to ask you about something. Can we speak then?"

I blinked in perplexed astonishment. What did she want

to ask that she could not ask now? Was it something that might distract me from the evangelistic work I hoped to do?

"I am in no hurry to go." I shifted to face her. "If you would like to talk now—"

"I cannot . . . yet." She smiled, but with an absent, inward look, as though she was waiting to hear a voice from the invisible realm.

I sighed and resigned myself to waiting. I had done what Yeshua wanted me to do, but apparently my task was not complete.

"I will look forward to seeing you tonight." I gave her a tentative smile. "And when we can find an opportunity to talk, I will happily give you my full attention."

"Wonderful." She pressed her hands together and stood. "I am sure you are eager to join Peter and John, so I will let you go now. But do not forget—tonight after dinner, we must speak. And *at* dinner, I hope you will tell us what you have been doing in Capernaum. Miriam and I look forward to hearing how HaShem has used you during the last few years."

"HaShem has been good to me. Thank you, Mary—Ima." I bade her farewell and departed.

FOUR

Mary

For a long time after Matthew departed, I sat in silence, overcome by a wave of memories that brought back sights, sounds, and images of people and places I had not seen in years.

Like a potter who creates an edge by pressing his fingers against soft clay, so certain events leave an impression on our future lives, shadowing every subsequent moment with the curves and edges of the past. Yeshua's crucifixion had been one of those events, as had His birth and His resurrection.

But situations like Yeshua's calling of Matthew tended to remain buried in a sea of memories until an unexpected fling of the net dredged them up from the deep. Hearing Matthew's voice, seeing his arresting face, took me back to Capernaum's town center, where Matthew had manned a tax-collection booth near the city well. I could close my eyes and feel the breeze off the Sea of Galilee and smell the odor of fish in the marketplace. Several children were running through the town square the day we visited, and one of them stopped to look at Yeshua, his eyes wide and his lips parted, as if he suddenly intuited the heavenly origin of the Man standing by the well . . .

Like many others, I was surprised when Yeshua invited a tax collector to follow Him. I was even more surprised when the young man, then called Levi, abandoned his toll booth and followed my Son without hesitation. He remained with us all afternoon, listening and looking, and then he invited us to his house for dinner. We were all surprised when he provided a sumptuous feast for us and several of his tax-collector friends.

But what I remembered most vividly was the look on Levi's face as he listened to Yeshua. The tax collector did not eat his own food but sat as if mesmerized by every word Yeshua uttered.

Why had he been so transfixed? Was it because no one in Capernaum gave him the smallest measure of compassion or kindness? Or was it because he saw no judgment in Yeshua's eyes, heard no censure in His voice?

The next morning, I was among those astounded when Levi left his home, his servants, and his expensive possessions behind. Though he had been accustomed to the finest things money could buy, he joined our group and never complained about the long walks, the missed meals, or the nearly constant criticism leveled at us by everyone from the poor and skeptical to the religious authorities. The next day, Yeshua called Levi aside and, in front of all the others, said he would no longer be called Levi, but Matthew, which meant "gift of God."

Compared to the untamed Galileans, Matthew was well-groomed, well-spoken, and compulsively organized. He was the first to rise every morning, the first packed and ready to leave a campsite, the first to finish whatever task Yeshua asked of His followers. Even after many months, he remained the disciple who watched much and said little. I never knew Matthew well, but out of all the disciples, I thought he would be the first to turn back or betray Yeshua's cause. Though Matthew was a son of Abraham, somehow the Romans had stamped him with their influence. Occasionally he uttered a foreign word or phrase, and sometimes he stood with a military posture . . . I cannot explain it, but I could not help but feel that Matthew had been tainted by pagan Gentiles.

I knew one of the Twelve would betray my Son, for David had prophesied it:

> "Even my own close friend,
> whom I trusted, who ate my bread,
> has lifted up his heel against me."

While I did not know Matthew's history, I felt sure he had come from a wealthy family, perhaps from a line of Sadducees. Yet the Sadducees tended to be tightly connected, so how could one of their sons become a tax collector for the hated Romans? A dog would be more likely to turn into a pig.

I was quietly surprised when Judas, not Matthew, betrayed Yeshua. I had misjudged the former tax collector and asked HaShem to forgive me for my mistaken assumption.

Perhaps one day I would learn Matthew's history, but for now I felt grateful he had agreed to speak with me after dinner tonight. I did not mention any details about my particular need because I was not certain he was the right man, but why else would HaShem send Matthew when I desperately needed a scribe?

Perhaps the Ruach HaKodesh saw my need long before I did.

FIVE

Matthew

I met John at his house, and together we waited for Peter, who arrived late as usual. "What are we doing today?" I asked, hoping to hear we would be going to a neighboring village where the Spirit would empower us to cast out demons or raise the dead.

Peter gestured for us to follow him into the street. "Today we are going to the home of Simeon bar Jonah, who has invited several of his relatives to join us. They are curious about Yeshua, so we will explain the Gospel to them."

I smiled even though Peter's plan did not sound as thrilling as I had hoped. John must have seen the disappointment on my face, because he laughed and clapped me on the shoulder. "Wait and see," he said, a grin overtaking his features. "There is nothing as wonderful as watching the Ruach HaKodesh quicken a man's spirit. When the Spirit of God opens a sinner's heart, not only do the angels rejoice but we do, too."

Simeon bar Jonah, a merchant, lived in the upper city, not

far from Herod's palace. Our host greeted us warmly, bade his servants wash our feet, and seated us in honored places at his dining table. His guests regarded us with open expressions, and as Peter told the story of Yeshua's life and death, comprehension flickered in several pairs of eyes.

Peter had engaged their minds. Now the Ruach would have to engage their hearts.

"Yeshua of Nazareth," Peter went on, "a man authenticated by God with mighty deeds and wonders and signs God performed through Him in your midst—this Yeshua, given over by God's predetermined plan and foreknowledge, was nailed to the cross at the hands of lawless men. But God raised Him up, releasing Him from the pains of death, since it was impossible for Him to be held by it. For David said about Him, 'I saw Adonai always before me, for He is at my right hand so I might not be shaken. Therefore my heart was glad and my tongue rejoiced; moreover, my body also will live in hope, because You will not abandon my soul to Sheol or let Your Holy One see decay.'"

I studied the men's faces—lines of concentration deepened along brows; mouths frowned in confusion.

Peter continued: "Brothers, I can confidently tell you that the patriarch David died and was buried—his tomb is with us to this day. So because he was a prophet and knew God had sworn an oath to seat One of his descendants on his throne, David saw and spoke of Messiah's resurrection—that He was not abandoned to the grave, and His body did not see decay.

"This Yeshua God raised up—John, Matthew, and others here, we are eyewitnesses! Therefore, being exalted to the right hand of God and receiving from the Father the promise of the Ruach HaKodesh, now the whole house of Israel may

One of the oldest men lifted his hand. "Are all the groups ministering to their poor and elderly? Are the children and widows being fed?"

James smiled. "I am pleased to say they are. The Hellenized Jews, who have been neglected in the past, are now content. I have heard no more reports of their people being overlooked." He spread his hands. "Any other concerns?"

When no one spoke, James nodded toward me. "Then let me introduce Matthew, who was one of the Twelve and is an eyewitness to Yeshua's ministry. He has been working with new believers in Capernaum, but he has come to Jerusalem to help us. We are happy to have him and will definitely put his talents to good use."

Every venerable face turned to me, their eyes glimmering with unspoken questions and undeserved admiration. I smiled in return, though my face burned. I had never been comfortable with such attention.

"Matthew"—James looked at me—"is there anything you would like to say?"

The eyes turned toward me again, and my face grew even hotter under their scrutiny. "I-I am grateful to be here," I stammered. "I was amazed when Yeshua called me so many years ago, and I am likewise amazed to find myself serving with you. But I will do whatever the Ruach HaKodesh leads me to do here in Jerusalem."

James gave me a bright-eyed glance, gleaming with confidence, and lifted his hand. "If there is nothing else, let us pray." He bowed his head. "We pray, HaShem, that you will lead us and direct our steps. Guide and support us. May you confer blessing on the work of our hands and grant us grace and mercy in your eyes. Bestow upon us abundant kindness and help us share that kindness and mercy with others.

Hearken to the voice of our prayer, for we pray in the name of your Son, Yeshua our Messiah. Amen."

When he had finished, James caught my attention and motioned that I should wait, so I remained seated until the rooftop emptied. Then James sat next to me while Peter and John sat across from us.

James spoke first. "I wanted to know if you have any questions about your duties here in Jerusalem. This would be a good time to ask."

I straightened my spine. "It would be good to know details. I know you need help with keeping records of gifts."

"Correct—the gifts of *many* communities." James folded his hands. "For instance, the large ecclēsia that used to meet at Solomon's Porch has disbanded several times. The first scattering occurred when Stephen was stoned several years ago. Others fled under threat of persecution from Saul the Pharisee."

I tugged at my beard. "What is the latest report from Saul? I heard he met Yeshua on his way to arrest believers in Damascus."

Peter nodded. "He is now a believer and feels called to minister to the Gentiles. He has spent the last several years preaching the Gospel in Arabia and Damascus."

"In any case," James said, "we have learned that HaShem works even when we fear for the well-being of the communities. Those who flee Jerusalem or Judea carry the good news to Samaria and beyond."

"Even to Rome," John added. "And while we cannot account for every assembly, we are responsible for those in Judea. Our people want to know their gifts are going to further the Gospel, and presently we have no way to assure them that we are distributing their gifts in the proper manner."

"Too many hands collecting contributions; too many hands distributing them," James said. "The right hand does not know what the left is doing. So what we need is a record of what each assembly gives, and where the money is sent."

"Sounds simple." Peter grinned. "But gathering the information will be a challenge. That's why we thought of you. We knew you could manage everything."

The man who used to collect taxes for Rome can certainly handle gifts for God's people. They did not mention my past, but I knew they had considered it.

I drew a deep breath. I wanted to serve Yeshua. I was willing to do whatever He wanted me to do. But I had hoped for a task that would not remind me of my past. I had hoped for a job that reflected my changed character. How could I be sure this was what Yeshua wanted of me?

I lifted my chin and met my brothers' eyes. "I am here, friends, because I love you and trust your leadership. I had hoped you would want me to serve alongside you in some way that did not involve counting money and keeping records."

The setting sun painted Peter in a golden glow as he looked at his hands, then raised his eyes to meet mine. "If you associate records and numbers with your past, Matthew, you must remember—you are no longer that man. No one thinks of you as Levi the tax collector. You have a new name and a new life." His voice softened. "But Yeshua needs skilled and educated people to help us spread the Gospel. No matter what you do, you are still a witness. You are the man we need, and I can think of no one who would do a better job."

"I felt so free when I set aside all thoughts of money to follow Yeshua," I said. "He liberated me from that sort of work."

"But He did not liberate your abilities, and I know you are still better at calculations than anyone I could name. Say you will serve as our accountant, Matthew. We will find you a house, a place where you can live and work. If you are in charge of collections and distributions, our people will trust that their gifts are being used for the glory of God."

"Have you not said you will do anything Yeshua asks of you?" John asked.

I drew another breath, then met James's determined gaze. "I must pray about it," I told him. "I will ask for guidance and give you an answer after dinner."

James rested his hand on my back. "Thank you, brother. I will look forward to our conversation. May the Lord reveal His will to you."

"Now," Peter said, rising, "I hope the women have finished preparing the food. My stomach is growling, and I know Matthew is hungry. His stomach is growling, too."

her gaze. "I always find what I need when I listen to His voice."

I caught Anna's eye. "You have a remarkable daughter. Beautiful, kind, and filled with the Spirit. Have you and Peter given much thought to her future?"

Anna shook her head. "I keep telling Peter it is time to think about Dina's betrothal, but he keeps saying he has not heard from the Lord. 'When I do,' he says, 'you will be the first to know.'"

"As long as you let *me* know." Dina entered the conversation with a coy look. "If I am to be married, I would like to know and respect the man who will be my husband."

"Then you had better keep an eye on your father." Anna slipped her arm around Dina's waist and gave her a teasing smile. "And pray that he listens carefully to the Spirit, lest he see a wealthy man and confuse his yearnings with the Spirit's voice."

Finally the men came downstairs—Peter, John, Matthew, and my son James. I embraced James, then greeted Peter and John. I sent Matthew a quick smile, then returned my attention to the women. I did not know how he was feeling and did not want to make him feel self-conscious before I had a chance to broach the subject weighing heavily on my heart.

While the men took their seats, Peter lifted his hands. "Thank you, brothers and sisters, for coming to dine at our humble home," he said, quiet joy shining from his eyes. "This is a wonderful reunion, is it not? If only Yeshua were here with us."

Peter bowed his head and recited the blessing: "*Barukh ata Adonai Eloheinu melekh ha'olam hamotzi lehem min ha'aretz.*" *Blessed are You, Lord our God, Ruler of the universe, who brings forth bread from the earth.*

Peter grabbed a boiled egg from the nearest tray and took a bite, our signal to eat. We women ate and exchanged small talk at our end of the table while the men did the same at their end. I do not know what the men talked about, but Mara told us about her work with the women's prayer group, and Dina shared about the three children she cared for next door. "Their mother is ill," she said, a trace of compassion lighting her brown eyes. "And their father spends nearly all day at the market, selling his wares."

"What does he sell?" I asked.

"Oil lamps," Mara said, her voice rough with age. "They are overpriced and undersized, but people buy them because they pity the man. Three small children and no wife."

I lifted a brow and looked at Anna—was this neighbor a possible match for Dina?

Anna read my meaning and shook her head almost imperceptibly. "Not a believer," she said, her voice so low I barely heard her.

"What's that?" Mara cupped her hand around her ear and leaned closer to her daughter. "What did you say?"

"Nothing important, Ima." Dina smiled. "Would you like more fish?"

When everyone had finished eating, Peter offered another blessing, then pressed his hands together and said, "I have asked you all here because Matthew has just agreed to join us as an accountant for all the Judean communities of believers. I want you to welcome him as a brother in Christ. We are happy to have him as part of our ministry—he is gifted as a scribe and accountant and will help us remain accountable to those who give so freely to spread the Gospel. He will be staying here with us until he finds a suitable place to live, and I trust you will do all you can to meet his needs." Peter looked toward his wife and lifted a brow. "He will need food, Anna, but I am certain you will not let him starve."

Miriam and I joined the other women as they laughed, but my laughter died when a voice, sharp and clear, spoke to my heart: *Matthew is the one.*

I had asked HaShem to show me who would be best suited to help me record my memories. Though I thought Matthew might be the man, now I knew for certain. He had come to Jerusalem to work with the other apostles, but surely he would not need to work with them every day.

I closed my eyes, remembering the lists he used to make for me to take to the market. He was a skilled copyist, he had a keen grasp of words and numbers, and he had been an eyewitness to Yeshua's ministry. He spoke Hebrew, Greek, and Aramaic. Matthew might have come to Jerusalem to answer Peter's call, yet he had also come as an answer to my prayers.

Matthew would be my helper.

I opened my eyes and sighed in relief.

As John and James said their farewells, Miriam and I sat in a quiet corner. Miriam did not approve of idle hands, so she pulled a bag of pistachios from her basket and began to shell them. I sat silently, taking slow breaths, trying to keep my heart from pounding out of my chest.

HaShem, you have led me to the man for the job. Now give me the words to help him see your will.

The idea had come to me after the women's prayer meeting. What lingered with me had nothing to do with the prayers or the reading of James's letter. No, what I could not forget was my conversation with the older woman next to me. While I found it comforting to believe I had not *lost* my memories, I could not deny that every year I found it harder to recall them. If memories were like garments packed in a trunk, my trunk was deep and crowded with both common and precious tunics.

I was a woman of flesh, and my body was beginning to feel the effects of the passing years. I had been uniquely honored by HaShem—how had my cousin Elizabeth phrased it? I was *blessed among women*. I could not deny it, but neither had I done anything to deserve it. Joseph and I were common, simple people; we had no reason to be proud.

When I held my first baby in my arms, I realized I would never be like my Son: my nature was human, not divine. As the years passed, that conviction grew sharper—Yeshua knew what I was thinking before I could speak and could repeat any Scripture within moments of hearing it. In the winding length of my memory, I could never recall His committing a selfish act, telling an untruth, or failing to honor me and Joseph.

In those early days, as HaShem's handmaid, I witnessed so many miraculous works. When I visited Elizabeth, who was also expecting a miracle baby, she knew what had happened to me before I could share the news. Joseph also experienced a visit from an angel, who assured him he should take me as his wife. In a dream, another angel warned Joseph to spirit us away from Bethlehem just before Herod's soldiers killed all the baby boys.

So many stories, with so many details. Would I ever remember them all?

When our children were small, I did not worry about forgetting because Joseph shared my recollections. But now he was gone, so the stories resided in my heart alone . . . and I would not live forever.

How could I safeguard our history? How could I ensure that the *world's* children would know what HaShem had done to provide us with a perfect atoning sacrifice for sin?

As I sat on my narrow bed that night, the answer sprang immediately to mind: I would have to write the stories. So the world would know . . . and I would not forget.

In the year following Yeshua's resurrection and ascension, we had been so involved with sharing the Gospel that it had never occurred to me that the stories ought to be written. We felt an urgency to spread the good news throughout the world before Yeshua's return. We had no idea when He would come back, but some insisted that Yeshua would return before John died. Peter later told me that Yeshua actually said, "If I want him to remain until I come, what is that to you? You follow me."

Still, we were almost a decade younger in those days. The Ruach HaKodesh had given us energy and enthusiasm, and we worked in the confidence that we were doing what HaShem had called us to do.

We were still convinced that we were doing Adonai's will, but we had begun to bury men and women who died in the faith. The Spirit had not bestowed the gift of immortality upon our earthly bodies, and I, as one of the oldest of Yeshua's followers, had begun to feel the bewildering effects of old age. I could no longer do the delicate embroidery that required a sharp eye; I could no longer hear Miriam call from the street, and my flesh hung on my bones. My face had become a map of fine lines and creases, and, most alarming, one of my breasts had developed an unusual swelling.

I chewed my thumbnail as the notion of writing persisted. I had to write the stories of Yeshua, but how? While I knew how to read and write, I knew more about keeping house than writing stories. I could write a letter, but to compile a complete scroll, to collect accounts of all Yeshua had said and done during His time on earth—how could I manage such a thing? How could anyone?

In the flickering light of my oil lamp, I stared at the trunk against my bedroom wall—a repository for my tunics, several headscarves, a few sheets of leather, a stylus, and a packet of ink powder purchased long ago in case I ever needed to send a letter.

Though I had never written anything longer than a shopping list, I desperately needed to share what I knew about Yeshua. Of all people on earth, I had been with Him the longest and knew Him best. I was at His conception and His birth. I felt His first stirring in my womb, later felt Him kick beneath my skin. I nursed Him, taught Him, tended His skinned knees and elbows. Joseph and I raised Him. We presented Him at the Temple and took Him to synagogue. Joseph taught Him the Torah, while I taught Him the daily prayers and blessings. I fed Him; I knew what foods He liked and disliked. I understood His heart and marveled at His wisdom, which surpassed mine long before He astounded the Torah teachers as a boy of twelve.

I stood and watched when He performed His first miracle. I traveled with Him in Galilee, Capernaum, and Jerusalem. I worshiped with Him at the Temple; I knew His disciples—the Seventy, the Twelve, and the three who were closest to Him. I helped prepare His last meal on earth, and I watched as His life's blood flowed from His tortured body on the execution stake.

I was with the women who discovered that He had risen, and I waited with the believers until the Ruach HaKodesh descended on us at the Festival of Pentecost.

felt as though He had just left the room. He promised not to abandon us and said He would give us the Spirit of truth, who would teach us what we needed to know and remind us of everything He had said.

So what was the Spirit saying to me? He did not speak like men; sometimes I could barely hear His voice. Waiting to hear from the Spirit made me long for the days when I could approach Yeshua, ask Him a question, and get an answer. Sometimes I received a cryptic answer, but at least I did not have to strain to hear Him. The Spirit, however, sometimes spoke in a voice so low that I wondered if I had heard correctly or if I had heard Him at all.

David had known the Ruach HaKodesh. The Ruach traveled in the midst of the Israelites when Moses led them out of Egypt. The Spirit of God protected Israel, filled the hearts of men, and grieved for Israel's sin.

Was the Ruach HaKodesh going to help me add rows of numbers? I could do that on my own, so had the Spirit brought me to Jerusalem or had I come because I yearned for excitement? Perhaps bored with teaching young believers and drawn by the promise of seeing my dear friends, I had listened to my own yearnings and attributed them to the Spirit.

But if the Spirit *had* brought me to Jerusalem, what did He expect of me in the Holy City? While Peter and John worked miracles, did the Spirit truly want me to spend my days working with soulless accounts?

At the conclusion of the meal, after James and John said their farewells, I walked into the front room where I could be alone. Mixed feelings surged through me, troubled feelings that waxed as the candles on the table waned. Why would the Ruach HaKodesh enable my brothers to work miracles and consign me to desk work?

"Matthew?"

I tried to swallow a rise of disappointment when I turned and saw Yeshua's mother in the doorway. She wanted to discuss something with me. I snorted softly. She probably wanted me to keep the records for one of her women's groups.

"Mary." I forced a smile. "It is good to see you again."

"Is it?" She tilted her head as if to better study my face, and her eyes softened with a touch of sadness. "I can see you are discouraged."

"I am fine. I am willing to serve Yeshua in any way I can."

Her eyes were like torches, pushing at the gloom that had filled my heart. "You say that . . . but you yearn for something more."

Abruptly, she gestured to a bench. "Sit, my young friend. Let me tell you what Adonai has placed on my heart."

EIGHT

Mary

Matthew sat next to me on a bench, an anxious look on his face. I smiled as a feeling of assurance rose from the center of my being. "You are probably wondering why I wanted to speak to you."

"Of course." A smile found its way through his mask of uncertainty. "Because I am one of the least of the Twelve, I assume you need an accountant—"

I laughed. "I would not say you are one of the least, Matthew. You may not have the gifts of Peter and John, but you have skills they lack."

He leaned forward, resting his elbows on his knees. "James has already asked me about accounting for the gifts of the Judean assemblies. Soon I will have to determine how many assemblies there are, so I am certain I will be busy in the days ahead—"

"You will be. But keeping the accounts will not occupy all your time. I know this because HaShem knew I would have need of you, but not as an accountant."

Surprise flitted across his face. "Not as—?"

"I need someone who is skilled with words—someone who speaks formal Hebrew and who can write with a clear hand. Most important, I need someone who traveled with Yeshua, who witnessed the things He did and heard the things He said. Someone who can validate my memories of certain events."

Matthew blinked. "Many men would fit that description."

"Yes, but not many of those witnesses are skilled and well educated. I have a project in mind, something we must soon commence. As I prayed for help, the Ruach HaKodesh brought you to mind. So I am asking—" I paused to grip his hand, forcing him to look directly at me—"I am asking if you will help me in this undertaking. I would be most pleased to have your assistance."

His mouth curved in a smile, yet in his eyes I saw confusion and something that looked like doubt. Did he think I was losing my mind? Perhaps he thought I was being womanish or excessively sentimental.

"Honored lady, you have not explained what you would like me to do."

I drew a deep breath and released his hand. "I am no longer a young woman, Matthew. The other day, as friends and I were discussing a letter James sent to all the believers, I realized that everything I know about Yeshua will die with me. Those of us who witnessed the events of His life are growing older, and memories are fragile things. Some of my recollections are vibrant and clear; others have faded with time."

Matthew nodded. "It is human to forget, but Yeshua said the Spirit would remind us of everything He said."

"Yes, but we are mortal. We will die, and who will the Spirit remind then? Surely you see the problem." I leaned forward, eager to make him understand. "Yeshua's human beginning occurred in my womb, after my conversation with the archangel. Joseph and I witnessed His birth and heard His first cries. We saw Simeon prophesy about Him in the Temple; we watched Anna weep with joy because she recognized the Messiah in a baby boy. But Joseph is gone. Simeon is gone, and so is Anna. My other children had not been born when those things happened. If I do not record those stories, if we do not leave a written testimony, the memories I have carefully guarded will never reach the world."

I searched Matthew's eyes and waited for his response. My words had taken hold of something in him; I could see he understood. Still, he was not convinced.

"So . . . you want me to write your memories and preserve them. In a scroll, I presume?"

"Scroll, papyrus, on a stone—it matters not. What matters is that we preserve the stories. I have them here"—I touched my breastbone—"but I have no idea how to organize my thoughts or how to record my memories so they are clearly understood. I will need help, and I believe you are the man meant to help me."

Matthew eyed me with a calculating expression. "How long would this take?"

"I do not know. But I would be willing to meet in the evenings, after you have completed your work for James. I think it would be useful to break the writing into several sessions. That will give me time to sort through my cluttered thoughts and revive my memories. To pull them out and dust them off, so to speak."

He fingered his beard a moment, then gave me a reluctant nod. "I am honored you would think of me, but I cannot consent until I speak to James and Peter. I came here to help the communities of believers. Surely you understand that my work for them must be my priority."

"Of course."

"And I must be honest with you, Mary—Ima. I have promised to help James and Peter with their accounting, but my chief desire is to preach. If I agree to help you, you must understand that my heart is yearning for an opportunity to preach the Gospel."

I leaned back, content with his answer. "Preaching is a noble calling indeed. But ask yourself this, Matthew—in fifty years, when we are silent in the grave, what will the preachers of the Way preach about? I am certain they will read from the Torah, but would it not also be appropriate for them to read the words of Yeshua? If they read Yeshua's words, who will provide them?"

He opened his mouth as if to answer, then snapped it shut. "I will have to let the next generation answer your question. But I will speak to Peter, James, and John, and I will pray about the matter."

I smiled, confident of the answer he would receive. "That is all I ask. Thank you."

I stood, bade Matthew farewell, and went in search of Miriam. The streets outside were dark, and the last two hours had drained me.

As we draped scarves over our heads, Miriam asked if I wanted to invite Matthew for dinner on the morrow.

"Not yet," I answered, tucking a wayward hank of hair under my head covering. "But I have a feeling we will share many meals with him in the days to come."

When she lifted a brow in unspoken question, I linked my arm through hers and drew her toward the door. "I will explain everything on the walk home."

I glanced at Peter, wondering if he was behind this feeble attempt at a jest, but Peter appeared as confused as I.

"Who is making inquiries about Matthew Levi?" I asked.

The man grunted and held out a scroll with an ornate seal. "If you are Matthew, the son of Alphaeus, an important official has written to you."

The words quickened my pulse. "An official?" I extended my hand. "I am the man you seek."

The man grunted again, and not until Peter fished a coin out of his pocket did I realize why the stranger hesitated to release the epistle. After being paid, the man dropped the scroll onto my palm and walked away.

Peter gave me a sidelong glance. "Have we just been robbed?"

"I do not think so. Few people know I am in Jerusalem. And fewer still would address a message to Matthew Levi." I broke the seal and scanned the heading. "It is from a man I studied with in Caesarea. After our training, I went to Capernaum, but he went to work for a Roman official."

Peter lifted a bushy brow. "Why would he write you now?"

"I do not know." I glanced at the small, neat writing. "I have not heard from Achiakos in eight or nine years. I met him in Capernaum and led him to belief in Yeshua not long after the resurrection, then he returned to Rome."

"Let us make our way to John's house," Peter said, easing back into the crowd. "You can read your letter once we arrive."

John's house was not far from the Temple Mount. Peter and I covered the distance with brisk steps, eager to begin our work. A young woman opened the door and bade Peter and me enter, so we slipped out of our sandals and quickly dashed water over our dusty feet. John, James the Just, and several of the elders were already in the front room, their voices rising in passionate debate.

Since we had entered into the middle of a discussion I knew nothing about, I lingered in the vestibule to read my letter.

Achiakos, a servant of Herod Agrippa.
To Matthew Levi, scribe, Torah teacher, and friend.
Regarding events in Jamnia, which should concern all who care for Israel:

Grace and shalom be unto you from Rome, where I serve King Agrippa.

I would have written you sooner, but my master has kept me occupied with maintaining his accounts, which are many and often in a state of indebtedness. I would write more often, but I am sure you are as occupied as I.

I am writing now because I know you love Israel, and because Adonai has placed me in a situation where I am privy to knowledge and events which might prove useful to you and other followers of the Way. I am trusting you will not reveal the source of this knowledge, for my life, small as it is, lies in the hands of a temperamental and powerful man.

My master Agrippa and his dear friend, Gaius Caesar, formerly known to you as Caligula, have recently received news of an event in Jamnia of Judea, no more than a day's walk from the coast of the Great Sea. You probably know the town—it is occupied by Jews and Gentiles who struggle to maintain peace among themselves. The Greeks of Jamnia, wishing to honor the imperial cult, erected a clay altar on which they could make sacrifices in Caesar's name, since he has declared himself divine. The Jews of Jamnia, being mightily offended by the Greeks' action, destroyed the altar, thus arousing the indignation of their fellow citizens. Those indignant men wrote Caesar, and two days ago their epistle reached the emperor.

You may not know Caesar's temperament, but I can assure you he is not a man one should test. He has not forgotten a recent occasion that occurred on his visit to Alexandria, when a group of Greeks spoke against the Jews, saying the Jews neglected the homage due to Caesar, refusing to erect statues in his honor or swear by his name. Caesar became wroth at the news and wanted to enact great mischief against the Jews. Considering it a heinous insult that he should be so despised only by the Jews and no other conquered people, he sent Publius Petronius to be president of Syria and successor to Vitellius. He commanded Petronius to have made a golden statue of his divine self and then to advance into Judea with a great body of troops to kill and destroy unless the Jews would willingly admit his statue and erect it in the Temple of God. If they proved obstinate, Caesar commanded, Petronius was to conquer them by war.

This news made me quake with fear and trepidation, but my master Agrippa says Petronius is a reasonable man and not inclined to destruction. He will do his best for the people of Israel, but he is commanded by Caesar and must eventually proceed in obedience.

I am writing to inform you of these events and pray you will do what you can to spread the word and urge caution. Many have assured me that HaShem has al-

ready set himself against Gaius Caesar, but until He acts, you and your brothers must with great care consider your reactions to the imperial provocation.

I have much to say to you, but can only write certain things with pen and ink. Yet I hope to see you soon when we may speak face-to-face.

Shalom aleichem. Greet my friends—if any remain with you—by name.

Achiakos

I sat on a bench and read the letter again as dismay siphoned the blood from my head.

Achiakos was not given to hysteria, nor did he suffer from an excess of emotion. For him to take the risk of sending a written warning meant the situation was grave indeed.

When I was certain I had a clear understanding of the situation, I rose and strode into the front room, brandishing the scroll.

"Forgive me for interrupting," I said, respectfully dipping my head toward the older men in the room. "I would not intrude if I had not just received word from an old and trusted friend in Rome. He, too, is a follower of Yeshua, and he has sent a warning for all who dwell in Judea."

One of the elders frowned and cleared his throat with a great harrumph. I recognized the man; the short, dour fellow had been at Peter's house last night. "Why would you have access to such a warning?" he asked, his voice as flat and dry as the desert. "Are you in league with Romans?"

The words stung, but I pressed on. "My friend," I said, taking care to steel my voice, "serves as a scribe to Herod Agrippa, who is a close friend to Gaius Caesar. At great risk,

Achiakos has written that certain Jews have offended the emperor, so he has charged Publius Petronius with assembling an army in Syria. This army will attack Jerusalem if we do not obey Caesar's edict. And it is an edict we cannot obey."

The frowning elder stroked his beard. "To which edict do you refer?"

"One that has not been published abroad." I looked around the room, meeting each man's gaze. "Apparently Caesar intends to erect a statue of himself in the Temple and command that we bow before it. If we do not agree, this Petronius has been given an order to attack and destroy the city."

Stillness washed over the room, shock followed by denial.

"Bah!" Another elder waved my words away. "Your friend, whoever he is, is jesting."

"He is sober-minded; he does not jest."

"Caligula should know better. Surely his advisors—certainly Herod Agrippa knows we would not allow such a statue into the Holy City. We would lie down in the street before we would allow a graven object to approach the Temple."

"That is why Achiakos has warned us." I turned to John, who would certainly believe this report. "My friend is a good man and a true believer. He would not send a letter—at the risk of his life, I am certain—unless the threat was genuine."

"His name is Greek," one of the elders pointed out. "He is not a Jew."

"Half the people in Jerusalem have Greek names," I countered. "His full name is Caleb Achiakos, and he is as Jewish as we are. I assure you, we cannot ignore this message."

James held up his hand, signaling for quiet, so I sat, my chest heaving with exasperation.

"Several of you met Matthew last night," John said, a gentle smile gleaming through his beard. "And those of you who have not had the honor, let me present my brother Matthew, who is also one of the Twelve. He has agreed to work with us as we minister to the various believing communities in Jerusalem. He is excellent with numbers, and you know we need a skilled accountant to keep our records."

The elders nodded, their faces brightening as they studied me. I was no longer an unknown who had rudely burst into a meeting; I was one of the Twelve, so I had walked with Yeshua and been filled with the Ruach HaKodesh.

But even men governed by the same Spirit often argued when human nature reared its head.

"I trust Matthew and his friend," John said. "I think we should heed this warning and share it with the high priest."

"Theophilus?" The dour man shook his head. "Why would we give such information to the religious authorities after they have persecuted so many followers of the Way?"

"They are still the leaders of Israel," John said, gentle reproof in his voice. "The Romans will parlay with the high priest, not with leaders of the Way."

"What good will it do to share the news?" Peter spread his hands. "We have no power against Caesar. And we know the high priest will never allow the emperor's statue into the Holy City. We can do nothing about Caesar."

"We can pray." James straightened his shoulders. "A wise man would not ignore this warning. Gaius Caesar is apparently intent on exerting his will on our people, so he will press forward."

John's mouth twisted into a cynical smile. "Once again, an enemy has set her face against Jerusalem, so once again we must ask HaShem to deliver us."

take action on her behalf but fell into company with a witch. That woman introduced her to dark spirits, and those spirits invaded Miriam's heart and mind, twisting her thoughts and perceptions. When the people of Tiberias cast her out of the city, she lived in a graveyard, stealing whatever she needed to survive and eating vermin and insects when she could find nothing else.

"And then," she said, her face brightening, "I met Yeshua, and He restored my soul."

I would have asked for more details, but Miriam excused herself, saying she had other chores. I reminded myself that I was telling *Yeshua's* story, not Miriam's, and picked up my stylus, ready to listen to Mary. Her words flowed more freely now, probably because she had relaxed. She told me about her kinswoman Elizabeth, a woman past the age of childbearing who had also conceived a miracle child after her husband, Zechariah, heard from an angelic visitor. This angel appeared when Zechariah, a Levite, was serving at the altar of incense, and Zechariah was so startled he could not speak. The angel prophesied the birth of a son, who would bring many of the people of Israel back to the Lord.

"In Elizabeth's sixth month," Mary added, "after the angel appeared to me, I went to visit Elizabeth. When I walked into the house and greeted her, she exclaimed, 'Blessed are you among women, and blessed is the fruit of your womb. Who am I, that the mother of my Master should come to me?'" Mary's mouth curled in a one-sided smile. "That is the only time I have ever heard those words with joy."

I looked up. "Why? I should think you would be happy—"

"I received Elizabeth's words with joy because they were confirmation of all the angel had said. But now when people bow before me as 'the mother of the Lord,' I am . . . uncomfortable." She looked away as a blush stained her cheek. "Pride is a subtle thing, as I am sure you know, and HaShem hates it. I take great pleasure in my Son Yeshua, but I am not *proud* to be the mother of the Messiah. Someone had to bear Him in order to fulfill the word of the prophets, and I will never understand why HaShem chose me."

"I am sure," I murmured, "HaShem had His reasons."

She shook her head, then released a soft laugh. "HaShem's ways are beyond imagining. In any case, Elizabeth went on to say that when she heard my voice, her unborn child leapt with joy in her womb." Mary gave me a quizzical look. "Even now, I am amazed. Her son, John the Immerser, was filled with the Ruach HaKodesh before his birth. For a long time I thought it was the same with Yeshua, but that was before I realized He was one with God, which was not the same as being filled with the Spirit."

"Wait." I lifted my hand. "You have not given me any details about Yeshua's birth. An angel came to visit you. I assume you and Joseph had married by that time . . . for how long had you been wed?"

Mary hesitated, then idly dragged her finger over the surface of the table. "I have not told this story to many people. Few would understand. But surely you must have wondered how Yeshua could be called the Son of God when he was born of a mortal woman?"

I lifted a brow, conceding her point. I had always assumed He was a normal child, but God had called Him, or indwelt Him, at some point in His infancy. But if John the Immerser could be filled with the Spirit before birth . . .

A drum began to pound at my left temple.

"I suppose the *real* beginning of the story is Yeshua's conception," Mary said, oblivious to my confusion. "He did

Temple, above the Ark of the Covenant. As it is written, 'The cloud filled the House of Adonai, so that the *kohanim* could not stand to minister because of the cloud, for the glory of Adonai filled the House of Adonai.'"

I made a sound of agreement; the passage referred to the dedication of Solomon's Temple.

"That is how it was. A thick cloud filled the garden and surrounded me, and then the glory of the Lord blazed about me so brightly I had to close my eyes. I cried out, surrendering to Adonai's will, and after a moment the cloud departed and all was as it had been. I was still on my knees, still clasping my hands, but I was weeping . . . because HaShem had approved of my willingness and entrusted me with His Son."

She turned to look at me, her cheeks wet with tears. "I am not a woman who often weeps, but after experiencing the glory of Adonai I could do nothing else."

I made no notes—this was a mystery, and not a story to be shared. I could only stare at Mary, because in that moment something akin to glory seemed to light her face from within.

That is when I realized that few men, if any, would ever experience what I had been granted—an opportunity to hear the history of Yeshua the Messiah, Son of God, from the lips of the woman who knew Him best.

TEN

Mary

On the second day, Matthew arrived at our house shortly after sunrise. Miriam offered him bread and honey while I finished my morning prayers and braided my hair. When I was certain my haggard face wouldn't frighten him away, I stepped out of the bedchamber and greeted him. "Shalom, Matthew. Thank you for coming so early."

He put down his bread and waved sheets of papyrus in my direction. "I went back to my room and started to write. After reviewing my notes, the words began to flow . . ." He lifted his hands, smiling. "The experience was amazing. I cannot wait for you to hear what I have written."

The young man was excited, probably too excited to notice I had passed a sleepless night. I lifted a hand to gently temper his enthusiasm, then sank onto the bench by the table. "Would you like honey water?" Miriam asked, bringing the pitcher and a cup. She lowered her voice. "You did not sleep, did you?"

"Not much. And yes, I would like some water." I reached for a bowl of figs. "Thank you, Miriam. You were up early this morning."

"Many things to do," she said, giving me a conspiratorial smile.

I had told her, with great reluctance, that I would probably be unable to do my share of the household chores for the next few weeks. I apologized, but Miriam dismissed my words with a wave. "I would do anything to help you and Matthew," she replied, her eyes snapping with joy. "You are right to undertake such an endeavor. Everyone who met Yeshua has a story about Him, and it would be a shame not to record those tales for those who will come after us. They need to know who He was, and the many ways He showed us His Father."

I sipped the honey water, bit into my first fig, and nodded to Matthew, who looked as if he might burst from anticipation. "All right," I said. "Read."

He picked up the papyri, cleared his throat, and began:

> "'Yeshua of Nazareth. Yeshua ben Elohim. The Light of the World. The Bread of Life. The Living Water. The Son of God.
>
> Those of us who knew Him while He dwelled on earth discovered who He was in myriad ways—some of us believed immediately because we beheld miracles, signs and wonders only a man with the power of God could perform. Others of us needed no miracle, but saw in Him the Shekinah glory of God, hidden beneath a veil of humanity. Some of us came to Him early; others came late. But we came, we walked with Him, we talked with Him. We laughed and wept with Him.
>
> Then, when He rose from the dead, we fell to our knees and worshiped Him.'"

Matthew lifted his gaze. "Well? What do you think of this beginning?"

HaShem, give me wisdom.

I drew a deep breath and forced a smile. "You write beautifully, Matthew. You are talented and skilled. But this—this is not what the beginning should be."

Disappointment flooded his eyes as he lowered the papyri. "I do not understand."

I pressed my hand to my heart. "I want these stories to be . . . simple. Plain. What you have written is too polished. And *you* are there, in the words, and neither you nor I have any right to be in the story. This should be Yeshua's story, not ours."

His face went blank with shock. "What do you mean, I am there? I never mentioned my name—"

"We," I said. "You wrote *we*, and you are present in the *we*. In the *us*."

"It is an accepted way of writing." Matthew lifted his chin. "I have read many scrolls by Greeks and Romans, and most of them are written in this style. It is personal, the writer speaks directly to the reader. This form is intimate and has great power to pierce the heart and mind—"

"No." I struggled to find the right words. "This writing draws too much attention to the writer and not enough to Yeshua."

"Not enough to *Yeshua*?" Disbelief echoed in Matthew's voice. "The entire papyrus is about Yeshua. The first line is His name and a list of His titles. The following lines are only about Him and how we followed Him—"

"There it is again," I said, whispering. "*We*."

Matthew gaped at his neatly written pages as if the words had somehow rearranged themselves, then he dropped the papyri to the table and lowered his head onto his hands. I glanced at Miriam, who turned from her dishes and looked at both of us with compassion in her eyes. "Not an easy task," she murmured.

"No. But I know how this should be written."

Matthew lifted his head. "Let me . . . give me a moment, please, to gather my thoughts."

I sipped my water and waited.

"You asked me to help you," Matthew finally said, pressing his hands to the table, "because you said I had skill. I used that skill to write a page you described as beautiful. I *know* it is beautiful, because I felt the words flow in a spirit of beauty. But you say it is not right; it has too much of me and not enough of Yeshua."

He looked at me, frustration evident in the line of his jaw and the heat of his eyes. "Mary, how are we to work together if you do not trust me to use my skill in the way I think best?"

I reached across the table and rested my fingers on his clenched hand. "I understand why you are irritated with me. And you are right—I did say your writing was beautiful, and I meant it. But our work should not be modeled after a Greek poem or a Roman memoir because it is not Greek or Roman. Our work should be the simple, unadorned truth of Yeshua and the Gospel. You and I should not be evident in the writing, only in our stories. You and I are observers, witnesses to the truth, that is all. We will not embellish His story, nor will we turn it into an elegant tale that contradicts Yeshua's simplicity. He lived and worked among common people, so why should we write as though He were born in a king's palace?"

"He is the Son of a King," Matthew mumbled. "The King of the universe."

"Yes, but we did not understand that until later. So we will write the story as we saw Him—simply and truthfully, with no airs or embellishments. Do you understand?"

A deep silence filled the room; the unearthly quiet seemed to absorb even the clatter of Miriam's dishes. I held my breath—would Matthew gather his papyri and leave? But as sound returned and a donkey cart rumbled past the house, Matthew nodded. "I understand."

"Good." I patted his hand. "You can rewrite the beginning later, but for now, let us keep talking. What story should we tell next?"

Matthew slid the papyri off the table, then opened his satchel and pulled out the scrawled page he had used for taking notes. "Tell me what you remember about Yeshua's childhood."

"Good." I took another fig from the bowl. "We are making progress."

let me accompany them and accustom myself to their approach to evangelism.

Except . . . the Spirit had not led me to talk to Peter. I had not heard either a still, small voice or a booming thunder. I had dreamed no unusual dreams and had no leading except that which Yeshua had given me when I arrived in Jerusalem: *Trust the Father, Matthew. He will use you in ways you cannot imagine.*

I had never imagined that I would be working with Mary, nor that she would be so difficult to please.

When we traveled with Yeshua, everyone talked about how wonderful Mary was, how blessed, meek, and mild. We disciples deferred to her, listened to her intently, and treated her with more respect than we would have given our own mothers. The people we met fawned over her even more than we did. I saw women too overcome to speak when they met her, and once I watched, stupefied, as a woman fainted when she realized she had accepted a basket of food from Yeshua's mother.

What they did not know—and what I did not know at the time—was that meek Mary could be as inflexible as a child and as abrupt as a recluse. The woman who had been unafraid to face her betrothed with an inexplicable pregnancy was likewise unafraid to challenge a professional scribe. The woman who was not intimidated by wise men from the East would not be intimidated by a meticulously handwritten papyrus. She who stood at the foot of the cross and watched, unflinching, as her firstborn Son suffered torture expected me to refrain from flinching when she held my first page to a lamp and consigned my hard work to the flame.

"Why, Lord?" I lifted my gaze to the thatched ceiling. "Why did you call me to this task? I would rather collect taxes than work with your mother. She is not who I thought she was."

The answer was not audible, but I heard it nonetheless. *She has always been obedient. She is obedient still.*

"But she has grown cantankerous in her old age. She is inflexible. When I suggest a better way to tell a story, she refuses to listen."

Listening is your *work. Her work is to tell the stories.*

I lay in silence for a moment, then slowly blew every bit of breath from my lungs. "All right. I will listen and I will write. If she does not approve, I will write again. And again. Until she is content."

I heard nothing after that, and finally I was able to sleep.

On the sixth day of the week, Mary stood, pressed her hands to the center of her back, and stared into the open courtyard. We had been working hard—she, telling her stories; me, pulling often painful details from her memories. Dark circles ringed her eyes, and she appeared paler than usual. Was the work too much for her?

"There is a story I have not shared," she said, her voice sounding as if it came from a faraway place. "I know it only because Yeshua shared it with me."

I lifted a brow. "Something that happened during His ministry?"

"Something that happened before." She stared into the courtyard a moment more, then turned and took her place at the table. "After Joseph's death, before Yeshua moved to Capernaum, He went to hear John the Immerser preach. After listening, Yeshua asked John to baptize Him. John refused because he recognized Yeshua for what He was, but

Yeshua said, 'Let it happen now, for in this way it is fitting for us to fulfill all righteousness.' So John yielded to Him and baptized Yeshua in the Jordan." She remained silent a moment, then lifted her head. "Many witnessed what happened next, but I am not sure how we could verify the story unless we ask Peter and Andrew. They were disciples of John, so they should have been there."

I nodded. "Sounds reasonable."

"In any case, after being immersed, Yeshua came out of the water and the heavens opened. He saw the *Ruach Elohim* descending above Him like a dove. A voice from the heavens said, 'This is my Son, the Beloved, in whom I delight.'"

I looked up because the words sounded familiar. "I have heard that phrase before, but in a different situation. Something someone else told me . . ."

"It may be so. But that is not the story no one else knows. What I am about to tell you is something Yeshua told me. I am not certain, but He may have told only me." She paused and pushed at a piece of hair that had fallen over her brow. "As His mother, I can attest that Yeshua was fully human—He hungered, as a child He fell and scraped His knees, and throughout His life He laughed and wept."

"I know."

"But He was also one with God. After John the Immerser baptized Him, the Ruach HaKodesh led Yeshua into the wilderness to be tempted by the devil. For forty days and nights He did not eat, and the ordeal exhausted His body. He lived in human flesh, with all its frailties, and forty days without food left Him ravenous."

I nodded as I made notes. "I understand."

"In his weakened condition, the tempter came to Him and said, 'If You are Ben-Elohim, tell these stones to become bread.' But Yeshua replied, 'It is written, "Man shall not live by bread alone, but by every word that comes from the mouth of God."'"

"Words from the Pentateuch."

Mary continued: "Then the devil took Him into Jerusalem and placed Him on the highest point of the Temple. 'If You are Ben-Elohim,' he said, 'throw Yourself down. For it is written, "He shall command His angels concerning you," and "with their hands they will lift you up, so you may not strike your foot against a stone."'"

"From a psalm," I murmured. "I know it well."

"But Yeshua said to him, 'Again it is written, "You shall not put Adonai your God to the test."'"

"From the Torah.'"

"Then the devil took Him to a high mountain and showed Him all the kingdoms of the world and their glory. And he said, 'All these things I will give you, if you fall down and worship me.'"

"But Yeshua said, 'Go away, Satan! For it is written, "You shall worship Adonai your God, and Him only shall you serve."' Then the devil left Him, and angels came and cared for Yeshua until He was strong enough to journey home."

"Again he quoted from the Torah." I jotted down the phrase. "No one can accuse Yeshua of not knowing the Law."

Moved by the story, and by the knowledge that Yeshua had been tempted by the same desires that enticed other men, I crossed my arms and looked over at Mary. "When you heard this story, did you wish you had been there to protect Him?"

She exhaled softly. "What mother would not give anything to feed her starving child? I would have crumbled at Satan's first offer. I would have said, 'Is it so evil to command stones to be made bread?'" She gave me a slow smile. "How easy it would have been to obey the devil instead of God. Now I see why HaShem kept me away from Yeshua's temptation. But it does us no good to speculate about things that did not occur. And this is not my story. We must keep our work centered on Yeshua."

I jotted another note on my page: *Keep the work focused on Yeshua.* A lesson I should not forget.

I pasted on a bright smile and turned to my co-writer, determined to make our partnership work. "What other stories do we need to include?"

"Let us allow HaShem to tell us on the first day of the week." Mary leaned on the table and gave me a small smile. "Shabbat shalom, Matthew."

Abruptly realizing that I had been dismissed, I stood and gathered my tools. "Shabbat shalom, Ima."

TWELVE

Mary

At the sound of the closing door, Miriam stepped out of her bedchamber and hurried to my side. "Is the pain bad?" She caught my hand. "Shall I make you an herbal tea?"

I lowered myself to the bench, then let my head drop to the table. "Let me sit here a moment." I closed my eyes and savored the cool kiss of the polished wood against my cheek. "I will feel better soon. I only need a little time to rest."

For an instant I feared Miriam would pull me up and beg me to go to bed, but she had lived with me long enough to know I could be stubborn.

"Then praise HaShem for Shabbat."

A moment later I heard the snap and pop of fresh fuel on the fire, followed by the sound of a crockery lid settling onto a clay pot.

"I will make you something to eat. The vegetables are already cut, so we shall have a Shabbat stew." Miriam's voice floated toward me. "After you eat, you will go to bed."

Through a haze of exhaustion, I managed to smile. "Yes, Miriam. After prayers, I will."

working out a peaceful resolution, if a solution can be found.

Petronius's last report to Caesar indicated that he will take his army to Ptolemais and winter there, intending to march on Jerusalem in the spring of next year. Caesar has approved Petronius's plan and applauded his apparent eagerness, so unless the Jews of Jerusalem obey Caesar's command, many will die in the coming months.

I know you have friends who have the ear of Jews in leadership positions. Please use this news as the Lord gives you wisdom, and do what you can to save our brothers, the children of Israel.

One more thought, which I share with great discretion: our emperor Gaius Caesar is but two score and seven years old. Imagine one so young with so much power.

Your faithful servant,
Achiakos

I held the scroll aloft and searched for the meaning behind Achiakos's last comment. I knew he held no love for this Caesar, nor did he admire the man. He could not write plainly, lest his epistle fall into the wrong hands, so what was he trying to say?

I closed my eyes as realization struck. Achiakos was warning me that we could not outlast this egotistical madman. Caligula was not sickly, nor was he aged, so he was unlikely to die before his determination to destroy Jerusalem passed away.

I felt the pressure of James's gaze as I rerolled the scroll. "Your friend sends good news, I hope."

I shook my head. "Achiakos writes that Petronius now has four legions under his command. He is in Syria, and he has hired men in Sidon to create that abominable statue." I gave James a wry look. "He has told the Sidonians to take their time and work with great care. In the interval, Petronius is marching his army to Ptolemais, where he will spend the winter. Apparently, we have six months to negotiate some sort of peace with Caesar's envoy."

John's shoulders braced and broadened, accepting the burden of this latest news. "I will alert the Temple authorities and the high priest. As far as we are concerned, we will continue to pray . . . and we will refrain from spreading this report. It may be that our prayers and Petronius's efforts may stave off this tragedy."

"Our prayers have been effective before," I said, trying to maintain a positive attitude.

"Yet the Maccabees were forced to pick up swords," James countered. "Let us hope that Caesar's order does not result in bloodshed."

As John walked away, I slipped the scroll into my girdle, then tilted it so my mantle would cover it while I visited Mary. The woman had enough on her mind. Our project seemed to be sapping her strength, and if our prayers did not work to stop Caesar, we had less than six months to finish.

Mary and I had spent many days talking, several hours arguing, and little time writing. By the time we finally reached agreement and prepared to finalize words on papyrus, time might be scarce indeed.

Mary was reading my draft of the story about Yeshua calming the storm when Peter and John arrived at her house.

All morning I had been distracted by thoughts of Achiakos and Gaius Caesar, so I barely heard Mary's comments about the writing.

Grateful for the interruption provided by Peter and John, I put away my tools and papyri. Miriam set barley cakes, pickled fish, stuffed grape leaves, and honey on the table. As the five of us sat and ate, our conversation centered on Petronius and Gaius Caesar.

"What will this threat mean for the new believers?" John asked, drizzling honey over his bread. "They are young in the faith—I would hate for them to fall away over a toothless threat."

Peter took the honey pot from John. "Yeshua warned us. Remember the parable of the sower? The seed that falls on rocky ground lasts only a little while because it has no root. When trouble or persecution comes, immediately that plant withers."

"The threat does not seem toothless to an earthly-minded man," I pointed out. "Though our eternal life is secured, some believers' faith goes only as deep as their earthly lives—and Caesar's armies could easily snuff those out."

"Then let us hope the situation is peacefully resolved." John lifted his cup. "James and I are praying that Caesar's edict will come to nothing."

"How?" I asked.

John shrugged. "HaShem knows."

"I have heard," Peter said, "that this Petronius is studying our religion. If this is so, surely he understands why we cannot allow a graven image in our Temple." He rested his arms on the table and looked at me. "Which reminds me—how goes the work on Yeshua's story?"

"Slowly." As Miriam cleared away the remains of our

meal, I reached for my satchel. "I am glad you and John have come by. Mary and I wanted to ask you about the time Yeshua went into Jairus's house to visit his sick daughter. You two went with Him; I did not, and neither did Mary."

"We are not likely to forget that day." Peter looked at Mary and chuckled. "Jairus, you may remember, was the leader of the Capernaum synagogue. When he approached Yeshua, tongues began to wag."

"While he was speaking to the Master," John added, "one of his servants approached and said the girl was dead, so there was no need to bother the Teacher. But Yeshua heard and said, 'Do not be afraid—just believe, and she will be healed.'"

"I remember that much," I said. "But when we reached the house, Yeshua allowed only you, James, and the girl's parents to go inside with Him."

Peter shrugged. "There was no room for anyone else. We had to wade through a sea of mourners to get to the girl's bedchamber. Once Jairus arrived, the mourners wailed mightily—he was a wealthy man, and they wanted to prove they were worth their wages. But Yeshua looked at them and said, 'Do not weep. She did not die but is sleeping.'"

"Their wailing turned to laughter." John shook his head. "They mocked Him—who was He to question what was obvious to all? I saw the girl, and I had to agree with the mourners. Her skin was pale, her lips blue, her chest motionless. The spirit of life had deserted her. But Yeshua took her hand and said, 'Child, get up.' In that instant, her spirit returned—I saw breath animate her body and her flesh colored. She sat up, and Yeshua told her parents to get her something to eat. Then He told them not to say anything about what had happened."

"Why?" I looked from Peter to John. "Why did He not want anyone to know?"

"He was hiding His face." Mary spoke so softly I wondered if she was talking to herself, but she was intently looking at me.

"He had worked miracles in public before," I said, turning away from Mary's penetrating eyes. "So people knew He had power."

"Not power over death." John tugged on his beard. "Do you remember how word of Lazarus's resurrection incensed the Temple authorities? I think Yeshua told Jairus to remain silent because if the authorities had heard of the girl's resurrection, they would have realized what we were just beginning to understand. HaShem alone holds the power of life and death, so Yeshua had to be the Messiah and Son of the Most High."

"The time was early," Mary said, her gaze drifting toward the courtyard. "He still had furlongs to walk, and others to lead into the kingdom of God. He knew His time would come soon enough. But"—she sent me a warning look—"we will not speculate in our stories. We will report what we saw, what we heard, and nothing else."

Quietly, I noted her words on my papyrus.

FOURTEEN

Mary

I lowered the papyrus Matthew had left on the table for me to read. "You have done a lot of work." I slid the page toward him. "You did not write on Shabbat, I hope."

"Of course not." The smile he gave me brimmed with confidence. "So, what do you think? Is it not a faithful accounting of Yeshua's temptation?"

I drew a deep breath. "Yes . . . and no."

His smile faded. "What do you mean?"

"Here." I ran my finger over the first lines. "You wrote, 'After Yeshua fasted for forty long days and forty nights, He knew hunger He had never known before. And when the wily tempter came to Him, the wicked one stepped forward and said—'"

"What is wrong with that?"

I lowered the page and sighed. "Forty long days? A day is a day; it is neither long nor short."

shepherds who came to see us in Bethlehem, and the wise men who brought gifts to sustain us during our sojourn in Egypt. I wish we could speak to Simeon, the old man who had been promised he would not die until he saw the Anointed One of Adonai. And Anna, the prophetess who worshiped night and day in the Temple. She took one look at our baby and gave thanks to God, proclaiming HaShem's faithfulness to all who were waiting for the redemption of Jerusalem . . ."

Matthew lifted his hand, his way of urging me to wait, so I remained silent until he finished writing. Then he looked up. "Anything else unusual happen when you offered your purification offering?"

My thoughts returned to the scene of that long-ago encounter. "Simeon said something to us," I said, uttering words I had not shared with anyone since that day. "He said, 'Behold, this One is destined to cause the fall and rise of many in Israel, and to be a sign that is opposed, so the thoughts of many hearts may be uncovered.' And then"—my throat tightened—"he looked at me and said, 'And even for you, a sword will pierce through your soul.'"

I lowered my gaze, unable to speak further as the words resonated in the space between us. Either Matthew would understand or he wouldn't, but I wanted the truth to be clear: from the beginning, I had known Yeshua would not be universally loved and exalted. Despite the prophecies about our coming King and an eternal kingdom and power and glory, I knew we would have to endure a dark season of the soul. Through Simeon, HaShem had warned me, perhaps to prevent me from later protesting my Son's fate.

A wave of conflicting emotions played across Matthew's face. "That is . . . terrible and alarming, and I cannot imagine how it made you feel. Did you wonder if HaShem had made a mistake? Or if you had misunderstood?"

I lifted my chin. "When Gabriel appeared to me, I told him I was a servant of Adonai. What right has a servant to question her master's will?"

Matthew made a clicking sound with his teeth and wrote on his papyrus. "Were there any other important developments that day?"

"Only one," I whispered, wondering if he would understand the realization I had hidden away for forty years.

Matthew looked up, his face expectant. "And that was . . . ?"

"Wrapped in the flesh of a baby, the glory of HaShem returned to the Temple."

FIFTEEN

Matthew

I sat at the table with an open scroll before me—the writings of Daniel, who had been taken captive to Babylon more than six hundred years ago. The archangel Gabriel, who also visited Mary, appeared to Daniel at the time of the evening offering. I had read the angel's message many times, but after praying for understanding, I read it again:

> *"Seventy weeks are decreed concerning your people and your holy city,*
> *to put an end to transgression*
> *to bring sin to an end,*
> *to atone for iniquity,*
> *to bring in everlasting righteousness,*
> *to seal up vision and prophecy,*
> *and to anoint the Holy of Holies.*
> *So know and understand:*
> *From the issuing of the decree to restore and to build Jerusalem until the time of Mashiach the Prince, there shall be seven weeks and sixty-two weeks.*

It will be rebuilt, with plaza and moat, but it will be in times of distress.

Then after the sixty-two weeks, Mashiach will be cut off and have nothing.

Then the people of a prince who is to come will destroy the city and the sanctuary."

Mary had worn a troubled expression when she told me she pondered this prophecy not long after she and Joseph presented the infant Yeshua at the Temple. "I do not understand all of it," she said, gripping her hands. "But since it mentions the Messiah, I knew it applied to Yeshua. And though the prophecy is about weeks of *years*, one afternoon Joseph and I counted the days—and, as always, the Word of the Lord is true and filled with patterns."

I shifted my gaze from the text to her face. "What do you mean?"

"From the day of the angel's appearance to Zechariah in the Temple," she said, "to the day Gabriel appeared to me was one hundred eighty days. From the day I was overshadowed by the Ruach HaKodesh to Yeshua's birth was two hundred seventy days. From the day of Yeshua's birth until the day Joseph and I went to the Temple was forty days."

I blinked, confused. "So from the day of the angel's appearance to Zechariah to the day you took Yeshua to the Temple was—"

"Four hundred ninety days," she had whispered, her face glowing. "Seventy weeks."

I stared at the numbers I had scratched on a scrap of papyrus: she was right. But all the Torah teachers knew the Daniel prophecy was about *years*, not days, and the decree to rebuild Jerusalem went forth in the time of Cyrus, in the month Nisan, in the twentieth year of Artaxerxes the king. Over four hundred years had passed since that decree . . .

Could Yeshua's death—when he was "cut off"—have occurred after sixty-nine weeks of years?

I sighed. "I regret I am not a better Torah scholar."

"Joseph and I could not fully understand it, either," Mary said. "Yet Joseph did teach me about patterns."

I frowned. The word echoed in my memory; some Torah teacher probably mentioned patterns in one of my lessons. Still, what had Joseph taught Mary, and how did it apply to Daniel's prophecy?"

"Tell me." I shifted on the bench to face her. "Tell me what Joseph said."

With her finger, Mary traced the figure of a man on the top of the table. "Adam," she said. "HaShem blessed him, told him to be fruitful, and to subdue the land."

I nodded.

She drew another figure. "Abraham. When HaShem covenanted with Abram, He blessed him, told him to be fruitful, and to subdue the land."

I stared at the table, then caught my breath. "We could say the same thing about Israel entering the Promised Land. HaShem blessed them, told them to be fruitful, and to subdue the land."

"Exactly." Her eyes sparkled. "It is a pattern. We see a different one when HaShem wanted to destroy Sodom and Gomorrah. He warned the people in those cities, He removed the righteous, then He destroyed the unrighteous because they had done nothing but evil."

"Like Noah," I said, grasping the pattern. "HaShem warned the people, He removed righteous Noah, and then He destroyed the people because they had done nothing but evil."

"Do you see?" Mary crossed her arms and dropped onto the bench. "Even if Daniel wrote about weeks of years, the prophecy holds true in weeks of *days*. It is a pattern."

I tugged on my beard, suddenly wishing Yeshua were with us. He had always been able to explain the Scripture, and He spoke with complete authority.

"Patterns." I transferred my gaze to the scroll of Daniel, which contained prophecies about the end of days, sealed books, and other mysteries. I rolled the scroll until I reached the "Son of Man" passage, then read aloud:

> "'I was watching in the night visions.
> Behold, One like a Son of Man,
> coming with the clouds of heaven.
> He approached the Ancient of Days,
> and was brought into His presence.
> Dominion, glory and sovereignty were given to Him
> that all peoples, nations, and languages should serve Him.
> His dominion is an everlasting dominion that will never pass away,
> and His kingdom is one that will not be destroyed.'"

I lifted my finger from the passage and looked at Mary. "Yeshua never claimed to be the Messiah when He was teaching in Judea. He told the Samaritan woman He was Messiah, but when among the Jews, He called himself 'Son of Man.'"

Mary held me in a thoughtful scrutiny. "I believe you are right," she said after a moment. "He spoke freely with the twelve of you, but with the people, He remained hidden."

"Why?" I asked. "I know you have said it was because His time had not yet come, but even at the end of His life,

He remained silent. When He brought Jairus's daughter back from the dead, He charged her parents to remain silent. When demons came out of the possessed, *they* called Him Messiah, yet He commanded them to remain quiet. Why?"

Mary stared at me a moment, then opened another scroll on the table, the writings of Isaiah. She put her finger on a passage.

"'He is despised,'" she read aloud, running her fingertip over the words, "'and left of men, a man of pains and acquainted with sickness. And as one hiding the face from us, He is despised and we esteemed him not.'" She lifted her head and looked at me. "Isaiah wrote of the suffering Messiah. Do you see it? He hid his face from us."

"But why?"

"I do not understand," she said, "but HaShem does."

To my surprise, when I arrived at Peter's house, I discovered he had guests. James and John were with Peter in the front room and so was Nicodemus, a believing Pharisee and a member of the Sanhedrin. I had met the esteemed scholar some years before, but because John, Peter, and James were deep in conversation, I greeted him with a silent nod.

"Matthew, we are glad you have come." James gestured to a spot at the table. "Nicodemus has brought disturbing news."

I lifted a brow as I joined them. "From Jerusalem?"

Nicodemus nodded. "From the high priest's household. Though John has been sharing your friend's information with Theophilus and his household, apparently the high priest has not taken the reports seriously—probably because they came from the community of believers. But a Roman centurion visited the high priest last week and confirmed that Petronius and two legions have recently arrived in Syria, where they have begun training exercises."

John frowned. "So the news from Achiakos is correct."

"Indeed." Nicodemus stroked his beard. "Furthermore, the camp prefect, a veteran called Severus, is actively recruiting Samaritans to serve in the auxiliaries. Theophilus is concerned that training Samaritans to wage war on Jerusalem will stoke the fires of long-held animosity between our peoples."

"Wait." I lifted my hand, wanting to better understand. "We have been open and forthcoming with Theophilus. Six years have passed since Stephen was martyred, and now we worship freely in the Temple. There should be no animosity between the high priest and those of us who believe—"

Nicodemus interrupted, his voice sharp. "Do not mistake silence for agreement." His gaze softened when he looked at me. "Have you met our current high priest?"

I shook my head. "I have been working in Caesarea."

"Theophilus is a genial man," Nicodemus went on. "Some say he is too gentle to hold the office, and that may be true. But he is only a shadow—the power behind the *cohen gadol* has not changed since Yeshua's day. Annas still rules the high priest's house, and he has learned he cannot resist the power of the Ruach HaKodesh. But he does not support us and never will. He tolerates us only because he fears a revolt among the people—a revolt Rome would feel compelled to crush."

I fell silent as the other men glanced at each other. "I know Theophilus," John finally said. "And Nicodemus is right.

While the high priest has been polite and even grateful to receive the information we have given him, I am certain he has taken that knowledge to his father."

"And Annas is not the sort of man who will sit back, trust HaShem, and pray," Nicodemus added. "He will try to manipulate the situation for his advantage, you can be sure of that. He will work behind the scenes, he will write letters to the powers in Rome, he will bribe and cajole, whatever he must in order to achieve his ends. So whatever we do, brethren, we must not think we are resisting Rome alone. Annas will work as well, and if he is clever, he will find a way to silence both his enemies."

I blinked. "Both enemies?"

The older man nodded. "Rome and the followers of the Way."

Silence filled the room for a moment, then a sudden thought struck me. "Say—" I looked around the circle—"have any of you noticed someone following you?"

Peter, James, and John looked at each other, then all three burst into laughter. "Why would anyone follow us?" Peter said, teeth gleaming in his beard. "We have nothing to hide from anyone."

Nicodemus, however, did not laugh. "Has anyone been following you, my young friend?"

I shrugged, feeling sheepish. "I thought perhaps, but I was probably wrong."

As Peter stood, ending our meeting, Nicodemus leaned forward and pressed his hand to my arm. "Be careful, Matthew. Jerusalem may be the Holy City, but a fair number of rats reside within her walls."

Several weeks later, in early fall, a visitor from Rome arrived at Peter's house. This was not the usual pilgrim, however, but Lemuel, assistant to Achiakos.

I found him reclining on a dining couch, a cup of honey water in his hand and a platter of honey cakes on the table. Dina stood behind him, earnestly asking if he needed anything else.

The sight displeased me for reasons I could not name.

When Dina looked up and saw me, her cheeks went the color of pomegranates. "Here he is," she said, backing away. "This is Matthew."

The young man on the couch abruptly stood, nearly spilling his cup. "Greetings, Matthew," he said, unabashedly meeting my gaze. "I am Lemuel, a servant of your friend Achiakos."

I nodded. "I have heard of you. Have things become so dire that Achiakos no longer trusts his messengers?"

Lemuel dipped his chin in a quick nod. "He sent me on the fastest, most direct ship and charged me to come straight to Jerusalem after landing at Caesarea. My master has given me explicit instructions about what I am to say to you."

I gestured to the couch he had so swiftly vacated. "Sit, Lemuel, and speak freely. You are among friends here."

I sat on a couch opposite the young man and crossed my arms, noticing that Dina did not leave the room. Again, displeasure rose within me.

Lemuel fumbled in his traveling pouch and pulled out a sheaf of papers.

"How is it," I asked, "that Achiakos does not trust a written letter, yet you carry a written message? Is it not possible that you could have been robbed and the message intercepted?"

"The speaker for the group—"

"Do you know who that was?"

Lemuel frowned. "I am sorry, but I do not. I know only that the man was a Levite."

I waved the matter away. "Please continue."

"The Jews' spokesman said that just as Petronius could not disobey Caesar's law, neither could they disobey their Law. Furthermore, their Law had been established by God for their advantage, and they believed they could face dangers with a good hope of escaping them because God would stand on their side. But if they submitted to Petronius and allowed the emperor's statue, they would incur the anger of their God, who was far superior and more powerful than Gaius Caesar."

"Their leader spoke well," I murmured, glancing up. I thought the young man would be looking in my direction, but his head had turned toward the kitchen, where Dina was helping Anna prepare a meal.

"Lemuel?"

The man's head snapped toward me. "Yes?"

"Is that the end of the matter?"

He seemed to search his memory, then lifted his hand. "There is one other matter. After Petronius saw their resolve, he took his retinue to Tiberias, where he could see how the ordinary Jews of the land regarded the matter. The contingent who had met with him at Ptolemais dispersed, but we have heard they plan to confront him again at Tiberias. My master Achiakos will also go to Tiberias, because King Agrippa wants a firsthand report of all that transpires when the Jews confront the governor a second time. Achiakos would like you to meet him in that city, if it is possible, because he would appreciate your insight."

I rested my chin in my hand and let my thoughts wander. I

would like to see Achiakos again, but I did not think I would be able to leave Jerusalem in the near future. Mary was intent on finishing the scroll as soon as possible, and Peter and John might need my assistance in preaching . . .

"Thank you, Lemuel." I stood, formally ending our visit.

"Do you have a reply for my master?"

"When you see your master again, tell him I am not certain I will be able to see him in Tiberias. But I will continue to pray that this situation will resolve without bloodshed."

Lemuel stood, dipped his head toward me in a sign of respect, and turned toward the doorway, but not without a quick glance into the kitchen.

I followed him to the door, eager to see him safely away.

As always, I shared the information from Achiakos with Peter, James Zebedee, John, and James the Just. John made notes and took them to the high priest, so the religious authorities could remain informed about the situation.

"The high priest's assistant thanked me," John reported when we met again at Peter's house, "and said Theophilus was responsible for sending the contingent to Ptolemais. The same men are now at Tiberias, waiting to be granted an audience with the governor. The group—and there are many thousands of them—has filled the city and will not leave until they have confronted Petronius again."

"Good." James the Just nodded, his mouth set in a grim line. "If it is HaShem's will that we perish, at least we will have been faithful to the end."

"I cannot believe the news has not spread throughout the city," I said. "If the delegation was really as large as ten thousand men—"

"Theophilus summoned leading scholars from throughout Judea," John said, stroking his beard. "I am sure he ordered them to keep quiet. He does not want to induce panic and fear among the people of Jerusalem."

Peter shook his head. "Yet I cannot forget what Yeshua said—'So when you see the abomination of desolation standing in the Holy Place . . .'"

"If these are the last days," James said, "then let us be busy spreading the Gospel. Nothing else is as important."

After Peter led us in prayer, our meeting broke up. As the others went out to the courtyard, talking among themselves, I leaned against the wall and thought of my family. I had not seen my mother and father in years, so the chasm between us was broad and deep. But if HaShem allowed Caesar to march on Jerusalem in the spring, would I ever see them again? As James said, these might well be our final days, our last opportunities to share the good news with our loved ones . . .

"Would you like some honey water?"

The soft voice startled me. I turned and saw Dina standing beside me, a pitcher and cup in her hand. "Oh! I did not see you."

A dimple winked in her cheek. "You seemed miles away."

"Not miles, years. I was thinking of my family."

"Do they live in Jerusalem?"

"In Sepphoris. But the fall festivals are approaching, and my father always comes to Jerusalem for Sukkot."

She poured water into the cup and handed it to me. "I am sure he will be happy to see you."

"Hmmm." I accepted the cup. "Thank you."

She lingered as if expecting me to say something else, but my mind had taken a dark turn with the mention of my father. She probably thought I parted from him when I followed Yeshua, yet we had parted long before that.

I would count it a miracle if my father wanted to see me at all.

"Levi? Wake, my son."

My eyes flew open, summoned from sleep by my father's rumbling voice. For an instant I blinked at the ceiling, stunned from the abrupt shift from dreams to wakefulness. Then my tongue recalled the words I was to speak: "I am thankful before you, living and enduring King, for you have . . . you have . . . mercifully restored my soul within me. Great is your faithfulness."

"Now wash. You do not know what you may have touched while you slept."

Blinking rapidly, I rolled out of my small bed and stumbled to the basin where I lifted the heavy pitcher and splashed my hands three times. When I had finished, I stood straight beside my bed, struggling to recall the next words I was supposed to say.

"You have forgotten to urinate."

The stern warning propelled me to the pot in the corner of the room. I stood before it, still drowsy, and felt the room sway until I commanded my body to cooperate. Finally, a stream of urine.

"And now?"

I turned and faced my father, who towered like a shadow before the door. "What?"

"To the basin."

I trudged to the basin where again I lifted the pitcher and splashed my hands three times. I turned and recited another morning prayer: "The fear of Adonai is the beginning of wisdom. All who follow His precepts have good understanding. His praise endures forever! Blessed are you, HaShem, our God, King of the universe, who formed man with wisdom and created many openings and cavities within him. It is obvious and known before your throne of glory that if any one of them were closed, or if any one of them were opened, it would be impossible to exist for even an hour. Blessed are you, HaShem, who heals all flesh and does wondrous things."

I closed my eyes and waited for Abba's correction, but none came. I opened one eye and peered at him as if he were a pot that might suddenly boil over.

"Abba?"

My father shook his head, coming back from wherever he had been, and glared down his nose at me. "What?"

"Did I say it right?"

He scoffed and turned away. "You are slow. You have so much more to learn."

Without another word, he left my chamber. Ima slipped into the space he had vacated. "You did well, Levi." She held out her arms and smiled when I ran into them. "You must not be hard on yourself. You will learn your prayers when the time is right. You cannot be faulted for your sickness."

"Will I ever catch up to the other boys?"

"Of course, dear one." She teased my tousled hair with her fingertips. "You are a smart boy, and you will learn everything in due time."

I tightened my grip around her neck. "I wish I had never been sick."

"No, son, you must not say that. For a long time we thought we might lose you, but HaShem spared your life. So if you are behind the other boys, know this: we count it a blessing to have you with us at all. Now stand up and let us get some food into your belly."

I followed her into the kitchen, where my father sat at the table and my grandmother sliced bread. I climbed onto the bench opposite my father and kept my eyes lowered until he had finished eating.

"Study, Levi," he said, standing. "Make us proud of you."

I clasped my hands under the table and watched him go, wondering if I would ever be able to please him.

I was bent over a sheet of papyrus at Mary's table when I heard the door open and close. Mary glanced up, and the startled look on her face compelled me to turn and see who had come in.

Miriam stood behind me, a water jar in her arms, her headscarf askew. She looked at Mary with wide eyes, then shot a glance at me before coming toward us. "I would not have believed it," she said, setting the heavy jar on the table, "if I had not heard it myself."

Mary put her hand over Miriam's. "Sit, have some water, calm yourself. What did you hear?"

Miriam sat, but I was sure it would take more than a cup of water to calm her. She glanced at me again, then shook her head. "I overheard women talking at the well . . . about you."

Mary lifted a brow. "They were talking about Matthew?"

"No, *you*!" Miriam blew out an exasperated breath. "I know you are not offended by what people say, but I cannot help being upset when I hear false rumors and stories. Those women have no business speculating, no reason to mistrust or criticize you—"

project, but a professional scribe was assisting her—assisting you." He frowned. "Is this true?"

I transferred my gaze to Damaris, who did not seem at all offended by the idea. "I am assembling a collection of stories about Yeshua's life. True stories, attested to by eyewitnesses."

Shimon leaned forward. "Have you actually employed a scribe?"

"Matthew is assisting me. We are working together to write and compile stories of the things Yeshua said and did."

Shimon looked at his daughters as if mentally calculating the risk of my work to their future betrothal contracts.

After a moment, he turned back to me. "What you are doing is dangerous. Must I remind you that the Temple elders once arrested Peter and John? Another time they arrested and *flogged* the Twelve. Stephen was stoned. What makes you think they will not arrest you?"

"They have not arrested followers of the Way in years." I shrugged. "And HaShem protects those who believe in His Son. If trouble comes, I am content to receive HaShem's will, whatever it may be."

Shimon waved my comments away. "I know the esteemed Gamaliel said the authorities should leave the believers alone and wait to see if Yeshua's movement was of men or of God. But the disciples were not writing scrolls! They were not recording papyri that could easily be carried to Jews of the Diaspora, papyri that could outlive this generation. A scroll is a dangerous thing, and you, venerable lady, should not be involved in such a risky undertaking. Besides, you are not a prophet. What led you to believe you could write a scroll?"

"I have never claimed to be a prophet." I shifted my gaze and smiled at my three granddaughters, who were intently following the conversation. "Prophets claim to speak for Adonai, and I make no such claim. I am simply recording true accounts of Yeshua. Someone must leave a record before the stories are lost."

Shimon shook his head. "You should rest in your old age and rejoice because you have been faithful to your mission from HaShem."

"I will rest in Paradise. And then—" A chortle cut off my words, emerging from someplace beneath my breastbone, bubbling up through my throat and finally erupting into rich laughter. Damaris gaped at me, and my granddaughters stared, eyes bulging from their faces, until they laughed, too.

Shimon did not see the humor in the situation. His posture stiffened and his face brightened. By the time my laughter trailed off into sighing, his lips had tightened and disappeared in his beard.

"Shimon—" I coughed, finding it difficult to catch my breath— "is it not possible that HaShem might give me another task? Did He call David only to kill a giant? Did He call Gideon to fight only one battle? Did He call Moses to perform only one miracle?"

Shimon sputtered, his eyes narrowing.

"No." I spoke before he could answer. "HaShem speaks as long as we are willing to listen, and I am willing even now . . . in what you see as my *advanced* age."

Damaris stared at me as if I had suddenly begun to speak a foreign tongue, and for once Shimon remained silent.

I stood and opened my arms to my granddaughters. "Come, girls, and let's get your father something to drink. He looks as if he could use some refreshment."

SEVENTEEN

Matthew

The next afternoon, James the Just came to visit his mother. Mary greeted him warmly, as did Miriam, then Mary took his arm and pulled him toward our worktable. "I know you have come for a friendly visit," she said, guiding him to a bench, "but Matthew and I would like to ask you about a few things. I hope you will be able to help us."

He sat, but looked quickly from his mother to me, a question in his eyes. "I assume this involves your project," he said, giving me a lopsided smile. "I hope I am not in any of these stories."

Mary sat across from him. "These are stories about Yeshua," she said simply. "That is our entire purpose. But I do not remember much about His youth because He spent most of His time with Joseph. You are only a year younger than Yeshua, so you were often with Him. Tell me, son—can you think of any story we should include in this collection?"

James leaned forward, pushed damp hair off his brow,

and frowned at the stack of papyri. "So much has happened since our childhood. Those years are vague in my memory."

"For me as well," Mary said. "That is exactly why I am eager to get these stories recorded. Think—surely there is something you remember."

He closed his eyes for a moment, then snapped them open. "The year we lost Him in Jerusalem—I will never forget that."

Mary nodded. "I knew you would remember something." She looked at me. "We went to Jerusalem for Passover, of course. That year Yeshua would have been twelve; James, eleven."

"We were traveling with a large group from Nazareth," James said, picking up the story. "There were nine in our family, and we were scattered among friends. After the feast, our group left the homes where we stayed and departed. We traveled a full day, then stopped to make camp for the night. Abba and Ima searched for Yeshua but could not find Him. They asked us if we'd seen Him, and none of us had. So Abba sent the rest of us home with neighbors while he and Ima went back to find our missing brother."

I smiled and scratched a few notes, imagining the confusion of a weary traveling party. Surely Yeshua was not the first child to be left behind.

I glanced at Mary. "Was it difficult to find Him?"

Her mouth twitched. "Is it difficult to find a coin in a mountain of sand? Joseph and I went everywhere—the house where we had stayed, the marketplace, the Temple. That's where we found Him. Out on the southern steps, near the mikvehs. There He stood before a dozen or so Torah teachers, answering—and asking—questions."

"How did you feel—?" I bit my lip, knowing Mary would tell me her feelings did not matter. "What happened next?"

Men shouted questions at the man on the stone, and that fellow lifted both hands to call for calm. "I am Nadiv ben Aaron," he said, placing one hand on his chest. "You all know me. I have just returned from the Temple, where the news is spreading like a fever."

"What news?"

"Are they increasing our taxes?"

"Did the high priest die?"

"Out with your report! Be it good or bad, let us hear it!"

Nadiv lifted his hands again. "If you will all be quiet, I will share what I heard this morning. After that, you will have to go to the Temple to see if there is additional news."

The group fell silent, but even from where I stood, I could feel a palpable tension in the air.

"The high priest," Nadiv began, "sent a delegation of Levites to meet with Gaius Caesar in Rome. By all reports, with great respect these ambassadors explained that we Jews worship an invisible God who cannot be represented by a graven image. We would consider any graven image blasphemous if it were erected on the Temple Mount, and we would defend the sanctity of our Temple with our lives. Yet Caesar, who wants to erect his statue in our Temple—"

Like blood out of a wound, furious cries poured into the morning air.

"What?"

"He would desecrate our Temple?"

"HaShem, this is too much! Why do you allow us to suffer under the Gentiles?"

I heard the sound of tearing garments, then Nadiv held up his hands again. "Why does Caesar want to do this thing? Because he heard about what happened at Jamnia."

A hush fell over the group, and men cast knowing looks at

one another. I knew Jamnia as a city between Joppa and Ashdod, a town with a large population of Greeks. But I did not know what the people of Jamnia had done to anger Caesar.

I turned to Matthew and spoke in a low voice. "What happened at Jamnia?"

He bent closer. "The Gentiles erected a statue to honor Caesar, but the Jewish residents destroyed it. Apparently word of the destruction made its way to Rome."

"Of course it did. The city is near the port, so word was probably on its way the next day."

Matthew tugged at his beard as the man on the stone clapped for attention.

"Because Caesar had heard about the actions done by the Jews of Jamnia," he said, "he looked at our delegation and proclaimed that as the divine emperor, *he* deserved our worship, not some unseen God. Then he informed them that a golden sculpture of his likeness would soon be transported to Jerusalem, along with two legions of his army. We will bow before his likeness or we will die."

"Is there nothing to be done?"

Nadiv shook his head. "Theophilus sent an even larger delegation to meet with Petronius, hoping our men could persuade the governor to disobey Caesar's order, but they have not been successful. Petronius, while receptive to our situation, knows he will perish if he does not obey Caesar's command to destroy us."

A flutter of alarm rippled through the listeners, and even though I knew about the situation, the icy hand of fear touched the base of my spine. News of this threat had not yet spread throughout the city, yet nothing would stop it now. People would talk of little else. While no one wanted war, the alternative was unthinkable.

We had grown up hearing stories of the brave Maccabees, who fought against the pagan Seleucids who tried to outlaw our worship and our observance of our Law. After defeating the pagan army, the righteous Maccabees cleansed our defiled Temple and reestablished our worship, but a few generations later another enemy came at us. The first Herod, backed by the Romans, lay siege to Jerusalem and killed our people until no one remained but old men, women, and children.

Herod entered and declared himself king with the Romans' blessing. Though Herod, an Idumaean, was bitterly resented, he did his best to endear himself to the Jews. His greatest effort to win our favor was the restoration and renovation of our Temple. We did love the new Temple, but we never loved Herod.

Now Rome ruled Judea through a system of procurators, governors, and puppets. We resented them as earnestly as we had resented Herod, but this new Caesar, this Caligula, was reportedly more intemperate and volatile than his predecessors.

I clutched Matthew's sleeve. "What will happen now that the people know?"

Watching the assembly disperse, Matthew pressed his lips together. "Families will begin to make choices—some will flee Jerusalem, and some will stay, depending I suppose on the depth of their faith."

"Faith in HaShem?"

"Faith in HaShem's determination to save His people."

We went back into the house, but I could not shake a sense of foreboding. What if those women at the well were right? What if I was wasting my time? What if all this work amounted to nothing? Yeshua could come back before we were finished . . . or, if we did finish, the Romans could attack the city and destroy us before we could distribute our completed work.

I sat, chin propped in my hand, and moodily stared at the surface of the table. Joseph had built this table before we married. As a baby, Yeshua sat on this table while I ground grain. James studied Torah here, and Damaris sat on this bench while I taught her to sew. Everyone in my family had worked, eaten, and relaxed around this simple piece of furniture. Now Matthew and I labored at it, striving to complete a record of Yeshua's life before we ran out of time. Before I ran out of life.

Matthew did not know about my illness, nor did Peter or John. Miriam knew, and my physician. My son James knew, and he had prayed over me, asking HaShem for a miracle that did not come.

I did not fault HaShem for His silence. Long ago I learned that His ways were not my ways, and His ways were inexplicable.

Let it be done to me according to your will.

I looked over at Matthew, who was preparing his ink and papyri. "I am nearly sixty," I reminded him. "If the Romans descend on Jerusalem, I may not live even threescore years."

"Do not let your faith waver." He lifted his chin. "We have put our hands to this work, and we know the Spirit of God has led us to do it. So we will not stop, nor will we doubt. We will trust HaShem to give us what we need to continue."

I inhaled a deep breath, then folded my hands and smiled. Young Matthew, formerly Levi, had just reminded an older woman of what he had learned from Yeshua.

"May it be as you say, my young friend."

hair and a clean face, at first glance I could be mistaken for a Syrian or even a Greek.

By the second week, another man was missing five coins, and desperation filled his eyes as he searched frantically around the barracks. Oddly enough, the trainee who had been missing one coin no longer complained about his lack.

We should not have been surprised when other trainees began to work together. Twice we were challenged by rival alliances, who accused us of stealing from their purses, and both times we were able to repel their attacks. Yet I could not have prevailed without Achiakos, who possessed nearly twice my size and strength.

Every day Achiakos and I counted our coins, then buried our purses in the hard clay beneath our beds. Taking turns, so we did not leave our purses unguarded, we stripped down to loincloths and sweated in the sun, throwing the hasta and wielding heavy wooden swords designed to build muscle and strength. The legionaries of the Antonia Fortress were only too happy to spar with us, effortlessly wresting our weapons from our hands, knocking us off our feet, and taunting us with ribald laughter and creative curses. Every night Achiakos and I counted our coins, then examined our bruised limbs and told ourselves we would be better off returning home to our fathers.

But every morning we rose, tied our coin purses to our belts, and took our place in the courtyard. I could not believe we were willing to spend another day sweating and groaning as professional soldiers bruised our bodies and deflated our egos.

At the end of the six weeks, Achiakos and I handed in our purses and watched like hawks as a clerk counted our coins and announced that we had kept Rome's money safe.

Not all the trainees were so lucky. Two came up short—one by six coins, another by two—and both were tied to a stake and flogged until their backs were bloody. Those two, Felix announced, would not be continuing to Caesarea with the rest of us.

With great relief, Achiakos and I shed our military tunics and prepared for the next phase of training. We would travel to the capital of Roman Judea, where we would spend two months learning how to keep Roman records, write in the Roman style, and collect Rome's share of taxes. "You will profit according to how much you collect *above* Rome's portion," Felix told us, his lips curving in an expression that hardly deserved to be called a smile. "Your income will depend upon your appetite for wealth."

Achiakos and I no longer looked like Jewish youths, we were no longer afraid to fight, and we no longer felt we were worthless. We were, however, fast friends.

When we finished our training in Caesarea, we would be skilled accountants, tax collectors, and scribes, familiar with Roman sensibilities and eligible for a number of coveted posts in the empire. Felix told us that Roman officials assigned to Judea desperately wanted Jewish servants because we were familiar with the language and the customs of the people.

On the journey to Caesarea, I imagined myself living the life of a wealthy man in Sepphoris, where my father could not avoid seeing how successful I had become.

I did not, of course, expect to meet Yeshua of Nazareth seven years later. Nor did I imagine that one day I would be poor and content, laboring on a scroll my father would never see, much less read.

I sighed and went back to work, determined to transcribe my notes before Mary woke.

TWENTY

Matthew

Mary and I made slow and steady progress as the weeks passed. Two of the fall festivals—Rosh Hashanah and Yom Kippur—interrupted our work, but time away from the project seemed to benefit Mary. I could not help noticing she was often tired, and I did not want the work to exhaust her. I had collected several pages of notes, so I was able to start writing at home, allowing her to rest and review the material later. We still had people to interview, but finally I could imagine the complete collection, beginning, middle, and end.

When we were not working, I made certain to keep up with my work for the ecclēsia. The believers' communities gave generously, and we were able to save much-needed funds for a journey Peter and John planned to take within a few months. They wanted to visit Samaria, where Philip was preaching, and then travel on to several Gentile cities. "Yeshua told us to carry the Gospel to the ends of the earth," Peter reminded me. "John and I are ready to fulfill that part of the Master's commission . . . as soon as we can afford the journey."

I estimated they would be ready to leave around the time Mary and I finished our story collection. Then, with John and Peter away, James the Just might allow me to preach in Jerusalem, and HaShem might permit me to work a miracle in Yeshua's name. Word of that miracle would spread throughout Judea, reaching even Sepphoris.

Mary had just finished reading part of the manuscript when Miriam came into the room, her arms filled with clothing. "I have a few tunics to repair," she said, dropping her bundle onto the table. "I want to get a drink of water, then I will be out of your way."

"Take all the time you need," Mary said, lowering the papyrus. "Matthew has just finished the story of how Yeshua fed more than five thousand with five loaves and two fishes. He did a wonderful job."

I did? I lowered my gaze lest the women see the blush of pleasure on my face. Mary and I had finally come to an understanding—I understood what sort of writing she wanted, and she trusted that I knew how to tell a tale. Perhaps the rest of the writing would progress more swiftly now, and we could finally finish the work.

Miriam left as quickly as she had arrived. Mary slid off the bench, then paused before standing. "Is your family coming to Jerusalem for Sukkot?" she asked, glancing at me.

I blinked. "I . . . am not certain."

"Do they *usually* come to Jerusalem for Sukkot?"

In all the years I lived at home, my father never missed a pilgrimage festival. "Yes."

"Then you should try to discover where they are staying.

Family is a precious gift, Matthew, and you should not allow yourself to lose them."

I sighed. "They do not know me as Matthew. To them I am Levi, the son who fell in love with Rome and became a tax collector. They are ashamed of me."

"You are no longer Levi, or have you forgotten who you are? You are Matthew, a gift of HaShem." She gave me a sweet smile with a good deal of confidence behind it. "You need to find your family and tell them about the change in your life."

"Perhaps." I returned her smile. "If it will make you happy, I will try to find them."

"You are a good man, Matthew. It is time to let your family see the man you have become."

With those words ringing in my ears, she slipped out of the room and left me alone with my papyri.

Sukkot, the Feast of Tabernacles, brought cooler weather and thousands of pilgrims, all of whom were determined to live anywhere they could construct a shelter to remind themselves of our ancestors' wandering in the desert.

I made inquiries, as I had promised, and soon learned that Alphaeus of Sepphoris and his family were staying with friends in the Upper City, near the palace of Herod the Great. I was not surprised that my father had migrated to the wealthiest part of the city—he had always appreciated exquisite beauty and fine possessions. His tabernacle was certain to be furnished with large cushions, fine tapestries, and a thick rug. Never mind that the entire idea behind Sukkot was to remind us of our time of wandering—for my father, the Feast of Tabernacles was about living outdoors in luxury.

Sukkot lasted seven days, with the most important ritual held on the last day. I decided to seek my family after that service, when they would be thinking about returning to Sepphoris. If they were happy to see me, they could invite me to visit, and my appearance would give them cause for rejoicing on the trip home. If they were not happy to see me, at least my visit would not have ruined their entire week. My father would shut me out of his mind the same way he had shut me out of his heart.

The morning of the final service, I rose early and went to the Temple with Peter, Anna, Mara, and Dina. Dina looked particularly lovely that morning. The entire city had been decorated with garlands and fragrant flowers, and Dina had woven fresh blossoms in her hair. As tradition demanded, each of us carried a *lulav*, a bundle of branches from a palm, a willow, and a myrtle. Anna carried a citron for the entire family. "Citrons were hard to find this year," she said. "The only citrons at the marketplace were small and puny. I decided to buy the biggest I could find and carry it for all of us."

At the Temple, we stood in the women's court and watched the priests march around the altar, which had been adorned with freshly cut willow branches. The high priest appeared with a ewer of freshly drawn water, reminding me of when Yeshua had attended this same service. He stood before the altar and loudly proclaimed, "If anyone is thirsty, let him come to me and drink. Whoever believes in me, as the Scripture says, 'out of his innermost being will flow rivers of living water.'"

At the time no one had understood what Yeshua meant, but now I understood completely. Yeshua had given us the Ruach HaKodesh, which flowed out of us and empowered us to do great things for the kingdom of God . . .

The chanting of the priests snapped me out of my reverie. "*Hoshiah na*," they chanted, "Please save us. Deliver us."

The people had chanted the same words when Yeshua rode into Jerusalem the week before His death. Great crowds had waved palm branches before the colt He rode; the same crowds either fled or turned against Him when it became clear Yeshua would not deliver himself from death on the execution stake.

"Deliver me," I murmured as the priests passed by. "Deliver me from the wrath of my father."

Dina looked up, a question in her eyes.

"Excuse me." I forced a smile. "I did not intend to speak my thoughts."

She turned her gaze back to the chanting priests as I closed my eyes and whispered another desperate prayer.

The sun had passed its zenith by the time I found my family. As I expected, the tent belonging to Alphaeus of Sepphoris was larger than most, with fine fabrics stretched over a frame of willow branches and a thick woven carpet to hide the pavement. The fabrics had been drawn back, creating a doorway, and through the opening I saw my mother sitting on a chair, her eyes wide and vacant.

I approached quietly. "Ima?"

Astonishment touched her pale face, then she glanced toward something in the tent, something hidden behind the fabric wall. Without speaking, she rose from her chair and stepped outside, then took my arm and pulled me into the street.

"Levi." She looked me over and then wrapped me in her arms. "Praise be to HaShem for keeping you alive."

I clung to her, surprised by the depth of feeling that welled within my chest. "It is good to see you, Ima."

"Let me look at you." She released me and stepped back, her eyes lighting with joy. "You have filled out—my boy is now a man."

I resisted the urge to shrug. "I have been away more than thirteen years. Many things have changed since we last saw each other."

"I . . . I do not know what to say. Are you well? Are you married? Have you children? Are you—have you—?"

"I am well," I said, pulling her out of the foot traffic and guiding her toward the opposite side of the street. "I am not married. And I am no longer a tax collector. Several years ago I met Yeshua of Nazareth and became one of His students. Since He left us, I have been working for those who follow the Way, keeping their books and assisting their leaders. Oh—I am no longer called Levi. Yeshua gave me a new name because I am a new man. I am now known as Matthew."

Her expression did not change for a moment, then she shook her head. "No. Not the Way. Your sister and her husband are followers of the Way, and I have enjoined them to say nothing to your father. He has contempt for that man and was glad when certain Pharisees were persecuting and arresting His followers."

My heart squeezed at the mention of my sister. "Jael is married? She has a believing husband?"

Ima lifted her hand as if I had uttered a curse. "Keep your voice down. Your father is not pleased with the situation."

I accepted this news in silence, realizing that my question had already been answered. Still, I had to ask. "Would Abba see me? I would like to speak to him."

Ima pressed her lips together. "You must not approach him."

"But this animosity between us does not please HaShem."

"He would say you have defiled yourself, so he cannot see you and remain righteous. Please, Levi, is it not enough to know he is well? Thank you for coming, but you must go before he wakes. Please, go. And may the Lord watch between us while we are apart."

Words clotted in my throat as I stared at my mother, who remained lovely despite the passing of so many years. I had hoped—prayed—my father and I could reconcile, but apparently the time was not right.

But the day had not been without blessings. My younger sister Jael was well, married, and blessed with children. HaShem be praised! Perhaps, if the Lord willed, our paths would one day cross.

I could only hope and pray for that miracle.

I had just finished recording the most recent gifts when Peter entered the guest chamber. "You must come downstairs at once," he said, his forehead crinkling with concern. "You have a guest."

"Who?"

"You will see."

Had my father come?

When we descended to the courtyard, I noticed a large pair of sandals in the entry. After removing our own shoes, Peter and I walked into the front room. A big man stood there, his back to us, and from the cut of his tunic I surmised he was a man of considerable status. Then he turned, and for a moment shock caused words to wedge in my throat. "Achiakos?"

I embraced my friend, who slapped me on the back with warmth and enthusiasm. When we pulled apart, I stammered the only words that came to mind: "Why are you here?"

"I could not come to Judea without finding a way to see you." Achiakos released me, then propped his hands on his hips and grinned. "When it became clear you could not come to Tiberias, I wrote my master and asked if I could visit Jerusalem before joining him in Rome. He granted me two days, so I hastened here to find you."

"I am glad you did. I would much rather entertain you than your assistant."

"Lemuel? Was he not a good guest?"

I winced, remembering the way he had looked at Dina. "He was fine. He served you well. But he is not an old friend."

I gestured to the floor cushions, while Anna came into the room and asked if we needed anything. I would have said we were content, but Peter was a thoughtful host. "Bring honey water and the little nut cakes," he said, waving his wife toward the kitchen. "Then let them talk without interruption. I am sure our new friend has important news."

"Do you?" I settled on a floor cushion across from Achiakos. "You could have written and spared yourself the journey."

"There are some things I should not write." He smiled up at Anna and accepted a cup of water and a cake. "Thank you. HaShem bless you."

After Achiakos had eaten, Peter and his wife left us alone. Achiakos's friendly demeanor faded, and his eyes darkened when they met mine. "I was aggrieved to hear you could not come to Tiberias."

"I have work here," I said, wincing at a sudden pang of guilt. "It is important work—as is yours."

Achiakos shrugged. "I would never have imagined that HaShem would place me in Agrippa's service, but there I am—and by HaShem's will, for I have news for you about Caesar and Petronius."

My pulse quickened. "I have shared your reports only with the Temple authorities and elders of our communities, but the news has begun to reach the people."

"I expected it would, eventually." Achiakos rubbed his chin, still clean-shaven, then rested his hands on his knees. "In Tiberias, Petronius has taken over the former palace of Herod Antipas. The Jews who sought his company in Ptolemais overcame their dread of the Gentile city and met him there, where they went to the palace and petitioned the governor daily."

"Did their petitions have any effect?"

Achiakos inhaled a deep breath. "The stalemate continues. Petronius cannot disobey the emperor's command without forfeiting his life. The Jews risk their lives if they have war with Rome, but they will not transgress the holy Law. Petronius asked if they would make war with Caesar, and they said they would *not* make war with him but would die before they saw their laws transgressed."

I shook my head. "I am not surprised. They will not be dissuaded."

"Neither will Petronius," Achiakos replied. "After hearing that he could not disobey the emperor's command, the Jews threw themselves facedown and exposed their necks, saying they were ready to be slain. This they did for forty days, lying in the hot sun, abandoning the fields they should have been tilling because it was time for them to sow their seeds."

I listened with rising dismay. "Is there no hope for a satisfactory conclusion?"

Achiakos's dark brows slanted downward. "Aristobulus, my master's brother, and Helcias the Great begged Petronius to write Caesar. They told him to write that the Jews have an insuperable aversion to the statue, and they remain in Tiberias instead of going home to till their ground. They told him to say that the Jews are not willing to go to war with him but are ready to die with pleasure rather than allow their laws to be transgressed. Helcias pointed out that because the land remains unsown and infertile, robberies will increase, and the people will be unable to pay their tributes. They hoped Caesar might be moved to pity. They directed Petronius to conclude that if Caesar continues to bring a war upon them, he might as well set about it himself."

I drew in a deep breath, keenly aware of how that suggestion would have struck Petronius. One did not tell an emperor—particularly not *this* emperor—to "set about it himself." If any man said such a thing in Caesar's presence, the emperor would, without doubt, pick up a sword and kill the offender on the spot.

"And so did the advisors beg Petronius," Achiakos said, releasing an exasperated sigh. "Partly on account of the pressing opinions from them, and partly because he thought it a horrible thing to be a slave to the madness of Gaius Caesar, Petronius thought it better to write Caesar. He hoped to persuade the emperor, but if Caesar's dire resolution continued, Petronius decided to sacrifice his own life if necessary in order to hearken to the Jews' petitions."

"Blessed be HaShem," I whispered, amazed. "Our prayers have been answered!"

Achiakos held up a warning finger. "That is not the end of the story. Petronius again called the Jews to the palace, and they came, all ten thousand of them. To test their resolve, he

in his voice. "HaShem be praised! This will be a comfort to all who live in Jerusalem."

"Remain in prayer." Achiakos gripped my shoulder. "I will send word when I have other news to report. Until then, may HaShem keep you and those laboring with you in the love of Yeshua our Messiah."

Encouraged by the good news from Achiakos, I returned to my work with renewed energy. One afternoon, while I finished making notes about the story of Yeshua's cursing the fig tree, Mary poured fresh water into two cups, then set one before me. "There is another story you have not mentioned," she said, taking her place at the table. "I was not there, but I would like to hear about it."

Trepidation prickled the back of my neck as I sipped the water. I had a feeling I knew what she would ask but wanted to be sure. "Which story is that?"

"Gethsemane." She lifted her cup with both hands and looked at me over the rim. "If you are trying to avoid causing me pain, Matthew, you need not worry. I watched my Son die in the most agonizing way possible, so I do not think the story of His arrest will upset me overmuch."

I shuffled my papyri, picked up my pen, then lowered it. No sense in delaying; the stories of Yeshua would not be complete without that account.

And Mary already knew how I reacted when the enemy came to arrest Him.

I met her gaze head-on. "I remember seeing you at the Last Supper."

"Yes. I was working with the women, preparing food. Afterward, I remained to help them clean up. Yeshua led all of you outside . . . and I knew nothing about what had happened until the next morning."

I searched for words. "Did—did you suspect trouble?"

Her chin dipped in a barely discernible nod. "Before we set out the food, Yeshua sought me out. He pulled me away from the others and looked at me . . . and in that moment I knew He was trying to tell me something, something unspeakable. I asked if everything was all right, and He said everything was as it was supposed to be. Then He squeezed my shoulder and bent to kiss my cheek."

Her hand rose to that cheek now, and her chin quivered at the memory. "Somehow I knew He was trying to share something profound, but I could not grasp His intention. I watched Him walk into the dining room, my child from God . . . my child of God." She looked down, cleared her throat, and looked up again, her eyes focusing as she returned to the present. "Later, I heard Yeshua say that someone would betray Him, and I saw Judas leave. Then I heard Peter declare that he was ready to go with Yeshua to prison and even to death."

I snorted, but then none of us had been heroic that night. Except Yeshua. "Did you hear Yeshua tell us to get a sword?"

Her brow arched. "No."

"He said if we had a purse, we should take it with us, and if we did not have a sword, we should sell our cloaks and buy one. He quoted the prophet Isaiah: 'And he was counted with the lawless.' Then he looked at me and said Isaiah's prophecy would be fulfilled in Him . . . and I understood Him to mean it would be fulfilled that night."

Mary sat motionless, waiting for me to continue.

Unable to meet her piercing gaze, I looked down at my hands. "Yeshua led us out of the room. We left Jerusalem through the Eastern Gate and walked over to the Mount of Olives, to the garden He loved. As we were about to pass through the gate, He turned and said, 'Pray that you will not enter into temptation.' He waited until we all found a place to sit, then He asked Peter, James, and John to go farther into the garden with Him. They walked about a stone's throw from the rest of us, knelt, and began to pray. Yeshua did not recite the traditional prayers but rather spoke as a Son to a loving Father. From where I sat, I could not hear everything He said, only the tone of His voice. He was . . . passionate. Pleading. At one point I heard Him say, 'My Father, if this cup cannot pass away unless I drink it, let your will be done.'"

Tears glimmered in Mary's eyes when I looked at her again. "And then?"

"I remember waking up and shifting into a more comfortable position. I looked over and thought I saw something—someone—a man I did not recognize standing near Yeshua. I was groggy with sleep, but I became alarmed when I saw streams of blood running down Yeshua's face. The stranger, who wore a white robe, wiped the blood away, so I knew he was not dangerous. I remember wondering if the man was an Essene, then I fell asleep until Yeshua woke us again and chided us for sleeping. Three times He begged us to stay awake, and three times we failed Him."

I wiped perspiration from my brow; even now, the memory sent guilt surging through my veins. "I am ashamed—" my throat clogged—"because I failed Him that night. You must think me worthless for not supporting Him in His hour of need."

"I do not blame you," Mary said, her voice soft. "You were confused and exhausted. If I had been with you, I might have slept, too."

I did not believe her, but gratefully accepted her compassion. "While Yeshua was speaking to us," I went on, "Judas walked into the garden with a group of Temple guards. 'Master!' he said. He grabbed Yeshua by the shoulders and kissed Him on both cheeks. Yeshua gave him the saddest smile I have ever seen and asked, 'Judas, do you betray the Son of Man with a kiss?'

"That's when the pieces came together—Yeshua's comment at dinner, Judas's abrupt departure, Yeshua's grief in prayer. The rest of us scrambled to stand, Peter drew his sword, and someone shouted, 'Master, should we strike?' Peter did not wait for permission but struck wildly at the first man he met, who happened to be the high priest's chief servant. The man was called Malchus, and Peter cut off his ear."

Mary made a small sound in her throat as her hands tightened around her mug. I realized with some surprise that this information was new to her.

"Yeshua would not fight," I hastened to add. "He yelled, 'Stop this now.' He picked up Malchus's ear and put it back, healing the wound with a touch. The guards must have seen this, but they did not marvel. They had come for only one purpose—to deliver Yeshua to the high priest.

"Yeshua looked around at the ruling priests, officers of the Temple guard, and the elders who had come against Him. 'Have you come out with swords and clubs as you would against a revolutionary?' He asked. 'Every day I was with you in the Temple, yet you did not lay a finger on me. But this is yours—the hour and the power of darkness.'

"Before we knew what to do, the guards closed around Him. From out of nowhere I saw a young man in a nightshirt—I thought I recognized him from the crowds that followed Yeshua, and I believe he lived nearby. I do not know for certain, but I think he may have heard the crowd on the road, looked out his door, and realized what was happening. Perhaps he ran through the garden, trying to warn us. I do not know. But when the guards lay hold of Yeshua, one of them grabbed the young man, too. The lad was so terrified he shimmied out of his nightshirt and ran away naked. I can't blame him, for we were all terrified. We fled, some of us climbing the walls, some hiding among the trees. The guards took Yeshua away and that was the last most of us would see of Him . . . until later."

Silence engulfed the room as my courage faltered. The shame and sorrow of that hour, and my part in it, came rushing back, and I could no longer look at the woman whose Son I had utterly failed.

"Matthew—" Mary's voice broke—"I am tired. Shall we continue tomorrow?"

Unable to speak, I nodded, then gathered my tools and papyri.

TWENTY-ONE

Matthew

Several weeks later, Mary and I went to the Temple precinct for a meeting with Nicodemus, a highly respected member of the Sanhedrin. He had asked us to meet him outside the Hall of Hewn Stone, on the south side of the great court.

I spotted him before Mary did, and as soon as I caught the man's attention, he whisked us off the street and through the doorway of a nearby building. I glanced at Mary—was Nicodemus intent on hiding us from others of the Sanhedrin? Though the Pharisee was well known among the believers, I did not know how many Pharisees knew Nicodemus was a believer in Yeshua.

After exchanging the customary greetings, Mary sat next to me as I asked the elderly Torah teacher about his first meeting with Yeshua. He had quietly inquired after our group and sought a chance to speak with Yeshua while we were in Jerusalem. Finally, he arranged a meeting after sunset, when he could slip through the darkened streets unnoticed. Yeshua

"It *is* her!" someone shouted. "Mary of Nazareth! The Lord's mother!"

The stubborn line of Mary's jaw softened as she greeted those who eagerly blocked her path. She smiled and touched every outstretched hand, moving slowly through the crowd with the grace and humility I would have expected from Yeshua's mother. I followed, careful to stay out of the press of people but ready to defend her if necessary.

After a few moments, I saw a narrow alley and caught her eye. I threw my mantle over her, covering the bright color of her tunic, and together we darted into the alley and left the crowd behind. When we finally turned onto her street, I expected her to sigh in relief, yet the hard glint had returned to her eyes.

"Mary?" I fell into step beside her. "Are you all right?"

"Not now, Matthew," she said. We had reached her courtyard, so she opened the gate and stepped inside, then went into the house without glancing back. I hesitated, not certain I should follow, then reasoned that I was a grown man and more than capable of facing an irritated woman.

I straightened my spine and went after her.

TWENTY-TWO

Mary

I was determined to give Matthew a thorough scolding, but when I entered the house, Miriam hurried over and gave me a sealed scroll. Distracted, I broke the seal and discovered a message from Chiram, husband to my daughter Pheodora: "The baby is expected soon, and Pheodora is not well. Can you come?"

Being with my daughter was more important than rebuking Matthew, so I went to my bedchamber straightaway and began to pack for the journey to Nazareth. But I knew Matthew had come into the house and could sense his silent, befuddled presence.

"He looks like a scolded child," Miriam whispered, stepping into my room. "What happened?"

I lifted a woven blanket from my bed and put it in a basket. "Nothing we need to discuss now."

She glanced at the scroll on my dressing table. "Will you go to Nazareth tomorrow?"

"As soon as possible. Pheodora's baby is due."

Miriam folded a tunic and handed it to me. "We can borrow a donkey from James. I can go with you, if you want company."

"While I would enjoy having you with me, you are needed here." I stopped and looked around the room, trying to focus on my task. "I will ask James to find a group traveling to Nazareth, and I will go with them. Considering that it took at least four days for this message to reach me, I should not waste time."

Out in the hallway, Matthew cleared his throat. "You are leaving Jerusalem? Before we have finished?"

I raised my voice. "Our project will wait. My daughter needs me."

"Very well. I will work on my accounting while you are gone. When you return, we can begin again."

"Fine." I turned. "I will let you know when I return. Shalom."

"Mary." He squared his shoulders, signaling his intention to remain. "I cannot leave if you are angry with me. I believe you are, and I do not know why."

I braced myself against the doorframe and closed my eyes, inhaling deep breaths. I sensed Miriam's anxious presence and was suddenly grateful she had remained nearby. I would not lose my temper with her next to me.

"Matthew." I opened my eyes and faced him. "Why did you take me with you to see Nicodemus? You did not let me speak. I would have liked to ask a question or two, but you behaved as though I were not in the room. As if I were invisible."

He blinked, then spread his hands. "I have—women usually do not—you are always so humble, and you do not like it when people make much of you—"

"Nicodemus was not making much of me; this was an

entirely different situation. We are co-laborers together. I am not your wife, your mother, or your slave, so do not take me for granted. I am your sister in faith, yet today you refused to see me. Yes, I am angry, yet I am glad you stayed to let me speak my mind. We are partners, Matthew—let it be so, or let me find someone else. Because today you did not treat me as a partner."

A flush ran up from his throat, and his Adam's apple bobbed as he swallowed. "Forgive me," he said, his shoulders sinking. "You are right. I was thoughtless."

"That is a common problem with men." I waved my hand at an invisible host of indifferent males who had never fully appreciated their female counterparts. "Yeshua came to liberate *all* of us, but too often you men refuse to grant women the liberty Yeshua intended for everyone."

Matthew lowered his head. "I apologize. I hope you can forgive me."

I exhaled slowly, then walked over and placed my hands on his shoulders. A rush of maternal feeling swept over me as I looked up at his troubled face. "You are forgiven, Matthew. I respect you as a man and a leader . . . and trust you will never again ignore a woman who labors by your side."

"I will not. How could I after being rebuked by Yeshua's mother?"

I tightened my grip on his shoulders. "Do not respect me because I am Yeshua's mother, but because I am your sister in faith. We once stood together at the door of the empty tomb, so never forget—the ground there is level for everyone."

With my heart in my throat, I gathered my courage and uttered a terse command: "Pheodora, look at me."

My daughter's pain-filled eyes swept the room, then settled on my face. "Ima, I can't do this."

"I know about childbirth—I had seven babies, remember?"

I gripped her hands and lifted her to a standing position. "You should not squat until you feel the baby's head. I know the pains are strong, but you can bear them. You have borne four daughters; you know the pain is temporary."

"But this one feels different." She bit her lower lip, and the eyes she lifted to meet mine brimmed with anxiety. "This time everything felt different. The baby rode lower in my belly, it kicked more, and it would not sleep—"

"All babies are different," I said, shifting my position so I could massage her lower back. "And you have not carried a baby in years, so you have forgotten how it feels. Now another child reminds you that with great joy comes great pain. But only for a moment."

Her face twisted as another birth pang seized her. She closed her eyes and endured it, then relaxed and forced a laugh. "This baby wants to make sure I do not forget my lessons."

"Rest now." I helped her onto the bed, then pushed sweaty hair from her forehead. "Relax, if you can."

When Pheodora closed her eyes, I turned toward the open doorway, where a host of family and friends had gathered to await the birth of Chiram's fifth child. Pheodora's daughters—Judit, Eden, Jordan, and Shiri—moved among the guests, offering bowls of honeyed figs, cups of lemon water, and slices of freshly baked bread. Judit, who had married and would soon have a baby of her own, kept casting nervous glances toward the room where her mother travailed in labor. Eden, a new bride, averted her eyes from that doorway, while Jordan and Shiri, who were as yet unwed, ignored the looming event altogether.

I sank onto a bench and smiled at my son-in-law. "Your wife is doing well. I am sure the baby will arrive before morning."

Chiram blew out a breath and managed a smile. "Good. I only wish I did not feel so helpless. If Pheodora were a ewe birthing in the field, I could lead her to shade and—"

An ear-shattering screech interrupted his comment, and Chiram went pale. "Is that normal? I am sorry, but I was out with the sheep when the other children were born."

Torn between concern for my daughter and the desire to comfort my son-in-law, I gave him a fleeting smile. "I will take care of Pheodora. You take care of your guests."

While he stammered in helpless confusion, I hurried back into the bedchamber, where Pheodora was crouching over a pool of blood.

My heart nearly stopped beating.

After urging Pheodora to lie down so I could examine the birth canal, I immediately surmised the problem. Instead of seeing the top of a baby's head, I saw white flesh, probably a buttock or part of a limb.

"The baby is turned the wrong way," I said, wishing I knew more about midwifery. "I will send for help. While I am gone, do not push. Try to relax until I find someone who can help us."

"Relax?" Pheodora reached for me, caught my hand, and squeezed my fingers until I thought they might break. "Ima, what if the child dies? What if I die? Chiram would be lost, and he would not know how to care for a baby—"

"HaShem is faithful to provide," I assured her. "Now let me go. I will return as quickly as I can."

I went into the other room and found Judit, who stood at the table, her face flushed and troubled. "Judit, does the butcher's wife still practice midwifery?"

Judit frowned, then found her voice. "Not her, but her daughter does. I have heard others call for her when a woman labored too long."

"Hurry to her house, then, and see if she will come. Tell her the baby is turned the wrong way, and—" I hesitated, considering Judit's expectant condition—"never mind, stay here. We may need your help with the guests."

I turned instead to Eden. "Run to the butcher's house and ask if their daughter will come help your mother. Tell her to hurry."

Eden did not hesitate, but grabbed a headscarf and flew through the doorway, her husband trailing after her. I watched them go, then turned unwillingly to look at Chiram, who sat motionless, his eyes vacant and his hands twitching on his knees.

"Elazar." I walked over to the young man Judit had married. "Why not lead us in a prayer? Pray for the health of your baby and your wife. Pray for Pheodora and her child. Pray that HaShem will be merciful to all of us tonight."

Elazar pulled his prayer shawl over his head, and several of the other men followed his example. As their voices mingled and rose to heaven, I went back into the birthing room, where Pheodora lay on a blood-soaked mattress, her face streaked with tears.

"I did not want another baby," she whispered, her hand clutching mine. "I was surprised when I realized HaShem had sent us another child. I thought I was too old—"

"You are but thirty-six," I reminded her. "That is not old."

"Still, I have four girls. My womb went to sleep, and I thought it was the time of life, then I felt the child move. I was disappointed and had to confess my sin to the Lord. How could I regret something as special as a baby? How could I deny that HaShem had chosen to bless us again? Chiram was thrilled, of course, and wants a boy, but perhaps HaShem is judging me for my reluctance. Perhaps this is His way of showing me I was wrong to resent this baby, wrong to consider it an interruption in my plans—"

"Such things are between you and HaShem," I told her. "Right now you are confused and in pain. You must rest, gather your strength, and wait for the midwife. She will help, and HaShem will work His will tonight."

Pheodora's eyelids fell. "I am glad you are here, Ima. It was good of you to come. I know it is a long journey—"

"Hush." I brushed dark strands away from her forehead and wiped tears from her cheeks. "I have missed so many things in your life; I would not miss your child's birth. I do not want to be anywhere else."

Her eyes filled with tears, and in their brilliance I saw my reflection—an older woman, bowed with care, her face indelibly creased by age and sorrow. But I had also known great joy, and that joy gave me the confidence to sit beside my daughter and assure her all would be well.

"Tell me," she whispered, her cheeks flushing. "I have often wondered but did not have the courage to ask."

"What?"

Her flush deepened, then her face contorted in a grimace. "Another pain."

"Do not push."

"I am trying, Ima."

She waited until the urge passed, then shifted her weight and drew a deep breath. "It is better now."

"You wanted to ask me something."

"Yes." She gave me a faint smile. "When you gave birth to Yeshua . . . did you feel pain? Or did He . . . was it some sort of miracle?"

I squeezed her hand and laughed. "Yeshua came in human flesh so He could experience what all men experience. Why would His mother be excused from the pain all mothers endure? Even Eve suffered in childbirth."

Pheodora smiled. "You had enough pain bearing the rest of us. I thought HaShem might have shown mercy as you bore His Son."

"Oh, daughter. He did grant me mercy . . . though it was mercy most severe."

I closed my eyes as memory closed around me and filled me with a longing to turn back, if only for a moment. I could almost smell the straw, hear the cow's clanging bell and the bleating lamb searching for its mother in the small lean-to. I could almost hear Joseph's gasp and cry of wonder, his laughter as he caught the child, the squalling miracle begotten of God . . .

"I felt pain," I whispered, "but I felt wonder most of all. I had never borne a child, and no one had ever borne a child like Yeshua. So yes, I travailed with my labor, but the pain barely registered on my dazed senses. I watched in amazement as your father took the baby from between my legs, cleaned him with my headscarf, and lifted him high, as if showing HaShem that the child had been safely delivered. I saw all this before drifting away on a tide of exhaustion, then woke to the sound of voices. Joseph and I were no longer alone."

"Who?" Pheodora panted the word. "Who was with you?"

"Shepherds," I said, "and their herding dog." I chuckled at the memory. "The dog kept trying to sniff the baby. One of the shepherds tried to hold the dog back, but Joseph said to let it approach. HaShem had protected the baby for months, and He had arranged a safe place for us. He would certainly not allow a dog to harm the child. Not that night."

Pheodora moaned as another pain twisted her body. I fell silent, wishing I could take her agony into my own flesh. I felt the same urgent desire when I stood before the execution stake, watching Yeshua's face contort as He shifted His weight to His impaled feet, struggling to breathe, to endure the scrape of raw wounds over the splintered wood at His back. Watching from below, I begged HaShem to let me bear Yeshua's pain, but I knew His agony could not be shared. He was the atoning, unblemished lamb, who was wounded because of our sins, crushed because of our iniquities. He bore the chastisement that made us whole, and by His bruises we were healed.

No one could do what only He could do. Not even His mother.

I lifted my head at the sound of footsteps. Eden opened the door, followed by a young woman I did not recognize. She dropped her headscarf and went straight to work, running her hands over my daughter's swollen belly, manipulating the tight skin with fingers that seemed to work independently of one another.

"Pheodora," she said, speaking with an authority that belied her youth, "I am going to move the child within you. This may cause you some discomfort, but it is the only way to get the baby in the proper position."

Pheodora lifted her head, looked at the young woman, then shifted her gaze to me. "Who is this girl?"

I cast her a reproachful glance. "She is the midwife's daughter, and she will save your child. Trust her and do what she says."

Pheodora reached for my hand. "I hope you are right," she said, fixing her eyes on the ceiling. "Because otherwise I fear this baby will not be born."

TWENTY-THREE

Matthew

Oddly enough, I found it difficult to work when Mary was away. I had expected to turn pages of notes into polished prose during her absence, but instead my thoughts kept returning to how she had chastised me, how her chin quivered when I told her of the night Yeshua was arrested, and how earnestly she had entreated me to help her write these stories.

I had already written the story of how Gabriel appeared to announce Yeshua's upcoming birth. I planned to make it the first story in the collection, but then a thought kept niggling at my brain, something Yeshua had said . . .

He had been teaching in the Temple when a group of Pharisees came over to confront Him. They exchanged words, and Yeshua ended the conversation by saying, "Your father Abraham rejoiced to see my day; he saw it and was thrilled."

Then the Judeans—who had always looked down on Galileans—said to Him, "You're not even fifty years old and you've seen Abraham?"

Yeshua answered, "Amen, amen, I tell you, before Abraham was, I am!"

The other disciples and I were as taken aback as the Pharisees, but when they picked up rocks to stone our Teacher, the twelve of us hurried Yeshua away. So much was happening at the time, we barely had time to consider what Yeshua had said.

But I had time now.

"Before Abraham was, I am."

HaShem was the great *I am*. He had identified himself with those words when He spoke to Moses out of the burning bush.

I left Peter's guest chamber and went downstairs, where I found Dina shelling nuts. "Do you have a copy of the Tanakh?" I asked. "I need to refresh my memory about certain writings."

She smiled and pointed to a carved wooden trunk in the room. "You will find it there, along with the other books."

I thanked her, opened the trunk, and found several scrolls inside. The five books of Torah, thirteen books of the prophets, four books of hymns and wisdom, as well as the books of Enoch and the Maccabees. Peter must have been preparing for his work with the Gentiles because he also had Greek versions of each scroll.

I opened the scrolls and began to read. Before an hour had passed, I realized that both Mary and I were wrong. The story of Yeshua did not begin at His conception.

The Scriptures revealed His presence through all the writings. But if I had asked any man in Jerusalem if HaShem could come down from heaven in the form of a man, the answer would be a resounding *no*. Our God was not like the supposed gods of the Romans, who were forever coming to earth to sire children and create trouble. The Scriptures clearly stated that HaShem was not a man; He was Spirit. Moses reminded the children of Israel that they saw no form, no *temunah* of any kind the day the Lord spoke to them at Horeb, so they should be careful never to make an image and call it their God.

Yet when Moses, Aaron, Nadab, Abihu, and seventy elders of Israel went up on the mountain, they *saw the God of Israel.* They saw pavement under His feet, and they ate and drank in His presence.

The Torah also spoke of a time when Abraham was visited by two angels and a third being who ate and drank and had His dusty feet washed. The angels went on to Sodom, but Abraham remained "standing before the Lord." For years Torah teachers spoke of this being as *Malach panav*, the Angel of His face, and acknowledged that He was God. How could anyone deny it, since Abraham called Him *Adonai*?

Jacob wrestled with a Man one night, a Man who wrenched Jacob's hip from the socket and then blessed him. Jacob saw God face-to-face. He saw the temunah, the form of HaShem.

David yearned to see the temunah of HaShem after death, writing, "I in righteousness will behold your face! When I awake, I will be satisfied with your likeness." Job expressed the same desire: "Even after my skin has been destroyed, yet in my flesh I will see God."

The prophet Micah, who declared the place where the Messiah would be born, also declared that Messiah existed before His birth: "But you, Bethlehem Ephrathah—least among the clans of Judah—from you will come out to Me One to be ruler in Israel, One whose goings forth are from of old, from days of eternity."

And who could forget the mysterious Melchizedek, king of Salem, the city now called Jerusalem, built on Zion, the place where HaShem chose to dwell? Abraham met this king of peace, a priest for the King of Righteousness, and paid him tithes. Later David prophesied, "Adonai has sworn and will not change His mind: 'You are a *kohen* forever according to the order of Melchizedek.'"

Yeshua was from the tribe of Judah, not Levi. Yet He could be the Messiah-Priest we expected, an eternal priest from the order of Melchizedek. Yet how could these things be? How could HaShem be one and yet appear to men in the form of flesh?

Every Jew I knew uttered the Shema upon waking: "Hear, O Israel: the Lord our God, the Lord is one." In that passage, the Hebrew word for *one* was *echad*, the same word used to describe a night and day as one day, a husband and wife as one flesh. Echad was a unity of parts. If HaShem were *yachid*, on the other hand, His being would hold no plurality.

But HaShem was echad. One with plurality. Elohim. A plural God.

A rock of truth was somewhere beneath this sea of confusing thoughts, and I struggled to plant my feet on it.

How did the Torah teachers reconcile the Shema with reports of HaShem physically appearing to Moses, Abraham, and Jacob? They said that although the entire earth was not large enough to contain HaShem's glory, He could concentrate His being to fill one small space—the Tabernacle, for instance, or the Temple.

Or a body made of flesh.

Cold, clear reality swept over me in a powerful wave, a realization so stunning I sat dumfounded for several moments. Yeshua was the Malach panav, the Angel of HaShem's face, the temunah David and Job longed to see, the Divine Word made flesh.

Gabriel told Mary to name her son *Yeshua*, the word used by Moses and the prophets whenever they wrote of salvation. In the Greek scroll I held, a phrase from a psalm had been translated "I will exult in thy salvation." Yet David wrote in Hebrew, and the original text said, "I will rejoice in Thy Yeshuah."

I opened the Greek scroll of Isaiah and searched for a familiar passage.

> "Behold, my God is my Savior;
> I will trust in him, and not be afraid:
> for the Lord is my glory and my praise, and is
> become my salvation.
> Draw ye therefore water with joy out of the wells
> of salvation."

But when I looked at the words in Hebrew, the truth was obvious. How had I missed it?

> "Hinei, El is my Yeshuah;
> I will trust, and not be afraid;
> for Hashem G-d is my strength and my zemirah;
> He also has become my Yeshuah.
> Therefore with sasson shall ye draw mayim
> out of the wells of Yeshuah."

The truth was clear and had been written in the Scriptures for hundreds of years.

Yeshua was God. Yeshua became salvation for sinners. And Yeshua was the provider of living water that satisfied men's souls.

Patterns. Had not Yeshua stood in the Temple and proclaimed that for whoever believed in Him, "out of his innermost being will flow rivers of living water"?

My pen scratched over the papyrus, filling page after page with thoughts and realizations, and I could not wait to share what I had learned with Mary.

Yeshua's story did not begin with His conception. His story had no beginning at all.

TWENTY-FOUR

Mary

Night had fallen by the time a baby's cry filled the house. Leah, the midwife, took the child, wrapped it in fresh linen, and carried it into the other room, presenting it to Chiram, who seemed to have aged ten years since my arrival.

"You have a son," Leah said, giving him a satisfied smile. "And your wife is well, but she needs to rest."

I do not know which news delighted Chiram more. He looked at me, his face splitting in a wide smile, then he held up his son and spun around, displaying the boy to everyone. "I have a son!" he shouted, beaming with joy. "After four daughters, HaShem has seen fit to bless me with a son!"

He carried the child into the bedroom, where he spent a few quiet minutes with Pheodora before coming out and handing the baby to me. "I do not know what to do with him," he said, happily helpless. "And Pheodora is asleep."

"Let her rest," I said, taking the infant. I studied the tiny fingers at the edge of the swaddling blanket. "We should let this one sleep, too. They have had a busy day."

Judit and Eden offered the midwife food and drink, and as Leah sat and enjoyed the refreshments, I set the baby in the cradle Chiram had built from olive wood. The men who had come to pray with him relaxed, settling onto couches as Judit and Eden served honeyed figs and lemon water.

Chiram sat next to me. He leaned toward me as if he wanted to talk, but I think he simply wanted to be closer to his baby.

"I never thought we would have another child," he confessed, his voice filled with awe. "And to think HaShem has blessed me with a son." He gave me a shy smile. "You might not understand, having had sons and daughters, but a man wants to feel that he is leaving something of himself in the world."

"Your daughters are part of you," I reminded him. "Each of them is like you in some way."

"But they marry and become part of their husband's family." Chiram shook his head. "This boy—my son—will bring his wife to live in my house, and he will follow in my trade."

"Not always." I shifted my gaze to my tiny grandson. "Yeshua learned Joseph's trade, but He had a different calling. James, Jude, Joses, and Simeon were all trained as carpenters, but not one of them works with tools now. They are all involved in spreading the good news, and James lives in Jerusalem."

"About Jerusalem." Chiram's expression grew serious. "What is the latest news about Caesar? I am sure you hear more in Jerusalem than we do in Nazareth."

I lifted a brow, not certain I wanted to alarm him on this wonderful day. "What have you heard?"

He glanced around, then lowered his voice. "I would not

upset the others, but from travelers I have heard that Caesar is determined to erect a statue of himself in the Temple. Surely he knows this could never be permitted."

"I cannot say what Caesar knows," I said, looking again at my sleeping grandchild. "But for the sake of this boy, I am praying for the peace of Jerusalem. I know the Syrian governor has written Caesar in an attempt to change the emperor's mind. Petronius is a righteous man who has said he would gladly die rather than kill so many innocent men."

"Do you think this man means what he says?"

"Who can say what a man will do when he is facing a sword? But Matthew has a friend who believes Petronius is honorable. Even if he is not, God has defended us before. Perhaps He will defend us again."

"He has also allowed us to face judgment," Chiram countered, his long face furrowing with sadness. "With the Babylonians, the Seleucids, and Herod. If Caesar erects this statue, the history of our forefathers would repeat itself. The Temple must never be defiled again."

"Then let us pray Caesar changes his mind." I lowered my fingertips to the baby's forehead and brushed away a few strands of dark hair, amazed at the sweet little face beneath my hand. If HaShem was merciful, He would not let this innocent one die in a wave of Roman wrath.

"Why does a ruler like Caesar care so much about Judea?" Chiram crossed his arms. "He has temples and fortresses throughout the empire. I heard he recently sent troops to a place on the edge of the world. Why does he not erect a statue of himself in this Britannia?"

"I do not know what HaShem will do, but I will say this—until the issue has been settled, you should keep your family away from the Holy City."

TWENTY-FIVE

Matthew

After a week without Mary, I went to her house, hoping to at least hear that she was on her way home. Miriam welcomed me and bade me enter, then told me she had heard nothing from Mary or anyone in Nazareth.

"Do you think she is all right?" I asked. "She seemed tired before she left."

"There is nothing like family to refresh the heart," Miriam said, smiling. "I am sure she is well and would not want you to worry. She probably cannot bear to tear herself away from that new baby." Miriam gestured toward the table. "Why don't you work here? I have to go to the market, so I will not disturb you."

"Thank you." I walked over and dropped my satchel onto the table. "I enjoy being a guest in Peter's house, but he is not the quietest of men. And the desk in his guest chamber is small—I have grown accustomed to having space to spread out my notes."

"Then make yourself at home whenever you like." Miriam

took a basket from a hook on the wall, then covered her hair with her headscarf. "I will leave you to your work."

I mixed my ink, sharpened my stylus, and organized my papyri. I had written several stories in the past few days and keenly felt Mary's absence. I missed the sound of her voice as she read the pages aloud, and I earnestly desired her feedback. I could ask Miriam to read my latest work, but she *liked* me and would probably say the writing was good even if I had missed the mark.

Mary would never do that.

Writing without an audience seemed pointless, yet I would keep working because Mary could not stay away forever.

To get back into the flow of writing, I turned toward the basket where Mary kept the papyri I left for her to read. Before we went to meet Nicodemus, I had dropped the story of Gethsemane into the basket, hoping she would read and approve of it, but the pages were no longer there.

Ghost spiders seemed to dance up my spine as I called for Miriam. She did not answer, and I knocked my hand against my head when I realized she had gone to the market. She had told me so, right before leaving the house.

Had Mary taken the pages with her to Nazareth? I did not think she would risk losing them on the journey, but perhaps she was confident in her ability to manage a few papyri. Miriam might have taken them to read, then left them in her bedchamber. When she returned, I would ask her about the pages and she would blush, embarrassed to be caught in a moment of forgetfulness . . .

All I had to do was wait until she returned. I would ask her, she would tell me where the pages were, and I would not have to worry about rewriting one of the most difficult sections of the scroll.

I sat at the table and prepared to write, but I could not focus. My thoughts kept drifting to the missing pages and what might have happened to them. If Mary did not take them, or Miriam, then who? The two women hosted a prayer meeting once a week, so perhaps one of those ladies had seen the pages and inquired about them. But surely neither Mary nor Miriam would have given anyone permission to take them from the house. Those papyri were original, unique, and unfinished; I would not consider them ready for reading until after Mary approved them. So where were they?

I stood and paced the length of the room, then moved to the door and looked out at the courtyard. The day was sunny and bright, a perfect day for the market. Miriam might be gone a few moments or an hour, who could tell? While I waited, I might as well get some writing done.

I went back to the table and picked up my stylus. Rather than compose another story, why not write about Yeshua's lessons? Mary and I had focused on events, but Yeshua taught people with parables, so why not transcribe those? On some occasions the parables were easy to understand, but at other times we disciples had to pull Him aside and ask for an explanation.

Once we asked why Yeshua taught in parables—would it not be easier to simply say what He meant? He gave us a cryptic answer: "To you has been given to know the secrets of the kingdom of God; but to the others it is given in parables, in order that 'seeing, they may not see, and hearing, they may not understand.'"

I did not understand what He meant, but later John identified Yeshua's reference. "He was quoting the words of Isaiah," he told me and Peter. "Adonai told Isaiah that the people were not ready to hear, understand, and be healed."

"Why not?" I asked.

John shrugged. "HaShem had His reasons."

In those days, Yeshua said a great many things that puzzled us. One thing I never understood was why He often told people *not* to share the news that He, the Messiah, had come. The first time I heard Him issue this warning was when He raised Jairus's daughter from death. The girl's parents were astonished, realizing that the man standing beside them had power over death, yet Yeshua charged them to say nothing.

A few days before, however, Yeshua had told us to get into a boat and sail across the Galilee to the country of the Gerasenes, a Gentile community. As we stepped onto land, a naked demoniac met us, and the demon recognized Yeshua immediately. He cried out, dropped the man to the ground, and with a loud voice shouted, "What's between you and me, Yeshua, *Ben El Elyon*? I am begging you, do not torment me!"

I looked at Peter, who was as stunned as I that the demon not only knew Yeshua's name but also recognized Him as the Son of God Most High.

Yeshua asked the demon's name, and the demon replied, "Legion, for we are many." They knew He would cast them out, but rather than be cast into the abyss, the evil spirits begged to be allowed to enter the bodies of pigs feeding on the mountain. Yeshua granted their request. The demons left the man and entered the swine, whereupon the entire herd rushed over the cliff, fell into the sea, and drowned.

The delivered man sat on the ground, amazed and grateful for his freedom. Yeshua asked us to give the man some clothing, so Peter surrendered his mantle while John offered his head covering.

When the terrified swine herders went into town and reported what had happened, the townspeople came out to meet us. So great was their awe that they asked Yeshua to leave their shore. Yeshua agreed, but when the former demoniac wanted to come with us, Yeshua told him to return to his home and to tell everyone what God had done for him.

Yeshua did not shy away from displaying His power there, and everyone, from the demoniac to the people of the town, understood that Yeshua had the authority to wield the power of God.

So why did He allow the restored demoniac to share the news but not Jairus?

I considered another example of demonic possession. When we were in Capernaum, we visited a synagogue where another demon-possessed man recognized Yeshua. "What have we to do with you, Yeshua of Nazareth?" he shouted. "Have you come to destroy us? I know who you are! You are the Holy One of God!"

I thought Yeshua would confirm the demon's words, but instead He told the evil spirit to be silent and to come out of the man.

Without protest, the demon threw the man on the ground and fled, leaving the man unhurt.

Another time Yeshua was praying on a hill while the rest of us sat around a fire not far away. When He finished praying, He came down and asked an odd question: "Who do the crowds say that I am?"

We responded with various answers: "Elijah." "John the Immerser come back to life." "An ancient prophet resurrected for our time."

Then Yeshua sat on a stone, leaned forward, and looked earnestly around our circle. "Who do *you* say that I am?"

As usual, Peter was the first to speak: "You are the Messiah of God."

I leaned back, certain that Yeshua would congratulate Peter for his insight, but instead Yeshua ordered us not to repeat Peter's answer to anyone. "The Son of Man," He said, refusing to call himself by the other title, "must suffer many things and be rejected by the elders and ruling kohanim and Torah scholars, and be killed, and on the third day be raised."

We were so shocked by His talk of suffering and killing that we barely noticed the warning about not calling Him *Messiah*.

As far as I knew, Peter never again referred to Yeshua as the Messiah until the day of Pentecost, when the Ruach HaKodesh came from heaven and filled all of us with power from above. Then Peter stood on the southern stairs of the Temple and proclaimed to Jewish pilgrims from all nations of the Roman Empire: "Therefore let the whole house of Israel know for certain that God has made Him—this Yeshua whom you had crucified—both Lord and Messiah!"

Why did the Ruach HaKodesh allow Peter to announce Yeshua as Messiah after His ascension? Why were we not to tell some people but allowed to tell others?

I smacked the side of my head as understanding dawned. The people we were instructed *not* to tell were Jews—people at the synagogue, the people with Jairus. The people Yeshua freely told were Gentiles—the former demoniac and the Samaritan woman at the well. Though Yeshua had told Gentiles who He was, He had kept the news from His own people.

Why?

The Ruach brought another memory to mind, of Cleopas and Benami, two men who left Jerusalem shortly after we received reports of Yeshua's resurrection. They had been puzzled by the events of the past few days and were joined by another traveler, a man they did not recognize. When He asked why they were downcast, they explained everything that had happened to Yeshua, from His arrest to His crucifixion and rumored resurrection.

The stranger chided them: "O foolish ones, so slow of heart to put your trust in all that the prophets spoke! Was it not necessary for Messiah to suffer these things and to enter into His glory?" Then, beginning with Moses and all the prophets, He explained to them the things written about Messiah in all the Scriptures.

But their story did not end there. When Cleopas and Benami approached their destination, the stranger made as though He was going to keep walking, but they entreated Him to eat dinner with them. When they sat at the table, the stranger—unexpectedly exercising the authority of the host—took the matzah, blessed it, broke it, and handed it to them.

In that instant their eyes were opened. When they recognized Him, He vanished.

Comprehension began to bloom in my chest. Yeshua was visible, but hidden when he was with Cleopas and Benami. They should have recognized Him, but HaShem put blinders over their eyes. The moment HaShem removed the restraints, they recognized Yeshua, their Messiah.

I sat in the silence of Miriam's kitchen, my mind spinning as I considered the inescapable truth. Some of us had seen Yeshua for who He was, but most Jews had not.

Would HaShem remove the blinders? If so, when?

I was so caught up in my thoughts that I did not hear Miriam enter the house. Not until she set her basket on the table did I blink and look at her, startled out of my thoughts.

She frowned. "Are you all right? You look ill."

"Where are the papyri?" I pointed to the basket on the floor. "Before Mary and I met Nicodemus, I put several papyri in that basket. Mary was to read and approve them."

"I know." Miriam smiled and moved around the table, then stopped and stared. "They were there—I know they were; I saw them after Mary left for Nazareth."

"So she did not take them with her."

Miriam shook her head, then sank to the bench, her face growing pale.

I leaned toward her. "Think, Miriam. Did you pick them up to read them? Perhaps you left them in your bedchamber?"

"I would never," she said, recoiling from my suggestion. "I have not read a word of your writing, not even when Mary said I could. I want to wait until you are finished, then read the entire scroll from beginning to end."

"All right." I drew a deep breath and pressed my palms against the table. "If Mary didn't take them with her, and if you didn't take them out of the basket, then who did? Perhaps someone who attends your prayer meeting?"

Miriam's brow furrowed, then she shook her head. "Only two women came to pray this week. We met in the front room and did not venture near the table."

"Did you serve refreshments? Perhaps they came in for lemon water or one of your delicious cakes."

Her eyes narrowed. "I served them in the front room. I remember it clearly."

"Then what could have happened to those pages?"

My voice sounded sharper than I had intended, and pain filled Miriam's eyes. "I am sorry, Matthew, but I do not know. Perhaps you took them home without realizing it."

"I did not." I pointed to the satchel on the table. "I have

looked through those pages at least a dozen times, and the Gethsemane story is not there."

Miriam blew out a breath, then leaned on the table and stood. "Then I suppose we have two choices—we can wait for Mary to return and hope that she has them, or you can write that story again."

I dropped my forehead to my palm, not willing for her to see my disappointment and frustration. So much work, and for what? Miriam was even older than Mary, and Mary frequently mentioned that her memory was slipping. Miriam must have taken the pages without realizing, and then misplaced them—or burned them in the fire.

One thing, however, was clear: I would have to write the Gethsemane story again.

TWENTY-SIX

Mary

I did not intend to remain in Nazareth for three weeks, but even after Pheodora recovered her strength, I could not help but think I might never see my daughter and grandchildren again. Life, as sweet as it was, had never seemed more uncertain. Despite the hopeful news from Matthew's friend Achiakos, Rome remained a constant threat. And many times during my visit, sharp pains in my chest and back reminded me that I was nothing but spirit and dust.

I put the pain behind me because I was happy to visit with my family. Pheodora's difficult labor left her weak, so I prepared meals when her daughters allowed me to cook. Jordan and Shiri kept me company, and I delighted in the opportunity to get to know them as young women.

All of Pheodora's children, I was happy to see, believed that their uncle Yeshua was Israel's Messiah and Ben-Adonai. They seemed reluctant to ask about the family history, so after Pheodora nursed the baby in the evenings, I would tell my granddaughters stories about the childhood my children experienced in Nazareth.

"In this very house," I began one night, "while Joseph, he of blessed memory, led the boys in Torah study, the girls helped me clean. Damaris would frequently boss Pheodora around. She was the oldest, you see, but your gentle mother did not argue. She always loved the animals, so when Damaris began to order her about, she would slip down to the courtyard to care for our goat and chickens. I was not surprised when she married a shepherd. Joseph, of blessed memory, was wise to accept Chiram's betrothal contract. Your father is a good man."

The girls glanced at their father, who turned away and flushed.

"Tell them," I urged him. "Tell them about the night your father saw the angels at Migdal-Eder."

Chiram cleared his throat, then launched into the story I had heard only a few times before. I picked up a tunic that needed mending, threaded a bone needle, and repaired the ripped seam while Chiram's voice boomed like thunder, drawing exclamations and ahhhs from the girls' upturned faces.

Chiram was a wonderful storyteller—a skill honed, no doubt, in the hours he and his fellow shepherds entertained each other while keeping watch over the flocks outside Bethlehem.

"And lo, the sky brightened," Chiram continued, looking first to Jordan, then to Shiri, "and my father saw a host of angels, all of them praising God and saying, 'Glory to God in the highest, and on earth, peace, goodwill to men.'"

"We could use some of that peace now." Judit's husband, Josu, nodded as he entered the house. "Our messiah has come, but still Rome threatens us."

"The Messiah did not come to save us from our enemies," Chiram said, "but to save us from our sins."

"And He *did* bring peace," I ventured to add. "Not yet to the world, but to the hearts of men and women. I have known many people, some of them my children, who used to strive and worry about everything. But since believing in Yeshua, their hearts have found shalom."

"The little baby my father visited brought the kingdom of heaven down to us." Chiram smiled at his daughters. "When Yeshua is king of our hearts, we have peace and hope and joy. Rome can never take those things away."

"And that," I whispered to my grandson in his cradle, "is your inheritance. You cannot see Yeshua now, but one day you will."

TWENTY-SEVEN

Matthew

For several days, the question of why Yeshua told us to keep His identity secret hounded me. I thought about asking Peter, John, and James for their thoughts, but they were so busy caring for the communities that I did not think they would have time to give the matter careful consideration.

Time, however, was something I had in abundance. My accounting work barely took more than a day, since the communities collected gifts on the first day of the week and delivered them to me on the second. I entered the gifts in a ledger, made notes for the equitable distribution of funds, and gave my notes and the coins to James, who took care of everything else.

For the rest of the week, I had nothing to do but write, think, and pray. Yeshua promised that the Ruach HaKodesh would not only be our comforter but would also "guide us into all the truth." So that is what I prayed—that the Spirit would guide me into the truth, so I would not write one false word. If HaShem blessed this work, if it traveled as far as

Mary hoped, I did not want to be responsible for leading even one soul astray.

So when I sat down to work at Miriam's table on the third day of the week, something Yeshua said came immediately to mind. He had been talking about how no one lights a lamp and then hides it. "For nothing," He said, "is hidden that will not become evident, nor secret that shall not be known and come into open view."

Why then did He tell us not to let our own people know that the Messiah had come?

I lowered my head into my hands and massaged my temples, asking the Ruach to guide me. Yeshua's role as the Messiah was not hidden from everyone, for hundreds—no, thousands—of us had come to see Him as He was. But not the majority. And not those who were the most steeped in the Law . . .

I closed my eyes as my mind carried me back to a time when we were preparing to go to Jerusalem. Yeshua had gathered seventy of His followers and sent them ahead in groups of two. He told them to heal the sick and tell them the kingdom of God had come near.

After a few days, the seventy returned, jubilant and thrilled, and reported that even the demons obeyed when followers of Yeshua invoked His name. Yeshua was encouraged by their report and prayed aloud, "I praise you, Father, Master of the universe, that you have hidden these things from the wise and discerning and revealed them to infants."

At the time, I thought it odd that Yeshua referred to us as infants, but now I was beginning to understand.

Who accepted Yeshua first? Simple people. Shepherds. Galilean fishermen. The poor and hungry. The sick, blind, and lame. The outcasts—demoniacs like Miriam of Magdala, lepers, and tax collectors like myself. We were the marginalized, the ones who believed in HaShem but who were not caught up in observance of the Law. Some of us had not been to Temple in years. Others could not attend a synagogue because of some physical deformity or ritual uncleanness. We were the ones who needed a Savior, and He came to us. As He said in Capernaum, "Those who are healthy have no need for a doctor, but those who are sick do. I did not come to call the righteous, but the sinful."

We needed the Great Physician and we knew it. The Pharisees, scribes, and Sadducees did not consider themselves sick; they believed they were righteous on account of their adherence to the Law. Of all those who believed in Yeshua before His death, I could only recall two who were Pharisees—Nicodemus and Joseph of Arimathea. They believed because they were willing to admit they were sinners.

What had Nicodemus said when we spoke to him? "Now I see things clearly, but the night I met with Yeshua, I could not see at all."

He had not been able to *see*. But he was no longer blind.

The other religious leaders were expecting a messiah, but not one like Yeshua. Their strict adherence to the Law and their devotion to the Scriptures blinded them to the truth. They expected a messiah who would overthrow the Romans and sit on the throne of David. They could not accept a messiah who left the Romans alone and hung from an execution stake.

I stood and went into Mary's front room, where she kept her Tanakh scrolls. I opened the chest and searched through them until I found the scroll of *Yesha'yahu* or Isaiah. I smiled to see that Mary had a Hebrew scroll, not the Greek translation.

I unrolled the papyrus until I came to a passage Mary had mentioned before.

> "He is despised, and left of men,
> A man of pains, and acquainted with sickness,
> And as one hiding the face from us,
> He is despised, and we esteemed him not.
> Surely our sicknesses he hath borne,
> And our pains—he hath carried them,
> And we—we have esteemed him plagued,
> Smitten of God, and afflicted.
> And he is pierced for our transgressions,
> Bruised for our iniquities,
> The chastisement of our peace is on him,
> And by his bruise there is healing to us.
> All of us like sheep have wandered,
> Each to his own way we have turned,
> And Jehovah hath caused to meet on him,
> The punishment of us all."

I read the passage again as one line echoed in my head: *"And as one hiding the face from us . . ."*

Was it possible that HaShem intended to hide the Messiah from the majority of our people? If so, why?

I felt like an awkward child trying to make the pieces of a puzzle fit together. Then it occurred to me. The idea of a hidden Messiah felt familiar. Yeshua spoke often of hidden things, and the passage from Isaiah implied that our people would not recognize Messiah when He arrived among us. Was it possible that my people were not *supposed* to recognize Him? Had HaShem ever hidden other messengers or prophets?

Immediately I recalled the story of Joseph in Egypt. Years

after being sold as a slave by his jealous brothers, Joseph, dressed as a ruler, wearing a wig and clean-shaven, met his brothers again. He recognized his brothers immediately but continued as though he did not know them to test their hearts. After months, they passed the test and Joseph revealed himself to them, assuring them, "It was not you who sent me here, but God."

Though Joseph suffered slavery and imprisonment, he was elevated to a throne and reunited with his people. Between the imprisonment and reunion, Joseph saved nations from starvation.

And though Yeshua had suffered imprisonment and death, one day He would be elevated and recognized by His people. Did Zechariah not prophesy that Hashem would "pour out on the house of David and the inhabitants of Jerusalem a spirit of grace and supplication, when they will look toward Me whom they pierced. They will mourn for him . . ."?

Joseph's people did not recognize him because they saw him exalted and on a throne.

Yeshua's people did not recognize Him because they saw Him as a lowly Galilean.

But HaShem always had a purpose.

While Joseph was hidden, he saved nations from starvation.

While Yeshua was hidden . . . what?

I straightened my spine, rubbed my eyes, and saw the truth. Yeshua said it himself: "For God so loved the world that He gave His one and only Son, that whoever believes in Him shall not perish but have eternal life."

HaShem loved *the world*, not the Jews only.

Did HaShem not promise to bless the world through Abraham's descendants? Because our Messiah was hidden and not recognized by His people, a door of faith was opened to the Gentiles. Peter—whom Yeshua said would be a cornerstone of the ecclēsia—had been instrumental in leading Gentiles to faith. Through his ministry, the Ruach HaKodesh was poured out on Jews, Samaritans, and Gentiles.

To most of my people, the Messiah remained hidden. But Yeshua promised that nothing is hidden that will not become evident, nor secret that shall not come into open view.

The blinders *would* come off . . . in the fullness of time.

TWENTY-EIGHT

Mary

Pheodora's baby had arrived at the beginning of Kislev, so after three weeks I prepared to return to Jerusalem. Joses, my youngest son, volunteered to travel with me, and I looked forward to spending time with him. "We should have you home in time to light the menorah for Hanukkah," he said as we started out. "I know how you love that festival."

"I am glad I will be back in time—I would not want Miriam to celebrate alone. She will want to bake, and a baker needs an audience with a hearty appetite."

"Your appetite is not hearty. You barely ate anything while you were with us."

"How could you tell? Every night there were so many at dinner, the little ones barely got a bite."

I smiled as I thought of my friends and family in Jerusalem. "I doubt Miriam was ever lonely in my absence. James would have checked on her, and some of the women. And I think Matthew has become fond of her . . . we certainly see enough of him."

Joses sent me a sidelong glance. "I have heard that James's letter is being passed around to all the believers. We received a copy in Nazareth. Have you read it?"

I chuckled. "He asked me to look it over before he sent it out."

"They say many are distributing copies to travelers who pass through their towns. After all, he wrote it for the twelve tribes."

"Even the tribes that have scattered . . . as HaShem intended. I am glad they are making copies."

Joses frowned. "You think HaShem *wanted* our people to be dispersed by war and persecution?"

"Would so many believers have left Jerusalem if their lives had remained peaceful?" I glanced up as a flock of crows flew overhead. "I do not presume to know the mind of Adonai, but I do know He works in ways we do not expect. Because we were persecuted and scattered, James's letter will spread throughout the world. People will read it, and those who dwell in darkness may see the Light . . . and those who are already believers will be encouraged."

We walked in silence a moment, then Joses smiled. "James's letter contained a great deal of Yeshua's teaching, and yet I could see James in it too—especially when he cautioned the believers against showing favoritism. I have seen it so often in the synagogues—the wealthy are warmly welcomed and shown to seats down front, while the poor man is ignored or forced to sit in the back."

"James has always felt strongly about such things," I said. "Perhaps it is because we were never wealthy. No one ever made a fuss over us at synagogue, but when Damaris married Shimon, we certainly saw how differently the Torah teacher treated *him*. I do not think James has ever envied Shimon for being a wealthy man's son, but he has never approved of the way many Torah teachers bow and scrape before the rich."

"May his teaching spread far and wide," Joses said. "A miracle, really, that a scroll can travel farther than a man."

I nodded, thinking of the work waiting for me in Jerusalem. By now, Matthew must have finished turning his existing notes into stories. I hoped he would be eager to get back to work, because I was eager to read.

"I hear James is now called Camel-Knees," Joses said, one corner of his mouth rising in a lopsided smile.

I blinked. "What?"

"They say his knees are as callused as a camel's from continual prayer." Joses laughed. "That is almost as surprising as learning my oldest brother is the Messiah."

I waved his comment away but could not help but chuckle at his little joke.

TWENTY-NINE

Matthew

As the days of Kislev passed, I became convinced Mary would soon return. Surely, she would want to be in Jerusalem for the Feast of Dedication.

I sped through my work for the communities so I could devote myself to clarifying what I had learned about HaShem's mysterious plan for Yeshua. Because I began to write at night, Anna generously offered the use of her kitchen table, so I could spread out my tools and not have to go to Miriam's house. Anna's thoughtfulness spared Miriam the threat of gossip and meant I did not have to risk encountering Roman patrols after dark.

One night I was at the dining table, working by the light of a small oil lamp, when someone slid onto the bench next to me. I looked over, expecting to see Peter, but blinked in surprise to see Dina.

The lamp's glow painted her features in a golden light, emphasizing her eyes, her genial mouth, and the thick lashes that fanned her cheekbones as she studied the manuscript.

"You have been working hard," she said, her voice soft and melodious in the darkness.

I lowered my gaze as every coherent thought fled. "Um, yes."

"Still writing stories?"

"Actually, of late I have been formulating truths I discovered in the Tanakh."

The curtain of lashes rose, and I found myself staring into eyes like brown silk. "What sort of truths?"

I drew a deep breath to steady my nerves. "I have learned—the Spirit has revealed—that Yeshua is found even in the first book of the Torah. When, for example, HaShem says to the serpent, 'I will put animosity between you and the woman—between your seed and her seed. He will crush your head, and you will crush His heel.'" I fumbled with my papyri, searching for the page where I had written about the subject, but could not find it.

"In any case, Moses did something unusual by mentioning the seed of the woman, because genealogies are always traced through the line of the male. But now we can understand why Moses wrote those words. Because Yeshua had no human father, He was conceived in the womb of a virgin. So even from the beginning, HaShem revealed His plan to send One who would crush the devil, even though the evil one was allowed to 'bruise His heel.' To make Him suffer."

I looked at her again. "Do you understand?"

Her lips parted in a dazzling display of white teeth. "So . . . HaShem has always had a plan?"

"Indeed. Micah wrote that the Messiah's goings forth are from old, from eternity. HaShem foreordained that everything we have seen would happen. We expected a Messiah who would restore the kingdom to Israel, but Yeshua came to suffer. We should have seen the truth, for Isaiah gave us many details: the Messiah would not be overly handsome, He would be a man of sorrows, He would be pierced, He would be oppressed yet would not open His mouth, He would be assigned a grave with the wicked, He would lie with the wealthy in death even though He had done no violence or repeated a single falsehood . . ."

"Does HaShem have a plan for every man?"

I considered a moment, then nodded and searched through my papyri. "You are correct. Does the Scripture not say, 'The heart of man plans his course, but Adonai directs his steps'? And David wrote, 'Your eyes saw me when I was unformed, and in your book were written the days that were formed—when not one of them had come to be.' So yes, HaShem has ordained what will happen every day that we live." I glanced at her. "Was . . . was my explanation clear?"

She pointed to my pages. "I have a question and would be curious to know if you can find the answer for me."

"I will do my best to serve you." I smiled, pleased with her interest in scholarly matters. "What is your question?"

"Since HaShem has planned every day of your life, can you tell me when you will take a wife?"

I did not move, stunned by the sweetly determined expression on her face.

"My father says it is a young man's duty to take a wife and produce children," she went on, apparently not noticing my paralysis. "He says Yeshua did not marry because He devoted himself to prayer and teaching. But Yeshua's brothers are either married or betrothed, and so are many of the Twelve."

I stared at her, my heart pounding. "I-I do not know

HaShem's plan for the rest of my life. That is . . . that is why I—why all of us—must walk in faith."

"I see." She smiled again, then stood and moved away from the bench. "When your faith becomes sight, Matthew, I would be pleased to hear of it."

THIRTY

Mary

Matthew arrived early, clearly having heard I had returned from Nazareth.

"Shalom, good morning, and happy Hanukkah," he said, removing his sandals at our threshold. "Congratulations on the birth of your grandson."

I acknowledged his greeting with a smile and motioned him toward the cooking area. "Before we begin, would you like some honeyed figs? Miriam has been baking, and the entire house smells delightful."

Miriam offered Matthew a tray of *globi*, one of her specialties. She had spent hours rolling a mixture of semolina flour, honey, and ricotta cheese into balls, which she then rolled in sesame seeds.

"These look delicious," Matthew said, helping himself to the globi. "I am glad you are safely home, Mary. I have been eager to share everything I have written while you were away. And I have to ask—did you take any papyri with you to Nazareth?"

I blanched. "No."

Matthew shrugged. "No matter. I left the Gethsemane account here for you to read, yet the pages disappeared. But I rewrote the story, and I have a feeling the second version is better than the first."

"Good." I forced a smile. "I will join you in a moment."

As he sat to talk to Miriam, I retreated to the safety of my bedchamber and stared at my reflection in the looking brass. The pain was worse this morning—probably the result of the four-day journey from Nazareth. My bones ached, my stomach hurt, and my neck felt as though someone had driven a spike through the spot just beneath my head . . .

"Touch me, Adonai, and I will be healed," I whispered. "Save me, and I will be saved. For you are my praise."

When I was certain I could sit across from Matthew and not grimace with pain, I wrapped my himation around my shoulders and joined him and Miriam at the table.

"What did you do while I was away, Matthew?" I asked. "You said you were going to catch up on your accounting work."

He nodded as he bit into a fig, then swallowed. "During the first week I brought all the records up to date. Then I began to write about some of Yeshua's teachings. The Ruach opened the Scriptures for me and enabled me to see them with new eyes. I have learned so much; I cannot wait for you to read the pages."

I forced a smile. "That is good."

Matthew kept going. "When possible, I interviewed people whose stories you could not know. I spoke to Joseph of Arimathea because he was present at Yeshua's trial. I also spoke to the servant who worked at the high priest's house and confronted Peter that same night. I also met with Zacchaeus. He is in Jerusalem for the Feast of Dedication, and yesterday I spotted him outside the Temple. I knew him when I was a tax collector, so we had a good talk." He laughed. "He is no longer collecting taxes but sells olive-wood candlesticks outside Jericho."

I stared at him, annoyed at first, and then my irritation rose with each word that tumbled out of his mouth. "You did all that," I said, my voice flat, "without me. Even after what transpired between us."

He tilted his brow, gave me an uncertain look, and straightened his spine. "I did not ignore you, Mary; you were not here. I took advantage of opportunities, for how was I to know HaShem did not send them?"

I caught sight of Miriam's face—she was looking at me in alarm, her eyes troubled.

I lowered my head and struggled to understand my anger. Was it righteous, or was I upset because I was ill-tempered, exhausted, and unwell?

"I thought—" I forced myself to speak slowly—"I thought you were going to help me, not undertake all the work yourself."

His brows lowered. "*I* thought you were determined to make this Yeshua's story, not your own. You were not with us when we met Zacchaeus. You were not present at Yeshua's trial, nor were you at the high priest's house when Peter denied the Master. What should I have done, Mary, let those opportune moments slip away simply because you were not here?"

He was right, but I could not find the breath to answer. I leaned forward, my hand pressing against my ribs as an invisible shard stabbed my side with every breath.

"Mary?" Miriam slid toward me, the corners of her mouth tightening. "Should you lie down? Do you need food? Water?"

I held up my hand and shook my head. I took a painful breath, forcing air into my lungs, then exhaled slowly. Another breath and the sharp pain subsided a bit. Another breath. And another.

"I am fine." I flashed Miriam a quick smile, then lowered my gaze again. What was happening to me? From the beginning I wanted this to be Yeshua's story, so why was I so upset with Matthew? I involved him because I believed the work would bless him. But now he was taking over, asking the questions, doing the interviews, receiving instruction from the Ruach HaKodesh.

Yet Yeshua was *my* Son; the idea for these stories had been *mine*. What right had Matthew to move forward without me? I knew how the stories should be written, and I had stopped him from overstating them at least a dozen times . . .

Perhaps I could finish on my own.

"I have changed my mind." I lifted my head and glanced at Miriam, then looked at the eager young man across the table. "If you will leave your papyri, I can write the remaining stories and have them translated into Hebrew. I know exactly how they should read. Thank you for the work you have done, Matthew, but I no longer need you."

"Mary—Ima—"

"That is all." I stood and dismissed him with an abrupt nod, then slowly retreated to the solitude of my bedchamber.

THIRTY-ONE

Matthew

I covered the distance to Peter's house in a haze of irritation and relief. I was irritated because Mary did not appreciate all the work I had accomplished in her absence, and relieved because my responsibility had ended. I had done everything she asked but still could not make her happy. Fine. I would enjoy being free. I would finally be able to teach and preach with Peter, James, and John.

I thought I would walk away with a clean conscience, yet my thoughts kept returning to Mary's reaction to my report. I understood why she might be upset to discover that I had accomplished so much during her absence, but what else was I supposed to do while she was away? My bookkeeping tasks could not fill all the days in a week, and I would have been foolish if I had not stopped Zacchaeus when he crossed my path. We needed that story, and Mary knew little about the situation. She had not attended the dinner at Zacchaeus's house, and she had not heard him exclaim that he would repay anyone he had cheated four times over.

Neither could we omit the story of Yeshua's trial, so we desperately needed to speak to a witness. I suddenly wished she were standing in front of me so I could sputter out my defense.

Perhaps HaShem had led me to interview Joseph of Arimathea without her because his testimony would have caused her pain. Our merciful God had not allowed her to be present for Yeshua's scourging, His trial, or His interview before Pilate. Yeshua's story would not be complete without those episodes, and Mary knew it. She should have understood that I would have to interview others, and she should trust me to get the necessary details. I was fully capable of recording the facts and avoiding the sort of overwriting she despised . . .

When I arrived at Peter's house, I nodded at Anna and Dina, then went upstairs, dropped my satchel on the floor, and fell onto the bed. I lay flat on my back and stared at the ceiling. I was still quite awake when I sensed the voice of the Spirit: *Matthew.*

I caught my breath. "Lord?"

I sent you to help her.

"She said she would write the stories herself."

Go back.

"She dismissed me! She does not like the way I write, she does not appreciate the work I do, and she seems to think I ought to be able to read her mind."

Go back. And remain until the work is finished.

I heaved a sigh. I saw no vision, heard no audible voice, but I could not deny that the words came from outside my head—outside my *will*. If I had my way, I would join Peter and John tomorrow. I would go with them to preach, I could witness miracles, and HaShem might even use me to work a wonder—

Go back.

But I could never escape the insistent voice of the Spirit.

The next morning, I rose early, slipped out of Peter's house, and went back to Mary's. I did not knock at such an early hour but let myself into the courtyard and sat on the bench. Technically, I was trespassing, but Miriam would never report me. I could not speak for Mary.

I slumped against the wall and waited, my arms crossed and my gaze fixed on the goat, who stared at me with narrow, golden eyes. Around me, doors were opening and neighbors emerging, all of them heading to the Temple for the second day of the Hanukkah observance. Most of them did not see me slumped beside Mary's courtyard wall, and the few who did only looked at me curiously, then went their way.

Miriam stepped outside and gasped when she saw me, her hand rising to her throat.

"I apologize," I said, straightening. "I am waiting for Mary."

Miriam's startled expression softened to a warm smile. "You may be waiting a while. She is not happy with you."

"I know."

Miriam reached into the hens' nesting box and pulled out two eggs. "I am glad you are here, and she will be too—once she calms herself."

"Will that take long, do you think?"

Miriam chuckled. "She will feel the way she feels until the hurt fades. Then her heart will grow quiet, and she will hear the Ruach HaKodesh, who will remind her that you are her beloved brother . . . as well as Yeshua's."

request. Wine was a valuable commodity, and Yeshua's first miracle had involved wine. I could see why Shimon wanted Mary's approval for his new venture.

I had no trouble hearing Mary's clear reply. "HaShem did not call me to promote wine, but to do His will."

Despite the wall between us, Mary's answer filled me with pleasure.

On the final day of Hanukkah, I slid the last page of my notes into my satchel, leaned against the courtyard wall, and sighed. If she did not soon let me in, I would have to tend to my bookkeeping with this goat and the chickens. When I had finished that, I would have to ask Peter about some other trade to practice in this courtyard while I waited for the Spirit's permission to leave . . .

"Levi?"

I turned, surprised to hear a female voice address me by my former name, then nearly choked on an astonished cry. "Jael?" I leaned over the gate to embrace my younger sister, whom I had not seen in, how many years, fifteen? "HaShem is good," I said, stepping back to look at her. "You have grown into a woman."

"A married woman," she added, a smile ruffling her mouth. "With two children."

"Truly?"

She nodded. "Enough about me. Why am I hearing that you have been forced to stand outside this house?"

I waved the question away and sat on the courtyard wall. "Do not fret. It is due to a minor disagreement. How did you find me? Are Abba and Ima with you?"

Her smile faded. "They are at the Temple. I found you

because I have friends who follow the Way. One of them realized that the brother I always ask about is now called Matthew and was one of the Twelve."

I reached for her hand and squeezed it. "I was so happy to hear that you and your husband follow Yeshua."

"Abba and Ima do not approve, of course."

"Abba has not cast you out?"

"How can he? I live with my husband's family." She glanced over her shoulder, then lowered her voice. "Abba was greatly disturbed when David and I began to meet with the believers in Sepphoris. He might have publicly denounced us, but Ima convinced him I was no longer his problem. Yet something stronger than her words won the argument—Abba adores my children."

I folded my arms. "More than he adored his son, apparently."

"He is not the man he was when he cast you out of the house. He is still stubborn, but he is not as quick to make judgments that cannot be rectified." She hesitated, her eyes revealing a tenderness he had never seen in her before. "I think—I think Abba allows himself to love my children because he regrets not loving you better."

I swallowed the lump that had risen in my throat and studied the passersby. "I am glad you were not cast out of the family. Becoming a tax collector must be a more serious offense than following Yeshua."

She shook her head. "Yeshua was a Jew. And you were not cast out for becoming a tax collector. That came later."

"You are right, of course. But it happened so long ago."

"Let us not talk about the past." Her brown eyes brimmed with affection. "I have thought of you so often. Every night I pray that HaShem would keep you safe and well."

"Your prayers have been answered, then. I have been blessed far beyond my imagining."

"Are you married?"

I grinned. "Did your spies not report my lack of a wife?"

A blush shadowed her cheeks. "Perhaps I was hoping something had changed—or was about to."

I lifted my chin and laughed. "I have been busy. I have been back in Jerusalem for less than a year, yet I am working two jobs, both of them connected to the ministry of the Gospel."

"I am so happy for you."

"And I for you. David is a fortunate man."

She blushed and turned her head, revealing the purity of her profile. My little sister, who had been a child of twelve when I left home, had since grown into a beautiful wife and mother.

"Jael, do you think Abba would see me if—?"

"No. I love you, brother, and I would love to see Abba embrace you as a father should embrace a son, but he will not do it."

"But I am no longer a tax collector. I gave up that life when I followed Yeshua."

A melancholy frown flitted across her lovely features. "He knows—Ima told him about seeing you at Sukkot. His anger flared and he remains stubborn, and yet I do not believe he hates you. When people speak of Matthew the disciple, now he draws near to eavesdrop, though he pretends not to hear a word."

I crossed my arms, digesting this information. "So, he will not forgive the sins of my past."

"Not unless you renounce Yeshua and come home."

"And Ima?"

The grim line of her mouth relaxed. "Ima misses you,

but she will not disobey Abba's wishes. While she knew I planned to find you today, she would not let me talk of it. When I tried to ask if she wanted to come with me, she turned and quickly left the room."

"Are you staying in the Upper City?"

"Yes," she said, then understanding lit her eyes. "You must not look for us or Abba will know I came to see you."

"But—"

"Please." She lifted a hand. "I do not want trouble with Abba. As it is, we count ourselves blessed because he allows our children to visit him."

Not knowing what else to say, I sat and studied my sister, impressing every detail of her face in my memory. The usual sounds of street traffic wrapped around us, although we seemed to be cocooned within an almost palpable silence.

"Will I not see you for another fifteen years?" I asked, my voice breaking. "I want to meet your husband and hug your children."

She glanced over her shoulder and pulled her headscarf tighter around her face. "If you ever come to Sepphoris, you can stay with us. I might manage to invite Abba and Ima to come visit the children."

"You are a brilliant woman." I caught her hand and squeezed it, my heart constricting when I saw tears glistening in her eyes.

Then she released me, turned, and disappeared into the crowd.

I was drowsing on the courtyard bench, arms crossed and eyes closed, when an odd sound startled me to wakefulness. I opened my eyes and saw Mary sitting at my feet, a look of concern on her face.

"For a moment I thought you might be dead." She offered me a small loaf. "How long has it been since you ate something? There is cheese, if you want it."

"I-I ate earlier," I stammered, feeling my cheeks burn as I sat up. "But thank you."

Mary set the loaf between us, crossed her arms, and stared across the courtyard. "You are a most stubborn man. Did Yeshua never teach about the sin of stubbornness? Perhaps when I was away?"

I smiled. "He told a parable about a woman who made a request of an unjust judge. The judge was unwilling to grant it, but because she would not stop pestering him, he finally did."

Mary snorted softly. "And the meaning behind that story?"

"If even an unjust judge will grant a persistent request, HaShem will surely do justice for His chosen ones who cry to Him day and night."

Mary sat in silence for a moment, then cleared her throat. "I am the unjust judge, then. I have wronged you, Matthew, and I am sorry. I was tired and not myself, but that is no excuse for the way I reacted. You were right, of course. You were right to go ahead and continue the work without me. You should probably finish the scroll yourself, for I have contributed all I have to give."

"Not so." I turned to face her. "I understand why you felt the way you did. The Spirit inspired the idea in you, and you invited me to work by your side. You did not expect me to charge ahead, and for my thoughtlessness I apologize. I made assumptions I should not have made. I was carried away by all the Ruach taught me . . . but I would never want to leave you behind."

She smiled, and the warmth returned to her voice. "We

should be a team. I supply what you could not know, you provide what I do not have, and together we learn about what neither of us could witness."

"Agreed."

We sat for a moment, content in our mutual peace, then Mary smoothed the wrinkles from her tunic. "Hanukkah is over, but Miriam has baked fresh honey cakes. Will you not come in and enjoy them with us?

Grateful my vigil had ended, I followed her into the house. Miriam must have known what was happening outside, because she greeted me with a smile and gestured to the table, which had been beautifully spread with barley cakes, chopped cucumbers, celery, carrots, olive relish, and cups of lemon water. I sat on the bench while the two women sat opposite me.

We had just blessed the food when Mary looked up and caught my eye. "I must know," she said, studying me carefully, "why you waited so patiently. Most men would have given up after the first hour."

I shrugged. "I could not go. The Ruach HaKodesh called me to this task, and He would not let me walk away."

She accepted my words with a knowing smile. "You love Him, so you obey Him."

"I will not disappoint you, Ima. As I serve Yeshua, so I will serve you."

She bit into a barley cake and ate in silence for a moment, then tilted her head. "I do not know much about you, Matthew—other than what I learned when we first met. You lived in Capernaum and you were Levi the tax collector. What were you before that?"

"The son of Alphaeus." I lowered my gaze. How much should I tell her? I did not think she would want to hear

a glance with Miriam, who had been silently listening with wide eyes.

"Your father disapproved of this Roman girl," I said.

Matthew barked a laugh. "I never told him about her, not at first. I knew he would never even hear of such an association. I knew I had no business speaking to a Gentile or a woman, but I forgot everything, including who I was, when I saw Aurelia in the marketplace. I spoke to her, I asked her name, and when we parted, I felt as though I had left some piece of myself behind. After that day, I spent little time thinking of Torah or HaShem, but countless hours dreaming of Aurelia."

"Let me guess." Miriam leaned forward. "Your father realized something was amiss."

Matthew folded his arms as tight as a gate. "Of course he did. I did not dare tell him about my preoccupation, but he noticed—how could he not? When he asked why I had been distracted from my studies, I confessed everything, thinking that perhaps he had experienced something similar in his youth. I hoped he would tell me I was caught in a simple infatuation, and it would pass soon enough."

I pressed my hands together. "But he did not."

A rueful smile curved Matthew's mouth. "When I told him I loved a Roman girl, he tore his tunic and demanded to know how I could let such foolishness enter my head. Why had I lost custody of my eyes? I should never have looked at her, he said, and I certainly should never have spoken to her. I should cut out my tongue before doing such a thing."

"I wept before him, asking what I should do. Abba said I must renounce her and vow never to see her again. To enforce my vow, I could not leave the house until Aurelia and her family left the city."

Matthew fell silent, either gathering his thoughts or revisiting his memories. Then he lifted his eyes, and in them I saw a mingling of grief and guilt.

"What could I do? I told my father I wanted to please him above all things, but I could not be false to my heart. So he cast me out of the house, declaring I was no son of his."

Miriam made soft sounds of sympathy, but I remained silent, understanding how Matthew *and* his father had felt. My Joseph would have been horrified if one of our sons had declared his love for a Gentile woman, and my tenderhearted Joses was the sort who fell in love with every girl who smiled in his direction. Young women often did not realize the power of such a smile . . .

"I spent that first night on the street," Matthew went on, "and I filled the hours with impractical thoughts of how I would speak to her the next day, I would declare my love, and she would agree to be my wife. I would visit her father and offer to work for him. He would accept me, and one day we would leave Galilee and go to Rome, where we would raise children and I would worship HaShem in gratitude for giving me such a beautiful and loving wife. So when the sun rose the next morning, I went to the marketplace, hoping for a glimpse of Aurelia."

Miriam cleared her throat. "Did she come?"

Matthew smiled without humor. "She did. I waited at the market for hours, then saw her walking with one of her father's friends, a Roman soldier in full uniform. She hung on his arm, and he bent and kissed her in full view of everyone. In that horrible moment I realized I could never love such an immodest woman. I shrank back, realizing too late that my father was right. I sank to the ground as my silly dreams crumbled into dust."

He lowered his head. "You must think me a complete fool. No Jewish man does what I did; no one defies his family for the sake of a Gentile woman." He glanced at me, his eyes filled with uncertainty.

"Go on," I whispered. "This is not the time to concern yourself with what I think. Finish your story."

Matthew drew a deep breath. "By the time the sun set that day, I realized I had destroyed my life in Sepphoris. My family would not forgive my foolishness, and I could not remain in the city where everyone knew Levi, son of Alphaeus. So I left and went to Jerusalem, where I learned the Romans were looking for Jews who would give five years in service as tax collectors and scribes for Rome. I was already an outcast among the Jews, so what would it matter if I worked for Gentiles? I had been willing to marry one.

"That is where I met Achiakos, and where I learned I was good with numbers. After my training, the Romans set me to work collecting taxes in Capernaum, where I cheated everyone—Jew, Gentile, rich, poor—everyone but the Romans, who did not pay Judean taxes. I worked the required five years and two more, amassing a great deal of wealth.

"Then Yeshua found me in my tollbooth, my hands filled with coins taken from poor Jewish farmers. When He said, 'Come,' in that one word I heard an invitation to leave tax collection and find my rightful place . . . to find myself."

"You heard *love*." Miriam reached across the table to pat Matthew's hand. "I heard the same thing when Yeshua spoke my name."

"I learned an important lesson," Matthew said, making a fist. "I learned not to trust my heart. It got me into trouble once, so I will not let that happen again."

"Oh, Matthew." Tears sprang to my eyes. "You must not

say that. Your heart is different now—it is filled with the Ruach HaKodesh. You must trust it, always."

"Tell me." Miriam leaned toward our young friend. "Have you felt the stirrings of love for any woman since Aurelia?"

Matthew went pale, then a deep red washed up his throat and flooded his face. "I have had no time for such foolishness."

"Love is not foolish, Matthew. Infatuation is, but loving the woman HaShem prepared for you is a blessing. So . . ." Miriam gave him an indulgent smile. "Have you seen a woman lately—a woman to whom you could be happily married?"

He glanced away and cleared his throat. "Perhaps. There is one. She is beautiful and she loves HaShem. But she is young."

"How young? Six? Seven?"

"Of course not." His brows pulled into an affronted frown. "She is not a child, but she is younger than me."

"In that case, age matters not." I slapped the table for emphasis. "I was fifteen when betrothed to Joseph, and he was thirty. A man must be able to support a family. As long as a woman is old enough to bear children—"

"I should not marry," Matthew interrupted. "I do not know where HaShem will lead me next. When we have finished this project, what then? I must do something, but I have no idea what that will be. It is not fair to ask a father to betroth his daughter to an unsettled man."

I glanced at Miriam and smiled. "Thank you for telling us your story, Matthew. I have always wondered how you came to be in that tollbooth."

"That story," Matthew said, "should not be included in our collection."

"Not all of it," I said. "But we will include the most important part."

I left Matthew writing at the table, took my headscarf from the hook on the wall, and told Miriam I would be back later. "Are you sure you should go out?" she asked, her forehead creased with concern. "You look tired."

"It has been a busy day, but I am fine." I shot her a twisted smile. "I will feel the way I feel whether I stay home or go out."

Miriam watched me like a mother hen until I stepped out of the house. When the door closed behind me, I inhaled a deep breath. "HaShem, bless this endeavor. May your Spirit lead me to the right people, and may your will be done."

I walked toward the wealthiest section of Jerusalem. During the festivals, every home in Jerusalem opened its doors to visitors, and Matthew's sister had said they were staying in the Upper City. But in which house? The Ruach HaKodesh would have to guide me, and quickly. Hanukkah had ended, so most pilgrims would soon be returning to their homes.

I crept down the street, rocking from hip to hip like an old woman. The pain in my bones would not allow me to walk at a normal pace, yet I did not mind. I kept to the side of the street so as not to hinder faster walkers and caught snatches of conversation from open courtyards and rooftop balconies. I listened, hoping to recognize Jael's voice or catch a reference to Sepphoris, but I went all the way to Herod's Palace without hearing anything significant.

I turned and made my way down another street of the Upper City, then paused at the mikveh. Kings and queens built mikvehs in their homes, but most women used the community mikvehs to purify themselves after the time of *niddah* or childbirth. I was past the age of childbearing, so I rarely needed a mikveh, but Jael was young, and her mother might still be of childbearing age. Even if they did not stop at the mikveh, this street was well-traveled, so I might catch a glimpse of them . . .

HaShem, let it be so.

I sat on a stone bench outside the painted door and studied the faces of passing women. The bench, which had not been designed for comfort, scraped against my bones, forcing me to frequently shift my position. I placed my weight on one hip, then the other. I was considering whether I should stand when I looked up and saw Matthew's sister. She and an older woman were coming my way, their heads bent toward each other in conversation, their strides confident and carefree.

With great effort I pushed myself off the bench and moved to block their path. "Jael?" The sudden movement left me breathless. "Please . . . wait."

The young woman stopped, shock flickering over her face, and the older woman looked at me with speculation in her eyes.

"Shalom," I said, struggling to catch my breath. "I am Mary. I saw you at my house. You were speaking . . . to Matthew."

Jael took a wincing little breath and glanced at the older woman, who did not seem surprised.

I turned to the second woman. "You must be Matthew's mother. Blessed are you to have such a fine son."

I do not know what I expected—a smile? A blush? But Matthew's mother looked as if her face had been carved in stone.

Jael placed her arm around the woman's shoulders. "This is my mother, Abigail."

I nodded. "I am pleased to meet you. I was wondering if you would like to come to my home for dinner. Matthew is working there, and I know he would love to see you again."

Abigail's mouth spread into a thin-lipped smile. "You are kind, but we will be unable to accept your hospitality."

"Are you certain?" I almost grasped her hand, but something in her chilly demeanor warded me off.

She lifted her head. "Do you know Matthew well?"

"I know him better every day. For more than a dozen years he has been like family, and I love him like a son. He is a fine man and brings honor to you."

Jael smiled to hear this, but Abigail remained indifferent. "Shalom," she said, stepping forward.

I blocked her path. "Please. I have lost a Son, so I know something of the pain you have endured. My Son was returned to me, and I would love for you to experience the same joy."

The woman lifted a single brow. "I am a pious woman." She spoke in a low voice, but within it I heard an undertone of desolation. "I will not dishonor my husband by disobeying his wishes. This Matthew you speak of—he is dead to us."

"Perhaps he was, but he has a new life now. If you will come, I will lead the way."

"Shalom." Without another word, Abigail drew her mantle closer and moved past me, leaving Jael behind. Matthew's sister gave me a bleak look and was about to hurry after her mother when I clutched her sleeve.

"If she changes her mind," I said, searching her face, "you know where I live."

Jael nodded, then took off after Abigail.

I watched them go, and in the silence I heard my heart break.

On the second day of the week, the day Miriam and I usually set aside to scrub the house and wash our clothing, I heard an unexpected knock at the door. I knew it could not be Matthew, since he would spend the day working for the communities, but thought perhaps one of my sons had come to Jerusalem.

I blinked in astonishment when I opened the door and saw Dina, Peter's daughter, carrying a basket.

"Shalom." The girl gave me a sweet smile. "I was hoping to find you home."

I opened the door wider and invited her inside. "Miriam and I are usually here this time of day." I lifted a brow, thinking she would ask for something. Instead, she simply walked into the house.

I turned and led the way into the kitchen. "Miriam, look who has come to see us."

Miriam looked up and smiled, then cut a glance to me. "Shalom! What a nice surprise."

"Shalom to you." Dina sat at the long table and pushed her basket toward me. "Ima baked bread last night, and these loaves are for you."

"Thank you." I picked up one of the loaves and sniffed at the dark crust. "It smells wonderful. We will have some for dinner."

"And now I don't have to bake bread." Miriam clapped imaginary flour from her hands. "Praise HaShem for your thoughtfulness."

Deciding to let Dina explain her presence at leisure, I moved to the folded garments that needed mending. If Dina wanted to talk, she could say anything she wanted while I sewed.

I threaded my needle and sat on the bench, then proceeded to repair a rip in a seam. Dina propped her chin in her hand and watched for a moment, then moistened her lips. "Is . . . have you heard from Matthew today?"

I lifted a brow. "Why, no. He usually spends the second day of the week at your house, recording gifts from the communities."

"Yes, he does." Dina pivoted to Miriam. "Do you cook for him when he is here?"

Miriam smiled. "I cook, and he eats whatever I set on the table. He is not very particular about his food."

Dina nodded. "Abba says that comes from traveling with Yeshua all those years. He says some days they were lucky to eat at all, so they learned to be grateful for anything, no matter how it tasted."

I glanced at Miriam and smothered a smile. Obviously, Dina didn't realize that Miriam and I had been among the women who cooked for the men traveling with Yeshua.

"Ima says I should learn how to cook," Dina went on, her gaze idly roving around the room. "Because I should take good care of my husband."

I cleared my throat rather than release the laughter that bubbled beneath my breastbone. "That is important, yes. A wife should know how to cook and keep a home—if she is to live in a house. My son Jude and his wife do not have a house because they are always traveling to spread the Gospel. Tasmin is an excellent wife, but she has learned how to be useful in other ways." I lowered my sewing and caught Dina's absent gaze. "May I ask—has your father been approached by a young man? Are you about to be betrothed?"

The girl's flush deepened to crimson. "No . . . Abba has not said anything to me."

"Really? You are certainly old enough." I went back to sewing. "I wonder if we know any young men in need of a wife. What say you, Miriam? Does anyone come to mind?"

Dina's blush receded, leaving two red spots on her cheeks. "I should probably go now. Thank you for seeing me."

"You are always welcome here." Miriam smiled and walked Dina to the door. "Please give our love to your parents and especially to Matthew. We hope to see him tomorrow."

Dina nodded stiffly. "Shalom."

"Shalom, Dina. And thank you for the bread."

Miriam waited until Dina left the courtyard, then came back into the room and shook her head. "Will you speak to Matthew or shall I?"

"I will." I tied a knot, then cut the thread with my teeth. "It is time we put those young people out of their misery."

THIRTY-THREE

Matthew

I arrived at Mary's house early on the third day of the week, my satchel bulging with pages I had written the night before. Like a camel that smells water long before a man can see it, I sensed we were nearing the end of our labor. Mary kept talking about including other stories, but she knew full well we would never be able to put every story into this collection. The scroll would be quite thick once I glued the pages together, and the cost of hiring a copyist would be considerable.

I knocked and was surprised when Mary answered. Miriam was usually the first to rise, but as Mary led me into the cooking area, she said something about Miriam going to the market for herbs.

I barely heard her. I was eager to show her the most recent pages, so I dropped my satchel onto the table and unfastened the leather ties.

Mary slid between the table and the bench opposite me, then braced herself against the tabletop. "Wait," she said, her eyes on my satchel. "I would speak with you before we begin our work."

Something—perhaps the tone of her voice—made my stomach drop. Had something happened?

"Sit, Matthew." She glanced up at me, and in that instant I noticed that her cheekbones had sharpened beneath a translucent veil of skin.

I dropped to the bench and waited.

"Matthew"—she lifted her index finger—"you must stop wasting time. Dina loves you, and you care for her. You must speak to Peter right away."

I stared at Mary in a paralysis of bewilderment.

"I know," she went on, punctuating her words with her fingertip, "you feel you do not deserve to be blessed with marriage because of your past. But you *do* deserve happiness because Yeshua was right—you are a gift of God."

"Wh-what?" I stammered, trying to regain control of the situation. "Mary, I have told you—"

"You have made a great many objections, and none of them are valid. What man is able to know what will happen to him? None of us knows what the future will bring, but we trust HaShem to work His will. The important matter, the *crucial* matter, is that we trust Him and obey when we are given instruction."

"I have not received instruction from the Ruach about marriage."

"Do you think the Ruach HaKodesh speaks only in that still, silent voice?" She laughed. "My son, the Spirit speaks to us through the Word of God and also through the voices of godly believers. Sometimes we refuse to hear the still voice, so someone else must shout in our ears."

I sat motionless, her words echoing in the room, and knew she was right. I was attracted to Dina and knew she would make a good wife, no matter how many years separated us.

"Some say Jerusalem is the center of the world," Dina gently remonstrated. "It is HaShem's home."

"Perhaps Jerusalem is the world's spiritual center," Lemuel said. "But Rome is certainly the center of the world's government. Without Rome, we would have no paved roads, no system of message delivery, no—"

"Lemuel." I nodded and smiled when the young man turned to see me. "I see Dina has entertained you while you waited, but we do not want to detain you. You have a message for me, I assume?"

"Yes." Lemuel stood and dipped his head in respect, then folded his hands. "From Achiakos, a servant of Herod Agrippa—"

"No coded notes this time?"

The young man flushed. "I have memorized the message."

I sank to a bench opposite Dina. "Then deliver it, please."

Lemuel cleared his throat. "Achiakos says, 'Grace and shalom be unto you from the imperial city.' My master Achiakos is well and wishes he could meet you face-to-face. He told his master Agrippa of all that happened in Tiberias regarding Petronius's letter to Caesar, but Agrippa did not believe any letter would prevail against Caesar's stubbornness. So he planned a dinner for the emperor, a dinner unlike any Rome has ever seen. He brought in the best foods, the finest furnishings, and the most outrageous entertainers. He spent more than he owned, more than Caesar himself has ever spent on a single feast. More, even, than the feast Cleopatra held to entice Mark Antony."

"Surely," I interrupted, "Caesar can afford his own dinners."

Lemuel shook his head. "Business in Rome is often conducted over dinners. The amount of wealth invested in a dinner demonstrates the affection the host has for the guest. Agrippa wanted to show Caesar how highly he esteemed his friendship, so he was careful to exceed all other banquets, both in expense and in preparations. This feast was so far removed from the ordinary that even Caesar himself could never equal, much less exceed it."

"I would hate to pay for that dinner." I smiled at Dina, who gave me an uncertain smile in return.

"During the event," Lemuel went on, "Caesar so admired Agrippa's magnificence that he proposed to do all he could to please Agrippa. So when Caesar had drunk much wine and was merrier than usual, the emperor said, 'I knew before how great a respect you have for me, and how great a kindness you have shown me, but you have not omitted anything in this banquet. I therefore desire to make amends for everything in which I have been formerly deficient. Everything that may contribute to your happiness shall be at your service, and cheerfully, so far as my ability will reach.' So said Caesar to Agrippa, thinking Agrippa would ask for some large country or the revenues of certain cities. Agrippa replied that it was not out of any expectation of gain that he paid his respects, nor did he now do anything in order to receive anything from Caesar.

"The emperor was astonished at Agrippa's answer and pressed him again, urging him to request something in order that he might show his gratitude. Then Agrippa replied, 'Since you, O my lord, declare such is your readiness to grant, I will ask nothing relating to my own happiness. But I desire something that may render the Divinity helpful to your designs.'"

I lifted a brow as Lemuel continued: "Caesar listened intently when Agrippa finally stated his request: all he wanted was for Caesar to think no longer about dedicating the statue he had ordered Petronius to erect in the Jewish Temple."

I gasped at Agrippa's request—Caesar must have been astounded. Agrippa had never been a particular friend to the Jews, but Rome had made him our king, so perhaps he simply wanted to maintain peace in his territory. If Caesar waged war against us and killed the fighting men, how could Agrippa benefit from ruling a land of women and children? He was wise to dread war and courageous to suggest that Caesar abandon his audacious plan.

I caught Lemuel's gaze. "I am astonished."

Lemuel's smile radiated pleasure. "When I heard the news, I was happy to be working for a man who worked for Agrippa. His request was simple, but if Caesar had not granted it, he certainly would have had Agrippa and his family executed."

"And?" The breathless question came from Dina, who had hung on every word of Lemuel's discourse.

He turned to her. "What?"

"What did Caesar say?"

"He granted Agrippa's request," Lemuel answered. "He wrote a letter for Petronius, telling him not to trouble himself about the statue but to dismiss his army, go back to Syria, and take care of the affairs that Caesar had first sent him to oversee. He said he had granted the request of Agrippa, whom he honored so greatly that he could not refuse him anything."

"Praise HaShem!" Dina clapped, her joy shining in her eyes, her cheeks the color of summer roses. The effect was not lost in Lemuel, I noticed, for his cheeks colored, too.

"I am sure you are eager to return to your master," I said,

steeling my voice, "so we will let you depart. Do you need anything before you go?"

Lemuel lifted his hand. "My master bids me tell you that we must remain in prayer about the situation. Petronius's letter—in which he informed Caesar that the Jews were ready to revolt regarding the statue, and that they seemed resolved to threaten war against the Romans—is still en route to Rome. Unless it can be stolen or otherwise destroyed before it reaches the emperor, who can say how Caesar will react?"

I sank deeper into my chair, troubled by the reminder. Gaius Caesar was nothing if not temperamental, and Agrippa's victory might well become Petronius's disaster.

Lemuel stood. "Is there any reply for my master?"

I stroked my beard a moment, then looked up. "Please tell Achiakos that we are grateful for the report and committed to remaining in prayer. With him, we will trust HaShem to work His will."

Lemuel nodded. "I will be sure to relay your message." He did not move toward the door, however, and I looked up when Dina cleared her throat. "Shall we not give him a blessing before he goes?"

"Oh. Yes." I stood to face the young man, then placed my hands on his bowed head. "May it be your will, Lord, our God and the God of our ancestors, that you lead this man toward peace, guide his footsteps toward peace, and make him reach his desired destination for life, gladness, and peace. May you rescue him from the hand of every foe, every ambush along the way, and from all manner of evil. May you bless his handiwork and grant him grace, kindness, and mercy in your eyes and in the eyes of all who see him. Blessed are you, Lord, who hears and answers prayer.

I ask these things in the name of Yeshua, ben Elohim, our Lord."

"Amen," Lemuel and Dina whispered unanimously.

I turned away, unwilling to see the smile that undoubtedly passed between them.

Without delay, I told Peter what I had learned from Lemuel, who urged me to share the news with John, James, and the elders of the Jerusalem ecclēsia. Peter summoned them, and by nightfall they had all gathered in Peter's front room.

They were elated to hear that hope had come from an unexpected source, for who would have supposed that assistance would come from a Herod? Still, the threat remained, as this Caesar was known to be temperamental, double-minded, and unstable in all his ways.

"I will share this report with the high priest's personal amanuensis," John said, "because thus far Theophilus has not been successful in his efforts to win Caesar's favor."

"What efforts?" Peter asked. "What has he done?"

John shifted his weight in his chair. "He has sent gifts, of course. Hundreds of barrels of our finest olive oil and wine, along with gold. Though Caesar did not return any of the high priest's gifts, neither did he change his mind about erecting that blasphemous statue."

Together we prayed throughout the night, and not until the sky brightened in the east did each man return to his home.

I went upstairs and crawled into bed, ready for sleep. Just before closing my eyes, I remembered I had promised to ask Peter about his daughter. But my eyes were heavy, my body tired, and the hour late, so I fell asleep.

Eager to tell Mary and Miriam about Agrippa's good deed for the Jews—and less eager, I must admit, to tell them I had not spoken to Peter about his daughter—I went to their house early the next morning. The day was chilly and bright, the sun a dazzling blur in the eastern sky.

I let myself into the courtyard and knocked on the door. A moment later, Miriam greeted me and let me in. I found Mary seated at the table, my papyri scattered over its surface.

"Shalom, Matthew." She looked up and smiled. "You have done fine work on these stories. And these lessons . . . they have come from the Spirit."

"If you want to make alterations, we can," I assured her, taking my place across from her. "I will have to recopy the altered pages, but that is no trouble."

"I would change very little." She lowered her gaze to the papyri, and I noticed that her hand trembled as she traced the writing on the page. Had she been up all night?

"You look tired." I glanced at Miriam. "You should not let her stay up so late. We have to write several more stories, but there is no need to rush—"

"I am fine." Mary gave me a quick, reproachful glance. "I am old; I do not need to sleep as much as younger people."

I sighed and crossed my arms. Miriam filled the silence by coming over and sitting with us. "Well? What happened last night?"

"Oh." I blew out a breath. "We received news from Achiakos about Caesar, so Peter sent for the elders of the community. We spent the night in prayer, so I did not have a chance to speak to him about Dina."

"You will not forget today." Mary pierced me with a sharp look. "Promise me."

"I will not forget—but I am no longer certain Dina would be pleased to accept me."

Mary's brows rose like the wings of a startled bird. "What happened?"

I averted my eyes, feeling foolish, embarrassed, and . . . old. "The messenger from Achiakos is called Lemuel. He has come to visit twice, and both times Dina seemed . . . overly friendly to him."

Mary's brows rose even higher. "Why would she prefer this young man over you?"

"He is young." I lifted my chin. "And I suppose she thinks him handsome."

"You are handsome enough, Matthew. Why else?"

I shrugged. "They were talking when I came in. He spoke freely and easily to her, something I have never been able to do."

"Perhaps you do not speak freely because you have much on your mind. This Lemuel speaks freely because Dina is simply a girl to him, nothing more."

I shook my head.

"Is he a believer?"

"Yes."

"Does he live in Jerusalem?"

I looked up. "Why should that matter?"

"Because." Mary sighed and folded her arms. "If you think Peter would give his daughter to a man who lives in Rome, you are mistaken. And have you ever considered the possibility that Dina was using this young man?"

I frowned. "I'm not sure what you—"

"She sought to make you jealous," Miriam said, one corner of her mouth rising. "She wants you to act."

I leaned back, considering this, then nodded. "I should speak to Peter soon, then."

Miriam chuckled. "The sooner, the better."

Mary smiled. "Good. So, what is the latest news from Rome?"

I told them what Agrippa had done, how HaShem had worked a victory, but that we needed to continue in prayer. "At the moment, at least, Caesar is no longer intent on defiling our Temple."

"Praise HaShem," Mary murmured, turning another page. "He is merciful."

Mary had just finished stacking the papyrus pages when we heard a knock on the door. Miriam went to answer it while Mary slid the papyri toward me. "You have done well," she said. "And though I know we have other stories to write, we should begin to think about a proper ending."

"We have the account of the ascension," I reminded her. "We were all with Yeshua on the Mount of Olives."

"But Yeshua has been seen since that time," she said. "Saul of Tarsus saw Yeshua on his way to Damascus. If we can find Saul, we should talk to him."

"I will make inquiries," I promised. "Peter or James might know where to find him."

Mary's attention shifted to something behind me, and a sudden smile lit her face. I did not turn, supposing one of her family members had stopped by, but then I heard a familiar voice.

"Levi?"

I took a quick, sharp breath. When I turned, I saw Jael standing in the doorway with my mother—and Ima was weeping.

I do not know which surprised me more—seeing my mother

in Mary's house or seeing her tears. I rose and wrapped my arms around her as she collapsed against my chest. I felt the trembling of her frame and heard the broken sound of her weeping.

I caught Jael's gaze. "I did not think she would come," my sister said. "Yesterday, when Mary invited us, Ima would not be persuaded. But this morning she said she wanted to see you before we left for Sepphoris. So, while Abba went to inquire about a cart for the journey home, we came here."

I released Ima and stepped back to better study her face. Beneath the softly lined flesh I saw a suggestion of motion, as though an underground spring were trying to break through.

"Thank you for coming," I whispered, knowing how difficult it had been for her to go against my father's wishes. "It is good to see you again."

"My son." She gave me a twisted smile. "Your father will be furious if he learns I came to see you. Things were bad enough when you became a tax collector, but now you follow that blasphemer—"

"Ima . . ." I did not want to chide her, but neither could I let her believe a falsehood. "Yeshua is Israel's Messiah."

"And how do you know this?"

"I witnessed His miracles. I heard Him teach the Torah with authority, not relying on other scholars, only HaShem and the writings of Moses and the prophets. I saw Him minister to outcasts and the poor. I heard Him prophesy of things that came to pass, and other things that *will* come to pass. He is the Messiah, and I would gladly die for Him because He gives His followers eternal life."

"Someday, son, you may die for Him." Her brow wrinkled, and something moved in her eyes. "I did not want to come here, but I knew it might be the last time I would ever see you. So here I am."

I closed my eyes and prayed Peter or John would come through the doorway. They always seemed to know the right words to convince men and women of the truth of the Gospel. While I had spent as much time with Yeshua as they had, and words came easily to my pen, they did not come as readily to my tongue.

What had Yeshua said? *"No one can come to me unless my Father draws him."* Would HaShem draw my mother? If so, perhaps I would have to say very little.

As I stood and searched for words, Mary rose and took charge.

"Abigail and Jael, you are welcome here. Please come and sit." When I opened my eyes, Mary was gesturing to the cushioned benches in the front room. Ima hesitated, and then she and Jael walked over and sat. Miriam hurried to prepare a tray for our guests while Mary sat near my mother and smiled. "I understand your husband is a Torah teacher."

Ima nodded. "Yes."

"Then of course you remember the story of Joseph and his brothers."

Ima snorted with exasperation, and I feared Mary would try her patience. Yet she had obviously read what I had written about the hidden Messiah.

"Joseph's brothers stood before him," Mary continued, "when he was vizier of all Egypt, yet they did not recognize him. Joseph wept at the sight of the brothers who had betrayed and mistreated him, but so great was his love for them that he forgave them and revealed himself."

My mother's expression hardened. "What has that to do with—?"

"Yeshua *is* Israel's Messiah," Mary answered, her voice now as gentle as a spring breeze. "You may not see the truth yet, but one day He will reveal himself to all. Ask your husband—the prophecy is found in the writings of Zechariah."

My mother looked away, her face darkening with unreadable emotions.

"As you and your family return to Sepphoris," Mary went on, "I will ask HaShem to reveal the Messiah to you. Your son and daughter have found Him, as have thousands in Jerusalem. But, mother to mother, I want you to know that HaShem has forgiven your son for every sin. If HaShem can forgive him, it should be a small thing for your husband to do the same."

A tremor touched my mother's lips as she stood in one fluid motion. With a tilt of her head, she commanded Jael to follow her, and together they moved toward the door. Mary stood and wished them shalom on their journey.

Ima said nothing to me as she left, but she had heard the truth of the Gospel. I knew my mother would ponder Mary's words on the long way home. She would ask Abba to explain the prophecy of Zechariah.

And then perhaps the Ruach would draw their hearts to Yeshua.

THIRTY-FOUR

Mary

I did not think I would ever be irritated with Matthew again, but when he did not speak to Peter about Dina after his second promise, my patience vanished. Yes, the letter from Achiakos was unexpected. Yes, the visit from his mother and sister was emotionally draining. But why did those things exhaust Matthew to the point that he could not go downstairs and speak to his host about his daughter?

The morning after his mother's visit, Matthew came to our house at the appointed hour and took his seat at our table. But as Miriam sat next to him, I leaned over the table and held him with a look intended to communicate that I would brook no foolishness.

"We are not working today," I told him, my words clipped. "We are going to Peter's house to arrange your betrothal."

"But by this time Peter has surely gone out for the day. He and John leave together every morning—"

"I sent a message last night, imploring Peter to wait at the house until we arrive. So, not only is he home, he is waiting for us."

Mathew looked at Miriam. "Are you involved in this?"

She nodded. "I delivered the message last night."

Sighing, Matthew crossed his arms. "I am not prepared. I need a betrothal contract, I need a witness, I need a gift for Dina—"

"Here is your bridal contract." I lifted a parchment from my bench, written on the fine leather I had been saving far too long. "I copied it from my own *ketubah*, changing only the particulars."

"Mary and I will be your witnesses," Miriam said, a smile tugging at her lips. "And here is your gift." She reached to the back of her neck and unfastened the gold necklace her late husband had given her.

"I cannot accept that. It means too much to you."

"It will mean far more to me if I see it around Dina's neck."

She polished the gold links with the edge of her tunic, then dropped the necklace into a fabric bag.

"A Torah teacher usually officiates," Matthew protested. "And do you see a—?"

"You are a Torah teacher," I interrupted, weary of his procrastination. "And so is Peter. So stand up, smooth your hair, and let us go. Peter and his family are waiting."

I stood, but Matthew did not. He turned away and quietly said, "I cannot go."

I was about to say something sharp, but Miriam gave me a warning look. "Matthew," she said in a hushed, tender voice, "what is stopping you from doing what we know you want to do?"

"A man should have his father with him," he said, his

voice heavy with sorrow. "A father is supposed to negotiate the betrothal for his son."

Miriam and I exchanged a glance. Matthew was right, but what could we do about it? Alphaeus would not even speak to his son, so he certainly would not handle Matthew's marriage contract.

I sat again, stretched my arms across the table, and took Matthew's hands. "I can imagine how you must feel," I said. "Yeshua had His Father with Him always, except for the worst hour of His life. Do you remember the story? He was on the execution stake, enduring extreme suffering, when the skies went dark and Yeshua cried, 'My God, My God, why have you abandoned me?'"

Matthew dipped his chin in a grim nod. "He was quoting from the psalm of David."

"Yes, but He was also mourning the distance between himself and HaShem. He was bearing our sins—the sins of the *world*—and for that brief time, sin separated Him from His father. Yeshua felt the pain of separation, just as you do. But He did not let that pain stop Him from fulfilling His plan. He did not lose His faith in HaShem."

I squeezed Matthew's hands. "Yeshua trusted HaShem to give Him strength, and you can trust HaShem, as well. Your father may always see you as Levi, never as Matthew, but you know who you are. Now is the time to act as Matthew, not as a sorrowful son. Do you understand?"

I was not sure my words would reach his heart, but after a moment he lifted his head. "I am Matthew. And I want to marry Dina."

"Praise HaShem." Miriam stood and gestured toward the door. "Let us not tarry when Peter and the bride are waiting."

Peter and Dina greeted us with great solemnity, then Peter grinned, clapped Matthew on the back, and led him into the house. "I have been praying for this moment ever since I began to follow Yeshua," he said, guiding Matthew toward the dining chamber. "I did not know you would be part of my prayers until a few weeks ago, but I have prayed many, many times for my daughter's marriage. I wanted her to have a husband who will encourage her to love Yeshua above all, and I know you are that man."

"I promise to love her," Matthew answered, meeting Peter's earnest gaze. "I will love her as Yeshua loves us—patiently, sacrificially, and faithfully."

"I could ask for nothing more," Peter said, "but let us see about the terms of this marriage contract."

We sat around the table—Peter, Dina, and Anna on one side, with Matthew, Miriam, and me on the other. Peter picked up the parchment and began to read the ketubah, a document at least as old as Abraham. The contract would become the wife's property and guaranteed she would be paid a certain amount on the occasion of her husband's death or if he divorced her.

My ketubah had been written and signed months before I was overshadowed by the Ruach HaKodesh. When I returned from visiting Elizabeth and told Joseph I was expecting a child, he was prepared to quietly pay the amount specified by the ketubah and set me aside. But, praise HaShem, that did not happen.

"Bring out your tools," Peter said, "because you are going to need them."

A sense of anticipation descended over us while we waited

for Matthew to pull out his writing implements. Dina, I noticed, bit her lip and clung to her mother's arm. Peter crossed his arms and tugged on his beard, appearing to be in deep thought.

When Matthew had finished setting up his inkwell, he nodded to Peter, who picked up the ketubah and began to read aloud:

"On the second day of the week, the tenth day of the month of Tebeth in the year 3801 since the creation of the world, here in the city of Jerusalem, how Matthew son of Alphaeus said to this virgin Dina, daughter of Simon Peter, 'Be my wife according to the Law of Moses and Israel, and I will work for you, honor, support, and maintain you in accordance with the custom of Jewish husbands who work for their wives, honor, support, and maintain them in truth. And I will set aside for you two hundred *zuz*, in lieu of your virginity, which belong to you according to the Law of Moses, and your food, clothing, and necessaries, and live with you in conjugal relations according to universal custom.' And Dina this virgin consented and became his wife. The dowry that she brought from her father's house, in silver, gold, valuables, dresses, and bedclothes, amounts to . . ." Peter glanced at Anna. "What is the value of Dina's garments and such?"

Anna smiled at her daughter. "I would say thirty pieces of silver."

"Good." Peter kept reading. "Thirty pieces of silver. And the bridegroom consented to increase this amount from his own property with the sum of . . ." He looked at Matthew. "How much are you bringing to the marriage?"

Matthew swallowed hard. "Um . . . I think I can manage thirty pieces of silver."

Peter nodded. "Thirty pieces of silver, making sixty pieces

of silver in all. And thus said Matthew the bridegroom, 'I take upon myself and my heirs after me the responsibility of this marriage contract, of the dowry, and of the additional sum, so that all this shall be paid from the best part of my property that I now possess or may hereafter acquire. All my property, even the mantle on my shoulders, shall be mortgaged for the security of this contract and of the dowry and of the addition made thereto.' Matthew the bridegroom has taken upon himself the responsibility for all the obligations of this ketubah, as is customary with other *ketubot* made for the daughters of Israel in accordance with the institution of our patriarchs. May their memory be for a blessing!"

Peter lowered the parchment and turned to Matthew. "By signing this document, you are saying you agree to everything I have read pertaining to the husband."

Matthew glanced at Dina, gave her a flickering smile, then nodded at Peter. "I agree."

"Then sign here."

Matthew dipped his stylus in the ink and signed his name.

Peter turned to his daughter, his expression softening. "Daughter, do you agree with everything I have read in this document as it pertains to the wife?"

Dina looked at Matthew, her eyes glowing. "I agree."

"Then you may sign."

Dina wrote her name beneath Matthew's, then Peter passed the ketubah to me and Miriam, the witnesses. I signed with great happiness, knowing the union would be a strong one. Miriam wiped sentimental tears away before taking the stylus.

When we had both signed in the appropriate places, Peter took the ketubah, rolled it, and gave it to Dina. "Congratulations, Dina and Matthew. You are joined by your vows to one another. We look forward to celebrating a wedding with you."

"And now," Miriam said, smiling broadly, "we must prepare for the betrothal feast. Send a message to John and James Zebedee, and James the Just—dinner today will be at our house, where Matthew will sit at the head of the table. I must get the food ready—oh, how I have looked forward to this! We will have roast lamb, lentil and barley stew, carrots with cumin, and leek salad. And for dessert, cinnamon pears!"

Matthew exhaled a long sigh of contentment while a blush of pleasure rose to Dina's cheeks.

My heart sang with delight, knowing that HaShem had brought Matthew and Dina together. The road ahead would not be easy, but no road worth traveling ever was.

THIRTY-FIVE

Matthew

After the signing of the ketubah, Mary and Miriam hurried away to prepare for the betrothal feast. Peter and Anna congratulated us again, then went up to the roof to share the news with Mara.

I found myself alone with the woman who would soon be my wife. "Well." I turned and smiled, not sure what I should do next. "Have you given any thought to when we should marry?"

She shook her head. "We should probably wait until after you have finished your manuscript."

"Definitely. The work occupies far too much of my time and energy. I think—I fear—I would not be able to give a wife the attention she deserves."

Dina's lips curved in a shy smile. "A wise wife would find a way to catch her husband's attention. I have watched my mother carefully. Many a night Abba has come home with his head filled with problems, but Ima has a way of taking care of him . . . and smiling at him. Rarely does he take his problems to bed."

I glanced away as heat seared my cheeks. I did not know how to speak frankly with a woman, but apparently Peter did. I would have to consult him about marriage matters before Dina and I were officially wed.

"Matthew?"

"Hmm?"

"Are you sorry? I do not want you to feel you were pressured into this betrothal."

I blinked. "Why would I feel pressured?"

"Well . . . I may have behaved unseemly. I liked you from the moment you came to live with us, you see, and have been praying that HaShem would bring us together. So when Lemuel arrived from Rome—"

Ah. Mary and Miriam had been right.

I looked at the rush of pink blossoming on Dina's cheek and felt my heart warm. "I did not think you behaved inappropriately, not once. As for Lemuel, I disliked him only when you smiled at him. And if I had known the subject of your prayers . . ."

"What?"

"I might have acted more quickly." I took her hand, kissed it, and led her into the garden.

THIRTY-SIX

Mary

Something in me feared that my newly betrothed partner might be so love-sick that he could no longer focus on our work, but my fears proved baseless. Matthew did arrive a bit later every morning because he wanted to break his fast with Dina, but otherwise he confined his discussions about their upcoming marriage to the hours after we finished our work.

As Matthew and I continued to write and interview, our stack of papyri grew higher. I studied the ever-increasing mound and felt gratified to know I was once again helping to carry the Gospel.

One morning Matthew said he'd been awakened by a horrible dream—he dreamt the papyri caught fire while he dozed by an oil lamp. "If you approve," he told me, his customary expression of calm replaced by distress, "I will employ another scribe to copy our completed pages. I will have him make two copies, one for you and one for James or John. If one of our copies is damaged or goes missing, we will have at least two others."

Impressed with his foresight, I agreed. We had invested too much to see our work go up in smoke or disappear due to malevolent mischief.

I was reading some of Yeshua's lessons from the Galilean hillside when I heard a knock at the door. Miriam hurried to answer it, and James of the camel-knees strode into the house. He greeted Matthew warmly, then stooped to embrace me.

"What brings you today?" I asked, knowing his work with the believers' assembly usually prevented him from making social calls. "Has something happened to one of your brothers?"

"My brothers are fine." He straddled the bench where I sat and faced me. "Ima, I have a friend on the Sanhedrin. I cannot tell you his name, but he wants me to warn you. The high priest and the elders have heard about your work. They want you to stop writing."

I shrugged. "They wanted Yeshua to stop teaching, but He did not. They also told Peter and John to stop preaching in Yeshua's name. They said they could not help speaking about what they had seen and heard." I looked back at my son. "I would say the same thing. HaShem has led and enabled me to do this, so I will continue."

"Ima." James leaned closer. "They do not want to arrest a woman for defying the Sanhedrin. To my knowledge, such a thing has never happened, but your persistence is testing their resolve. If Yeshua knew you were in danger, what would He tell you? Do you think He would encourage you to continue if He knew you could be arrested and imprisoned?"

"Stephen gave his life for the sake of the Gospel. Who am I to do any less?"

"Who are you?" James shook his head. "You are the mother of the Messiah. You are the virgin who gave birth to the Son of Adonai. You are revered in Nazareth and respected in Jerusalem."

"If I am revered or respected," I answered, "it is not of my doing, and probably not of HaShem's. I am a mother, not only to Yeshua but also to you, Simeon and Joses, Jude, Damaris, and Pheodora. I guided my children, loved and taught them, but now they are grown. So now I do what I can—I record Yeshua's stories so the world will learn of Him long after I am gone."

James slumped in defeat, so I reached out and caught his hand. "I appreciate your concern for me, son, but you need not worry. HaShem will protect me as I follow His will. I am not concerned about anything else."

THIRTY-SEVEN

Matthew

I had just set out my tools and prepared to write when someone called from the courtyard gate. My stomach twisted when I recognized Lemuel's voice.

Miriam hurried to welcome our guest while I lowered my head into my hands. I had a troubling sense that Lemuel's appearance foretold bad news—if Achiakos had good news to report, he would have written.

"Shalom," Lemuel said, crossing the threshold in his bare feet.

Miriam followed behind him, a towel on her shoulder. Concern shadowed her face as she watched Lemuel approach and sit at the table.

I drew a deep breath. "You have news from Achiakos?"

He nodded. "My master sends you grace and shalom."

"You have returned quickly, Lemuel. I assume you bring urgent news?"

He nodded again, more slowly this time. "Petronius's letter reached the emperor. Though Caesar had said he would forget his provocation against the Jews, when he read the epistle from Syria, his temper flared. Undeterred by Petronious's reasonable words, when Caesar read that the Jews would not bow to his will, he was greatly displeased."

I leaned back and folded my arms, bracing myself for the worst. "Tell me everything," I said, wishing Peter or John would drop by. I did not want to bear this burden alone.

Lemuel abandoned all sense of formality as words spewed from his mouth. "Gaius Caesar is a slave to base and vicious actions on the best occasions and holds no regard for what is virtuous and honorable. On the worst occasions, he does not allow himself to be restrained by any admonition, but derives the greatest pleasure from indulging his anger upon those who cannot lawfully resist."

I nodded. "The man is ungodly and unjust. What did he do after reading Petronius's letter?"

Lemuel's hands curled into fists. "After reading the letter, he wrote to Petronius—and I have knowledge of its contents because one of Caesar's scribes is a friend. Caesar told Petronius to ship the golden statue to Egypt, then take it to Jerusalem and install it in the Temple. After that, Petronius is to act as his own judge and kill himself, so he may become an example to all who would dare contradict the command of their emperor."

The wave of rage that had fired Lemuel's speech faded, leaving his cheeks pale and his voice in tatters. "I am sorry, Matthew. The bloodshed we hoped to avoid now seems inevitable. My master begs you to pray for the peace of Jerusalem. He hopes to see you again in peace and safety, but if HaShem does not make a way, then he will see you when you stand together in the presence of Yeshua, our King."

My heart twisted at the look of guilt on the young man's

face. "Do not blame yourself." I leaned forward and squeezed his arm. "You have served your master well, doing your part to preserve HaShem's people. Neither you nor Achiakos or even Caesar can stop HaShem's will in this matter—He will act as He chooses, and we will obey His direction, come what may."

I released him and looked up at Miriam. "Can you prepare some honey water and food for Lemuel? I need to find Peter and the others. This news will not wait."

"Of course." Miriam moved to the counter, and I put my writing tools away. But before I left the house, I leaned toward Lemuel and smiled. "Congratulate me, friend. If the Lord wills, Dina and I will soon be married."

He blinked rapidly. "Um, congratulations. You are most blessed."

"Indeed I am." I smiled again. "And I must thank you—if you had never come to Jerusalem, I might not be getting married at all."

THIRTY-EIGHT

Mary

I stood in the courtyard and checked the angle of the sun for the third time—the sun stood nearly overhead and Matthew had not yet arrived.

I shivered from the cool air and glanced at Miriam, who was milking the goat. "Did our dear scribe mention making other plans for today?" I struggled to keep a worried note out of my voice. "I expected him long before this hour."

She looked up, squinting, and shook her head. "I remember him saying he would be here early."

"Yet there is no sign of him."

"None I have seen."

"Have we heard *nothing* from him? No report from Peter or John?"

Miriam lifted the milk bucket. "Nothing."

"He has never been this late before." I followed Miriam into the house, then thought I heard a familiar voice. I stepped back into the courtyard, eager to greet him, but the man who had spoken was not Matthew, and neither was he in our courtyard.

I closed the door and sighed.

I joined Miriam by the cook fire and saw that a shadow of worry had darkened her eyes. "Do you think . . . ?" She lifted a brow.

I knew she was thinking about the warning we'd received from James. "I will go find Peter. Perhaps Matthew is with Dina." I pulled my cloak from a hook and threw it over my shoulders, then flung a headscarf over my hair. I paused to squeeze Miriam's hand before leaving. "Pray that I would find him. And pray for him, wherever he is."

My heart pounded as I set out. Matthew was not my son, but over the past few months he had become as dear to me as Simeon and James. Though I had not given birth to him, I had listened to him, comforted him, counseled, and rebuked him. I had signed his ketubah. In some ways, he felt more like a son than my own Jude and Joses, whom I had not seen in weeks.

I had not gone more than twenty paces when I spotted Peter, his face a portrait of worry. He saw me, then gestured for me to step into an alley, out of the street traffic. When we met, he lowered his gaze and spoke in a gruff voice: "Matthew has been arrested."

Fear blew down the back of my neck. "What? By whom?"

"The high priest's guards." He lifted his head, glanced around, and looked at me again. "I suggest you come with me instead of going home. I will send Anna to stay with Miriam, but you are not safe. They may send someone for you, too."

"They would not—"

"How do you know? Come." Peter's hand gripped my

upper arm. "Several members of the community have gathered at my home to pray. You can join them." I cast about for some alternative but could think of no better option.

I followed Peter to his house.

I prayed with the elders of the community and comforted Peter, James, and John. Before she left to stay with Miriam, I saw that Anna was especially worried about Matthew. She had been his hostess for months and had begun to think of him as family even before his betrothal to her daughter.

"I should not have let him go out so early," she told me, wringing her hands. "I should have made him stay to break his fast with Dina. They must have had men waiting outside the house, because I do not think they would take him once the street filled with people."

I told her not to worry, that HaShem would work His will in this situation as in all others. "You cannot surprise HaShem," I reminded her. "Perhaps someone will hear the Gospel because Matthew was arrested."

Privately, I wondered if the Roman procurator had learned of Matthew's correspondence with Achiakos. What if one of their letters had been intercepted? Agrippa would not look favorably on a scribe who sent word of his dealings to a friend in Jerusalem, and Caesar would not hesitate to execute both men if he learned they had conspired to keep the Jews informed of his plans.

I caught John, who usually knew everything that happened in the Holy City. "Do you know where Matthew is being held?" I asked without preamble. "Do the Romans have him?"

Something in me relaxed when John shook his head. If

Matthew was not at the procurator's palace or the Fortress Antonia, they had not accused him of breaking a Roman law.

John crossed his arms. "The high priest is holding him."

"Why? Of what crime is he accused?"

John exhaled in exasperation. "They are saying all sorts of things, none of which make sense. But I am certain they would not have arrested Matthew if they had not heard about your scroll."

"The scroll?" I spat the word. "Why should they fear a book? Those who follow Yeshua will believe the stories; those who do not, will not."

"A movement with miracles and eyewitness testimonies is not likely to die. Such a scroll may outlive a man."

"Why do you think we are writing it?"

John smiled. "They are threatened by your work, so they arrested Matthew. They see him as a man transformed from an odious tax collector to an esteemed disciple and a righteous son of Israel. They fear the power behind such a transformation."

I considered this. If only Matthew's father could understand —and respect—the power that changed his son. "They still fear Yeshua . . . even if they do not speak His name."

John nodded in silent agreement.

I waited until John and Peter were engaged in a conversation with some of the elders, then I slipped through the darkened streets until I reached my house. Miriam was certain to be concerned about me, and I knew Anna would rather be home with Peter.

Though I knew HaShem was sovereign over all circumstances and Yeshua had promised He would not leave us, my maternal nature struggled with the thought of Matthew in chains. Would they realize he was more suited to desk

If he wanted me to confess some crime, he would be disappointed. I smiled and met his gaze. "I have no idea why I am standing before you. Perhaps you should explain why yesterday I was accosted outside my home, dragged through the street, and thrust into a dark cell. In the last day and night I have received no food or water. I have not even been allowed to properly wash my hands before coming to stand before the high priest of Israel. Is this any way to treat the man who has freely shared information about Caesar's intention to destroy our Holy City?"

Frowning, Theophilus glanced to his left and right, where several members of the Sanhedrin stood to witness the proceedings. "Why was this man not treated with respect?" he barked.

One of the Torah teachers stepped forward. "We had nothing to do with him. He was in the custody of the Temple guards."

Theophilus sighed and returned his attention to me. "As soon as we have concluded this matter, you will be free to go and purify yourself for worship."

"Very considerate of you." I crossed my arms. "I am still waiting to learn why I am here."

Theophilus glanced at one of the Pharisees at his side, then clasped his hands again. "Did you know I have a granddaughter who once met Yeshua? Since you were one of the Twelve, you might have seen her."

"Many people came to see Yeshua."

"Her name was Joanna. She was quite taken with the man."

I did not know what the high priest expected of me, so I stood silent and still, a trick I had learned from my father. Whenever he wanted to make me squirm, Abba would call me into his chamber and stare until I began to confess failings both real and imaginary—whatever it took to persuade him to lower his disconcerting gaze.

"Yes, many people were fascinated by the Nazarene." Theophilus's eyes searched mine, but I saw no condemnation in his face. He might prove to be more tolerant than those who held the post before him, for his granddaughter's testimony had apparently left quite an impression.

Caiaphas, one of Theophilus's predecessors, had shown no tolerance for Yeshua's followers. Not long after Pentecost, he arrested all twelve disciples and put us on trial before the Sanhedrin. He had been infuriated to realize that Yeshua's death did not stop those who believed He was the Messiah. Only Gamaliel had been wise enough to calm the high priest's rage and bring about our release.

"I hear you are writing a story," Theophilus said. "About Yeshua."

I dipped my chin in a slight nod. "We are not creating a fiction—we are simply recording the acts and words of Yeshua."

"Who is working with you?"

"One who saw nearly everything—His mother, Mary of Nazareth."

Theophilus considered a moment, then tugged at his beard. "I might like to read this scroll when you are finished. Will you bring it to me?"

Did he think I was foolish enough to deliver our only copy into his hands?

I tempered my smile. "I believe you would enjoy reading the finished scroll. Others are also eager to read the collection, so we will hire a copyist. We will be able to send the scroll to anyone who desires to read it."

"I see." Theophilus fingered his beard a moment more, then waved me toward the door. "We are grateful for your service to our people, Matthew ben Alphaeus. You are free to go. Pray for the peace of Jerusalem."

Stunned, but grateful for HaShem's mercy, I left the high priest's chamber and hurried away.

After my release, I knew I ought to hurry to Mary's house—she and Miriam had to be worried, especially since I had not shown up for two days. Mary would have checked with Peter, who would have asked James and John if they knew of my whereabouts, and by now surely many of the believers were praying for me.

Abruptly, I changed direction. Dina deserved to know the news first, and the fastest way to let my friends know of my release would be to tell Peter. Once Dina and Peter knew I was safe, I could proceed to Mary's house and put her mind at ease.

A chilly breeze blew through the city, sending a shiver down my spine. Winter was upon us, a welcome relief from summer heat. The women would soon pull out their thick cloaks, especially women as thin as Mary and Dina . . .

The thought of my betrothed sent a shiver through my senses. I had never imagined that I would marry, but already I could see how Dina would complete me. She would be my companion through life, my helper in ministry, my confidante and counselor, and I could not wait to see her again.

"'Whoever finds a wife finds good and receives favor from Adonai.'" I spoke to the air, quoting a proverb I had never claimed before. "Praise you, HaShem, for sending Dina to me."

I hurried down Peter's street, head low, because I did not want to be recognized by passersby. Perhaps I was being silly, wanting to see Dina first, but sometimes I did not understand my own actions.

I opened the courtyard gate and rapped lightly on the door before entering the house. "Shalom! Anyone home?"

Dina released a cry of joy and flew into my arms, covering my face with kisses. I stiffened, then reminded myself that soon we would be husband and wife. Surely this behavior was appropriate, especially since Dina might have been convinced she would never see me again.

I kissed her lightly, then took her hand and led her into the work area. Anna dropped the pottery bowl she had been holding and shrieked. She ran toward me, then stopped a modest distance away. "Matthew," she said, wearing a smile as broad as a house, "praise HaShem you are safe."

"Matthew!" Peter hurried forward and wrapped me in a quick embrace, then stepped back to look me over. "Are you all right? Were you beaten? Were you with the Romans?"

"Have some water," Anna said, pouring me a cup. "You must be thirsty."

"And hungry." I slid onto the bench. "I was an unwilling guest of the high priest. I cannot recommend his guest chamber or his cook."

Dina slid onto the bench beside me, giving me a smile I would have accepted as my last view on earth.

"I have lentil-and-barley stew." Anna gestured to the cook fire, where a pot sat amid the embers. "You must eat until you are full."

"I can only stay a moment," I said, gratefully accepting the water. "I need to tell Mary and Miriam where I have been. And there is work to be done, of course."

"Who lives in this place? We walked past the gate to the high priest's house, but who lives here?"

"The *former* high priest," the girl said, lowering her voice. "The current high priest's father holds audiences here."

Miriam was right. I had not been taken by Theophilus or Caiaphas, but Annas, the old man who ruled Jerusalem through his sons and his son-in-law.

I thanked the servant, then leaned back against the cool marble wall. Though I sat alone in the vestibule, various sounds came to me—the rhythm of footsteps overhead, the creaking of a wooden beam, the shush of wind blowing through an evergreen outside the door. Male voices rumbled through the wall, accompanied by the soft swish of trailing robes over the tiled floor.

I closed my eyes, inhaled the faint aroma of incense, and allowed my thoughts to wander.

Before stepping outside to gather eggs for Miriam, I had been reading Matthew's account of the night Yeshua was arrested. When I finished, I sat in silence, stunned by details I did not know. I did not know the Temple guards had bound Yeshua's hands and brought him here—to Annas, not Caiaphas, who was high priest at the time. My Son, His hands tied as if He were a common thief, stood in this vestibule while John and Peter approached the door of the high priest's house. John went inside while Peter remained behind. The doorkeeper asked Peter about knowing Yeshua, and Peter denied my Son—the first time.

According to Matthew's report, some of the guards made a fire in the courtyard. Peter joined them to warm himself. He was sitting by that fire when he denied knowing Yeshua a second and third time. And after his third denial, the rooster crowed—not because of the sunrise, but because Yeshua had prophesied that it would.

When the guards finally took Yeshua into the former high priest's reception hall, Annas questioned Him about His disciples and His teaching. "I have spoken openly to the world," Yeshua answered. "I always taught in the synagogues and the Temple, where all the Jewish people come together. I spoke nothing in secret, so why question me? Ask those who have heard what I spoke to them. Look, they know what I said."

Though my Son said nothing but the truth, one of the guards standing next to Yeshua slapped him. "Is that the way you answer the cohen gadol?"

Even now, my lower lip trembled at the thought of the guard's blasphemy. He had acted to defend the high priest, but what sort of man dares to strike the Son of Adonai?

Yeshua had not remonstrated, but said, "If I have spoken wrongly, give evidence of the wrong; but if rightly, why hit me?"

Just then, a carved door squeaked on its hinges, hauling me up from the well of memory. A guard beckoned.

I rose and walked toward him . . . crossing the same tiles my Son traversed on His way to judgment.

I did not know how old Annas was, but the passing years had not been kind to the former high priest. The wretched man in the chair looked like a malevolent corpse. Thin webs of gray hair floated around his shriveled face, and his eyes had retreated into caves of bone. His hands, covered with thin and spotted skin, danced like spiders on the armrests of his chair while he hunched forward, his ornate robe draped over a skeletal frame and puddling on the floor.

"I am sorry, but I cannot. I must obey HaShem rather than—"

"I command you to be silent, woman."

He leaned forward, clutching his armrests, and shook his balding head like an enraged bull. "You followers of Yeshua are all the same, but what am I to do with you? Apparently, you are now a central figure in this false messiah movement. The people called him a king, so they see you as the queen mother, a person of authority. If we are to stop this nonsense, we must stop you."

For the first time, a flicker of uncertainty touched my spine. Was he threatening *death*? I did not think he would—our religious rulers did not have the power to execute prisoners; that is why they sent Yeshua to the Roman procurator. And even if Annas wanted me dead, I had done nothing unlawful.

And yet . . . My mouth twisted in a slow smile. Death had been approaching me for months, so I was prepared to face it. If HaShem wanted me to depart this life, perhaps execution would be a good way to die.

"I am but a humble woman," I said, my voice calm. "I have no disciples, and I have not promoted false doctrine. Everything Yeshua taught was a fulfillment of the Law and the prophets, including Moses. Adonai told Moses, 'I will raise up a prophet like you for them from among their brothers. I will put my words in His mouth, and He will speak to them all that I command Him.' Yeshua was that prophet, but did you listen to Him? Did you recognize Him?"

The vein in the old man's forehead twisted like a pinned snake. "I told you to be silent," he snapped, gripping his gilded chair. "If you desire mercy from me, still your tongue while I consider what should be done with you."

I closed my eyes, waiting for some prodding from the Ruach HaKodesh, but felt nothing. Silent I would be.

I did not believe Annas would kill me. HaShem had called me and Matthew to complete another important task, and HaShem would enable us to see it through to the end.

As if he had read my thoughts, Annas narrowed his eyes and snorted. "I have spoken to your young co-conspirator. Because he has been helpful to us, Matthew son of Alphaeus has been released with a warning to stop this work. Like you, he refused. But I am certain he will stop if you are no longer able to support him."

I stiffened at the menace in his words. Was he threatening me or Matthew?

"And why," I asked, my voice tightening, "would I not be able to assist him?"

The corner of Annas's mouth lifted in a rictus of satisfaction. "Because you will no longer be available."

Fired with a courage that erupted from within, I met his gaze head-on. "You might kill me," I said, squaring my shoulders, "but the Gospel will live on. Any opposition you enact will only fan the flames of devotion among Yeshua's followers, and the Spirit will empower them to proclaim the Gospel throughout Judea. My death will mean—"

"I do not intend to kill a woman," Annas interrupted, "because the people would not stand for it. Nor will I put you in prison, because our prisons do not seem capable of holding those who follow Yeshua. Since I can neither kill nor detain you, I must consider other options."

I had no idea what he meant, but the look in his eye did not bode well for my work . . . or for my future.

Spirit of God, deliver me.

FORTY-ONE

Matthew

Miriam and I stared at each other, both of us at a loss for words. Peter, John, and James Zebedee spoke in low voices across the room, while Anna, Mara, and Dina sat and held hands in a quiet huddle. We had finally received word of Mary: she was being held by Annas, the former high priest.

"He would not be so bold as to kill her," Peter said, his voice flat and final. "He is afraid of the people, and they respect her as Yeshua's mother."

"Then what will he do?" A spasm of grief knit James's brows as he looked from Peter to John. "Can he imprison her indefinitely?"

"On what charge?" John crossed his arms. "No one would dare accuse her of breaking the Law."

Peter began to pace, stroking his beard in time with his steps. "They could say she supported her Son, the man executed for claiming to be king of the Jews. They could find dozens who would attest to that."

A thunderous scowl darkened James Zebedee's brow. "But why wait years before arresting her? The people would not stand for it."

"There are other ways to eliminate a threat." I lifted my voice to be heard across the room. "During the time of the Maccabees, John Hyrcanus left the throne to his wife, but her son Aristobulus kept her in prison until she died from starvation."

Miriam whimpered softly, and Anna reached out and patted her shoulder. The air in the house vibrated, the silence filling with dread. Dina, pale and quiet, began to weep.

I should have comforted Dina, but I was too distraught. Apparently, Mary and I had been wrong. We thought only believers in Yeshua would care about our collection of stories, but we had underestimated our opposition.

The relative quiet shattered when Shimon, Mary's son-in-law, stormed into the house, his chest heaving. He looked around the room as if counting heads . . . and his countenance fell when he came up short.

"So it's true," he said, his confident expression withering. "Mary is not here."

"Annas has her," Peter said, turning. "But you knew this, did you not?"

I blinked, surprised by Peter's cutting words, though Shimon did not refute them. Instead, he wiped pearls of perspiration from his brow and sank onto a bench. "I was with members of my chaburah this morning," he said. "One of my brothers mentioned that Annas had spent the morning questioning Yeshua's mother. I thought I had misunderstood, so I asked for clarification. He told me Annas kept Mary of Nazareth overnight and questioned her today about the scroll she is writing."

John folded his arms and pinned Shimon in a sharp gaze. "How did your acquaintance know about Mary's work?"

A muscle quivered at Shimon's jaw. "I . . . I may have mentioned it in a meeting. I thought nothing of it, because who would expect the scribblings of a woman to amount to anything? But apparently the word spread . . . even to the house of the high priest."

Unable to remain silent a moment longer, I stood and approached the humiliated Pharisee. "Did you mention my name, as well?"

Shimon made a sound deep in his throat, then nodded.

"I knew it." I turned to the others, my hands clenching. "That is why I was arrested and taken to Theophilus. But I was released while Mary remains in the high priest's custody. Why would they keep her and release me?" I whirled around to face Shimon. "Since your Pharisee brothers are so careless with their words, what are they saying about Annas's plan for Mary?"

Shimon drew a deep breath and lowered his head. "I am not certain. But I have heard that Annas might send Mary to Rome."

"He might send her *where*?" I stepped toward the man, fury almost choking me. "He *might* or he *will*?"

Shimon swallowed hard. "Since Caesar has decreed war against Jerusalem, time is of the essence. It has been said that—"

"Get to the point, Shimon. Why would he send Mary to Rome?"

"Because the gifts of oil and wine were ignored."

For an instant we froze in a stunned tableau, then Miriam released a desperate cry. Peter slammed his hand onto the table in frustrated fury, and James the Just went as pale as death, thinking, no doubt, that he would never see his mother again. John moved to comfort Miriam, and Dina wept quietly into her hands.

I stared at Shimon, my body trembling as my chest and belly heated with rage.

We grasped the situation immediately. Because Caesar was moving against Jerusalem, Annas was desperate to preserve the peace. He could not allow Caesar's statue to be erected in the Temple, but neither could he win a war against Rome. So he was attempting to placate the emperor with a different sort of gift—a woman, neither highborn nor wealthy, but mother to the miracle-working Jew who had claimed to be the Son of God.

"What have you done?" Peter's brows rushed together. "What sort of evil have you set in motion?"

"Annas will offer Mary to Gaius Caesar," Shimon said, his words barely audible. "To satisfy Caesar's thirst for dominance over the Jews. He knows she is greatly beloved among the people. Annas hopes the emperor's anger will be satisfied."

John stood and approached Shimon, confusion in his eyes. "Why would the Roman emperor be interested in Mary? She is a humble woman—"

"The Romans are superstitious," James Zebedee interrupted. "Caesar has heard about Yeshua's miracles and His claim to divinity. The Romans believe that gods beget gods, so if Yeshua was a God, Mary must also be divine."

Peter shook his head. "Blasphemy."

"To us, yes," James answered. "But the Romans do not know HaShem."

A fresh wave of rage rose in my chest, fueled by righteous anger and my sincere affection for Mary. I trusted HaShem;

The worst aspect of this dark box was the utter loneliness. I had not been given an opportunity to send word to Miriam or Matthew or Peter, so no one knew where I was. Annas would probably prefer that few people knew what had happened to me, and I would almost certainly be on my way to Rome before anyone knew where I had been taken. Annas might well remain silent, leaving my loved ones to wonder if I had simply disappeared.

A wry smile twisted my mouth. Perhaps they would think HaShem had summoned me to the heavenly throne room, like Enoch or Elijah . . .

> *"Yet You are holy,*
> *enthroned on the praises of Israel.*
> *In You our fathers put their trust.*
> *They trusted, and You delivered them."*

I did not expect deliverance, nor did I deserve it. I was still the lowly handmaid of Adonai, and since His will brought me to this place, I would accept whatever happened. Perhaps I was meant to testify of Yeshua before Caesar, or perhaps I was meant to die in a place where my death would not be given undue attention. That would probably be a blessing. Despite the many occasions I had gently corrected those who sought to put me on some kind of pedestal, I remained nothing but the Lord's handmaid.

A quiet, insignificant death might be best for all.

> *"They cried to you and were delivered.*
> *In You they trusted,*
> *and were not disappointed."*

I would be delivered from this box; I knew it with absolute

certainty. Whether I remained in it another day, a week, or a month, HaShem would deliver me.

Before Yeshua died, we understood death was a gate to Sheol, a dark and torturous place of waiting. But as Yeshua hung on the execution stake, He told a dying thief that they would soon be together in Paradise, the Garden of God. Sin caused Adam and Eve to be expelled from Eden, but Yeshua's atoning sacrifice opened the gates to all who believed.

If I died tonight, tomorrow, or next year, I would find myself in the Garden with Him.

> *"From the womb I was cast on You—*
> *from my mother's womb*
> *You have been my God.*
> *Be not far from me!*
> *For trouble is near—*
> *there is no one to help.*
> *But You, Adonai, be not far off!*
> *O my strength! Come quickly to my aid!"*

And yet—I did not want to die. Matthew could probably conclude the work on our story collection without my help, but I yearned to see it finished. HaShem had called me to this task, and I did not want to depart before it was done. Was that a selfish request?

I pressed my ear to the wood and tried not to gag from the stench as I concentrated on listening. We had departed at midday, and though Jerusalem was experiencing the cool of winter, little outside air flowed into my enclosed box. Once or twice I thought I heard voices on the road, but this was a mule-drawn wagon, so we traveled at a faster pace than those who walked.

Even if I had been able to make myself heard from within this conveyance, what could anyone do? Armed Romans rode at the front and back, and only a fool would dare question them.

"I will praise You amid the congregation.
You who fear Adonai, praise Him!
All Jacob's descendants, glorify Him!
Revere Him, all you seed of Israel.
For He has not despised or disdained
the suffering of the lowly one."

I pulled my sweat-soaked tunic from my chest and fanned my skin, but the effort was futile. This box had been built for security, not comfort, and the Romans were rarely concerned with the well-being of their prisoners. Whether I lived or died, my life belonged to Adonai.

"I will fulfill my vows before those
who fear Him.
Let the poor eat and be satisfied.
Let them who seek after Him
praise Adonai.
May your hearts live forever!"

Amen.

FORTY-THREE

Matthew

I had hoped to meet James, John, and Peter by the Fish Gate within an hour, but I went first to Mary's house, realizing that Miriam would want to know how to pray. While she prepared a basket with bread, fruits, and small waterskins, I briefly described the situation. Before she handed the basket to me, she looked at me with an almost frantic urgency in her eyes. "Be careful with Mary," she said, clutching the basket. "She is not well."

I shrugged to hide my confusion. "Of course she is not well—she has been taken hostage."

"The situation is worse than you know. She is . . ." Uncertainty crept into her expression. "She would not want me to tell you."

"Tell me what?"

"She is dying."

I turned to watch the shadows lengthen across the wall as an incoherent thought rapped for my attention. "Is there anything else I should take with me?"

"Matthew, are you listening? Mary is dying, and the stress of this journey will severely tax her strength."

I shook my head, unable to understand why Miriam kept saying words that made no sense. Mary could not be sick. I had witnessed many of Yeshua's healings; the very idea of His mother dying was incomprehensible. Miriam had to be mistaken.

I took the basket and hurried out the door.

My friend Tobias, whom I met during my stint at the Antonia Fortress, lived with his family outside Jerusalem near the Kidron Valley. Their home lay in the opposite direction of the Fish Gate, but once I had the horses, I could make up for lost time by traveling over the road that led through the Hinnom Valley south of Jerusalem. I would skirt the city and arrive at the Fish Gate in good time.

I had not seen Tobias since my training days, yet he greeted me warmly and inquired about my health. "I am well, thank you," I said, keenly conscious of every passing moment. "And I would love to talk about all that has happened since we last met, but I have an urgent need for horses. A friend of mine—an important woman—has been taken to Caesarea, and I have to reach her before her ship sails."

Tobias lifted a brow. "A woman, eh? Are you in love?"

"I am betrothed, but not to this woman. She is beloved by many people in Jerusalem and is especially dear to me."

"Congratulations on your betrothal. Will I be invited to the wedding?"

"If you can loan me a few horses, you will be the guest of honor."

Tobias grinned and led the way to the stables. "How many?"

"Four," I said, then I wondered if I should take a horse for

Mary to ride home. But more important than comfort was speed, and traveling to the coast with a riderless beast would slow us down, especially if we rode in the dark.

As I breathed in the musky aroma of animals and manure, Tobias called for servants and told them to saddle four fresh geldings. "You are fortunate," he said, grinning. "These four are some of my fastest mounts, and they have not been ridden today. You can return them once you rescue your mistress."

"She is not my mistress."

"Whatever you say, Levi."

I drew a breath to explain that I was no longer called Levi, then decided to let the matter pass. I would explain everything once Mary was safely home.

Tobias crossed his arms and narrowed his gaze. "How long has it been since you have ridden?"

"Years," I admitted, "but surely one does not forget such a thing."

"The mind does not forget," Tobias said, taking the reins of a handsome gelding, "but the body does. Now, do your companions know how to ride?"

I pressed my lips together. "Are these gentle animals?"

Tobias snorted. "You can have gentle or you can have fast. You cannot have both."

I blew out a breath and considered my options. To my knowledge, James, John, and Peter had never even mounted a horse, much less ridden at a gallop. Could the Ruach Ha-Kodesh miraculously make them horsemen?"

"They will do whatever it takes," I said, nodding. "We are desperate to reach Caesarea."

"Very well, then."

Tobias led the gelding over to a stump and gestured for me to step onto it. I took a moment to tie my food basket onto the saddle, then gripped the front edge of the leather seat and heaved my leg over the horse's back.

I had forgotten how it felt to straddle a mountain. When the horse stamped his foot, the world swayed around me.

"Zeus is a good beast," Tobias said as he handed me the reins. "We will tie the other leads to the back of your saddle. "If you stay on the roads outside the city, you should have no problems. Fortunately, the moon is full tonight, so you should have no trouble seeing the road."

"That is good to know." My heart pounded within my chest as I watched the servants bring three other horses out of the barn and tie their long leads to my saddle.

"I—" I cleared my throat—"I will return them to you as soon as possible."

"Leave them at the Antonia," Tobias said. "I will pick them up when I bring out the next group of fresh mounts."

A lump rose to my throat. "Thank you. May HaShem bless you, Tobias."

"And you," he answered. Then he swatted my horse's flank with the flat of his hand, and the mountain beneath me began to trot.

The sun had balanced on the western horizon by the time I reached the Fish Gate. As shadows pooled and thickened around the city wall, I spotted a tree where I could tie up the horses. I rode toward it, then slid off the saddle and fell what felt like a long way to the ground.

Immediately I understood what Tobias had meant. I remembered how to ride, but my body now ached in areas I had not heeded in years.

I walked toward the Fish Gate, searching the shadows until

I saw James, John, and Peter standing just outside the city wall. They appeared startled until I pointed toward the horses.

Peter let out a long whistle when they reached me. "I did not think you could pull it off."

John tugged on his beard. "How did you obtain such wealthy friends?"

"My friends are not wealthy," I said, shrugging. "Tobias's family supplies horses and wagons for the Romans at the Antonia. Years ago, he taught me how to ride."

"These are Roman horses?" James Zebedee snorted. "Does your friend know we are *chasing* Romans?"

"I did not give him details." I managed a grim smile. "But he did ask if my friends knew how to ride."

"What's to know?" Peter reached out and stroked one of the gelding's flank. "You get on and go, yes?"

I groaned, but John had more practical concerns on his mind. He opened a leather pouch and handed each of us a small loaf. "We need to keep up our strength if we are going to be of any use to Mary. Anna has provided us with bread, cheese, and dried figs."

"What if we do not reach Mary in time?" A quaver filled James's voice. "How will we face Yeshua if we lose His mother?"

John shook his head. "We will not fail," he said. "We have the Ruach HaKodesh to show us what to do. He will send whatever help we need."

"But will He teach you how to ride?" I asked.

John clapped my shoulder and smiled. "Have faith, brother. In two or three days, Mary will be home, and all this will be nothing but an unpleasant memory." He grinned. "It will be of so little consequence that you will not even mention it in your writing project."

"It is Mary's project," I said, my cheeks burning. "And she will definitely omit this chapter. She insists that the scroll contain only stories about Yeshua."

"Regardless, let us hurry," Peter said, preparing to stuff the rest of his bread into his mouth. "The sun has set, and Mary must have reached Caesarea by now. Let us pray the ship does not sail tonight."

I untied the first horse. "Here," I said, holding out the leather reins. "Who is ready to mount?"

Peter, James, and John looked at each other, then John stepped forward. "Show me what to do."

I looked around, searching for something we could use as a mounting block. Roman saddles were little more than padded seats with horns, one at each corner, for attaching supplies or dragging captives. Leather belts at the side of the saddle fastened beneath the horse's belly but did nothing to aid the rider who wanted to mount the beast.

"There." I pointed to a large rock. "Step on the rock, and I will bring the animal over."

One by one, stars appeared in the heavens while John made several clumsy attempts to mount the horse. "This," he grumbled as he tried to throw his leg over the beast's broad back, "is why Abraham rode a camel."

John gave up and jumped from the rock. "I will stay behind," he said, motioning to Peter. "Why don't you go?"

Peter mounted the horse after only one attempt, but after positioning himself in the saddle, he took the reins, kicked the gelding into a trot, and promptly slid off, landing in the dirt.

My uneasiness swelled into alarm when I realized that teaching my friends to ride would take more time than we could spare. Every moment we spent in Jerusalem was a moment in which Mary could be boarding a ship.

"Brothers," I said, scrambling onto the stone as John helped Peter up. "Take these animals to the Antonia Fortress and tell the captain they are from Tobias. I will go after Mary."

From the frustration evident on each man's face, I knew my friends were disappointed, but apparently HaShem did not need four men to rescue one woman.

"Go then," John said, squeezing my arm. "We will deliver the beasts and join the elders in prayer for your success."

I had just swung myself into the saddle when I heard a cry from the gate. We turned at the sound, and in the distant torchlight we recognized James the Just.

"Matthew, wait!" He ran toward us, his tunic flapping against his legs. "Miriam has sent me to find you. She thought this—" he drew a ragged breath—"might be important."

"What is it?" Peter called.

Panting, James stopped beside John and held up a scroll. "You have received a message."

"Can it wait?" I glanced at John. "Perhaps you can read it for me."

"*You* must read it." James walked to my side, and one look at his face convinced me to linger. "Miriam believes the epistle is from your friend in Rome."

I took the scroll, broke the seal, and held the papyrus in a stream of moonlight to read it.

"Achiakos, a servant of Herod Agrippa.
To Matthew, scribe, accountant, and esteemed friend.
Regarding events in Rome, which should concern all who care for Jerusalem:

Grace and shalom be unto you from the imperial city, where I serve King Agrippa.

Our prayers have been answered in a most unexpected manner. On the twenty-fourth day of January, in the morning, Gaius Caesar was murdered. Caligula is dead."

I lowered the letter and stared at Peter, James, and John as my impatient horse snorted. "Caesar is dead," I whispered, my voice emerging as a rusty croak. "The tyrant is no more."

"Dead?" Peter looked at John. "What does that mean for Jerusalem?"

"I do not know."

John looked up at me. "Who reigns in Rome now?"

I squinted at the letter again and read aloud, "'My master Agrippa is helping the Senate negotiate the succession, but it appears the new emperor will be Tiberius Claudius Caesar. Certain forces in the Praetorian Guard and the Senate oppose any rule by emperor, preferring to return to the days of the Republic, but my master believes Claudius will prevail. If we must have an emperor, the Praetorian Guard would have Claudius.

"'In any case, my friend, this is good news for Jerusalem and Petronius, our champion. He need not kill himself to obey a dead ruler, and the statue en route to Jerusalem should be destroyed. Our next emperor, if HaShem wills that we have one, will not look kindly upon a statue of Caligula.

"'Rejoice, Matthew. I will write again when I know more. Your servant, Achiakos.'"

John's worried expression relaxed into a smile. "That is cause for rejoicing indeed. Praise HaShem for His goodness."

I tightened the reins on my horse, who had begun to prance in anticipation. "I will not rejoice until Mary is safely restored to us."

Peter gestured to the scroll in my hand. "That is your weapon. You need only to thrust that in the face of whoever is holding Mary."

"Praise HaShem, and may it be so." I rolled the scroll and tucked it into my belt, then gathered the reins and saluted my friends. "Until I see you again, brothers."

I kicked the young gelding's ribs and galloped away from Jerusalem.

FORTY-FOUR

Matthew

Though I did not expect to find the closed wagon on my journey, I watched carefully for such a conveyance in case the Romans had been delayed. I saw no wagon of any kind, not even when I neared Arimathea. I slowed the horse to a trot as I moved through that city, not wanting to wake the sleeping residents, and resumed my gallop once we reached the maritime plain. As I rode along the flatland bordering the Great Sea, I seemed to be the only person on the road, probably because no one willingly traveled in the dark because of danger from thieves and brigands. If I had been walking or even riding a mule, I might have attracted trouble, but no one wanted to risk his life by jumping in front of a galloping horse.

I sighed in relief when I finally saw the white limestone pillars of the Port Augusti, built by Herod the Great. I did not spend much time exploring while I was being trained in Caesarea, but I knew there were four harbors—the Inner and Outer Basins, the South Bay Anchorage, and the North Harbor.

I had been to Caesarea only twice before, once with my father and once for the weeks of my accountant's training. My father did not allow me to visit the docks, but while I was studying Roman taxes, Achiakos and I would often take time in the afternoons to sit by the seaside. We would study the different vessels and try to guess what sort of cargo they carried. We never sat long enough to see one unload.

I rode into the city and looked for a stable where I could leave the horse. I found one, pounded on the door to rouse the sleeping owner, and left my horse outside his building. The poor beast deserved a meal and a place to rest.

He lifted an oil lamp to study my face, then shook his head. "You should sleep in the town center," he said. "You will not find an inn at this hour."

"I did not come here to sleep," I answered, tossing him a coin. "This is for the horse's care. I will check on the beast tomorrow."

After leaving the stable, I wrapped my mantle around me as a defense against the biting wind and strode toward the Inner and Outer Basins. I did not know where Mary was, but if my memory proved correct, most Roman ships anchored in the Outer Basin. They traveled to and from shore by smaller boats, which traveled through a channel and were kept in the Inner Basin close to the docks.

I turned toward the docks, which appeared empty except for a few random seamen. Some huddled around a fire on the shore while others squatted in a circle, throwing dice and gambling away their wages.

I was about to speak to the gamblers when I spotted a group of uniformed Roman soldiers. They stood in a knot, their voices rising in what sounded like an argument. I looked in every direction and did not see a closed conveyance of any sort.

Girding my loins with courage, I approached and directed my attention to the man with the most ornamentation on his breastplate.

"Sir." I inclined my head in respect. "I have somber news—and a request, if you will permit it."

He looked at me with the eyes of a frustrated warrior. "What news could you possibly have for me?"

"First, a question: are you transporting a woman called Mary of Nazareth, destined for Rome?"

His eyes narrowed beneath the brim of his helmet. "If I am, what business is it of yours?"

"If you are, I am here on *your* business, sir, because my urgent message is this: Gaius Caesar is dead. Your order to escort Mary of Nazareth to Rome is now obsolete. If you will permit it, I will take the woman back to Jerusalem."

His hand rose to his belt as his gaze locked on mine. "Yes, Caesar is dead—we have just heard the news. On whose authority do you make this request? I am obeying a command from Marullus the procurator."

I drew a deep breath, uncertain how to proceed. I had no authority—at least none this man would recognize—but I had a scroll in my belt.

I pulled it out, unrolled the papyrus, and held it up long enough for him to see the salutation. "I have just received this epistle from a man who serves Herod Agrippa, King of Judea. Surely a king outranks a procurator. It would benefit your cause, sir, if you released the woman to me at once."

The news of Caesar's death, I realized, had probably been waiting for this Roman in Caesarea, so he had not yet decided how to proceed with his mission. Surely this was a heaven-sent opportunity.

"Please." I lowered my voice and abandoned my attempt at bravado. "The woman is innocent and beloved in the Holy City. Let me take her home. There is no need for you to go to Rome."

The commander shifted his gaze to the sea for a moment, then turned to me. "So Little Boots is dead," he said, his voice filling with relief. "Long live the next emperor, whoever he may be. Yes, you may have the woman. I have no use for a hostage."

I bowed my head. "If you will take me to her—"

"This way."

He led me away from the docks, past a row of buildings toward a lot filled with wagons, carts, and every kind of conveyance. We turned a corner and approached a large wooden box on wheels with two small holes cut above a hinged door. The commander produced a key and unlocked the door, then flung it open. "Come out," he commanded.

From the darkness of the closed conveyance, Mary's pale face emerged. I assumed she had been imprisoned for most of the day, for her features were pinched and her clothing stained. The space beyond her reeked with the odors of waste and sweat. This was no luxury conveyance, but a prison on wheels.

Mary's lips trembled when she attempted to step out, then fell into my arms.

Struggling to hold her upright, I glared at the commander. "Has she been given no water? No food?"

He shrugged. "We were ordered to bring her to Caesarea, so that is what we have done." He gave me an abrupt nod. "I hereby consign her to your care."

I shifted my attention to the trembling woman in my arms and realized I was crying only when I tasted the salt of tears on my lips. "You are safe," I murmured again and again. "Praise HaShem, you are safe."

The Roman left without another word. In truth, I no longer cared about him—my only concern and all my compassion were centered on the woman who slumped against me, barely able to stand. My partner. My friend.

"You there!" I gestured to a wide-eyed woman peering at us from behind her door. "Bring me a mantle and some water. Hurry!"

I did not know who the woman was or what she thought about the stranger shouting at her, but she closed the door and disappeared. Keenly aware that Mary would be mortified to be seen in such a disheveled condition, I shielded her as best I could, then carried her to a tree away from the nearest buildings.

What was I to do? I had no clean clothing with me, no water, and no place for Mary to wash and attend to her personal needs. I had the basket of food from Miriam, which would strengthen her, but she needed more than food.

"Is she alive?"

I turned to see the woman from the house, whom the moonlight revealed to be hardy and well-fed. She had brought a pitcher of water and carried a stack of clean linens beneath her strong arm.

"HaShem be praised." I moved aside so the woman could attend to Mary. "Thank you coming out to help us."

The woman knelt and lifted the pitcher to Mary's lips, urging her to drink. Mary responded, albeit weakly, and the woman murmured words of encouragement as Mary sipped the life-giving liquid. When Mary had taken all she could, the woman splashed water on a piece of linen and wiped Mary's face with a gentleness I would have considered contrary to her nature.

"There's an inn near the docks," she said, her voice flat and matter-of-fact. "They will open the door, even now, because they are accustomed to seamen who arrive at all hours. Tell the woman who comes to the door that Ashira wants her to spare a bed for a day or two. She will find a quiet place for this woman and attend to her needs."

I nodded, amused that she was now the one giving orders. "You are Ashira?"

"Who else?" She tossed me a warning look that put an immediate damper on my rising spirits. "Someone needs to take care of this woman, and it is not proper that a man do it. I will take care of her if you get the room. Hurry away and see to it."

I stood, ready to go, but then a sudden thought caused me to hesitate. "Do you—do you know this daughter of Israel?"

Ashira shook her head. "Makes no difference who she is. I am commanded by One who said I should tend even a Samaritan should I find him by the wayside."

"Your husband commanded you thus?"

She laughed. "My husband cares only for himself. I serve Yeshua, the Messiah of Israel." She jerked her sharp chin at me. "Now hurry to the inn, speak to the innkeeper's wife, and come back and help me carry this woman."

I smiled. HaShem had led me to a sister in Christ, one who could probably outwrestle Annas himself were she only given the chance.

After speaking to the innkeeper's wife, I carried Mary to a comfortable bed and left her with Ashira. The innkeeper's wife had me put Mary in a small but private chamber, and then Ashira ordered me out of the room and told me to entrust her with Mary's care.

"By the way," she whispered as I was leaving, "what is her name?"

I smiled. "Mary."

"She lives in Jerusalem?"

I nodded. "She does now."

"All right—go along now. You can check on her in the morning."

While the women tended to Mary, I went to the stable where I had left the horse. The stable master had gone to bed, but I found an oil lamp, lit it with a flint, and searched through the building until I found fresh water, feed, and an empty stall.

The gelding had been a blessing and might have saved Mary's life. He deserved whatever I could give him.

When I was satisfied I had taken good care of Tobias's horse, I went to the docks and sat on a bench, watching four drunken Roman seamen gamble away their meager income. When one man held all their coins, the remaining three boarded a small boat, rowed through the channel, eventually climbing aboard one of the larger ships. The fourth man went into the city, where he would probably pass out in the street.

My gaze drifted over the four ships anchored in the moonlit harbor. Two appeared to be vessels of the Roman navy, for they were armed with brass-plated ramming rods, boarding ramps, and ballistae. Through their windows I could see flickering lights, probably from the slaves' galley where men remained chained even in sleep.

The other two ships had to be trading vessels. Their long, wide bodies shimmered like silver in the moonlight. Powered by sails, not slaves, they carried no weapons.

I narrowed my gaze and imagined the sunrise summoning dozens of bare-chested, beardless pagans who would roll out of their hammocks and scurry over the decks, moving trunks and rolling casks from the ship's hold. The cargo would be placed in smaller boats, which would be rowed through the channel so they could unload at the dock.

If I sat here long enough, I might see all sorts of expensive imports arrayed on this dock—casks of cinnamon, tusks of ivory, pearls from India, peacocks, metals, marble, horses, and chariots for the Roman conquerors . . .

I snorted a laugh. For all I knew, some of those items might be delivered to Sepphoris or to Shimon's father in Nazareth. That man had made a fortune exporting Judean wine and importing expensive luxuries. His wealth made it possible for Shimon to devote his life to Torah study. Fortunately, I had found Yeshua, who made the Torah come to life in a way that years of study could never do.

Mary made the Torah come alive for me, too. In her insistence on telling the stories of Yeshua in simple terms, she had stripped the pretense and artificial styling from my prose. Her collection, when it was finished, would be spare and powerful, infused with nothing but the words, deeds, and power of the Messiah.

I leaned forward, bracing my elbows on my knees, and studied the star-spangled sea slapping against the side of the nearest boat. Why had I resisted Mary in the beginning? Was it because she was a woman or because I fancied myself some kind of expert with the written word? In any case, she was right—and the book would be better and stronger because she pushed me.

I was better and stronger because she pushed me. I was a better man . . . because, like Yeshua, she saw me as I was.

My father lived with me for years, but did he ever see me? As a child, I tried to be the clever, bold son he wanted, yet my efforts were never enough. But Yeshua saw me and called me. He saw me in a way my father never could.

A wave of self-pity threatened to engulf me, but I pushed it back. Yeshua saw me, Mary saw me, so it was time I saw myself.

I was not a fiery preacher like Peter, or a teacher like James the Just. I did not have the compassion of John the Beloved or the evangelistic fervor of Philip. What I had was a skill with words and numbers—a skill my uneducated brethren had not picked up in their youth.

Oh, how I had wanted to be like them! I moved to Jerusalem thinking the time had come for me to shine so brightly my father would hear and be impressed. Finally, he would approve of me.

But now I saw clearly: I was not responsible for winning my father's favor. I needed only to be approved by HaShem, and because of Yeshua's sacrifice, I was. I would always be.

I had settled down to work with Mary thinking I would teach her about the proper way to tell a story. Instead, during the past few months she had taught me, and not in the way I expected. I had to endure a period of grinding, cutting, and polishing before my gem-in-the-rough could be revealed.

Mary did all that, and what had I done for her?

Not much. I may have entertained her on occasion, but I frustrated her just as often.

And all the while, she had been ill . . . and I kept pushing, oblivious to her pain.

I hung my head as tears fell onto my tunic. *HaShem, forgive me. Yeshua, forgive this ignorant disciple.*

I lifted my head into the shrieking of sea gulls, their voices strident as they flew from their roosts to herald the rising sun.

Praise HaShem, we were not finished. We still had stories to write. Mary would recover from this ordeal, and I would do my best to find a good physician for her.

I stood and turned toward the inn, hoping Mary would soon be ready to go home.

We were back in Jerusalem before sunset the next day. Mary drowsed beside me on the seat of the wagon I rented, and her head fell onto my shoulder whenever we hit a hole in the paved road. I did not wake her—it felt *right* for her to be by my side. Since my own mother would probably never have occasion to ride beside me, I would welcome Mary anytime.

Once we reached the Fish Gate, I hired a litter to take Mary home. When she was safely situated inside, I paid the litter bearers and told Mary I would soon check on her safe arrival.

I had one more task—I turned the horse and wagon in the road, then drove to Tobias's home outside the city. "Successful journey?" he asked, squinting up at me.

"Yes." I dismounted and stretched my legs, taking several long steps along the path to the barn. I grinned at him. "You were right about the body forgetting how to ride. My legs are still aching."

He jerked his head toward the wagon. "You rented this at the docks?"

"I did. I can take it back, if you loan me another horse."

"No need. The Romans are always transporting goods to the docks, so I can easily arrange its return. Do not worry—and do not let so much time pass before we see each other again."

"I will invite you to my wedding." I clasped Tobias's arm. "I cannot wait for you to meet my bride. And if you ever need anything, I am staying at the house of a man called Peter."

Tobias's bushy brow listed. "Could you mean Peter the fisherman? I have heard of him."

I laughed. "Yes, Peter is well known in Jerusalem. And he will soon be my father-in-law."

Tobias smiled and clapped my shoulder. I thanked him again, then turned to walk back into the city. The weather was an interesting combination of brisk wind and warm sun, both feeling good on my skin as I strode toward the Fountain Gate. It would lead me to the Pool of Siloam, which was very near my destination.

I smiled at the thought of Peter as my father-in-law, a relationship I would never have imagined when we traveled with Yeshua. Then again, I would never have imagined marrying his little girl, who had grown into a lovely and mature young woman.

"I praise you, HaShem." I lifted my eyes toward the heavens. "Thank you for ordaining all things and revealing your will at your perfect time."

The skies did not open, nor did a voice speak in rolling thunder. But in my heart I heard the still, quiet voice that had not let me quit my partnership with Mary: *I will open up the windows of heaven and bless the work of your hands.*

FORTY-FIVE

Mary

Miriam rapped gently on my door. "Are you awake?" She slipped inside my room and smiled. "If you feel well enough to come out, someone is here to see you."

"On Shabbat?"

Miriam's smile deepened. "I cannot think of a better day. After all, HaShem rested when He finished creating the world."

I frowned, puzzled by her remark, but got out of bed and moved to my dressing table. A quick glance in the looking brass assured me that I looked about as well as a dying woman could look, but I took a moment to dip my finger in a pot of red ochre to tint my lips. Somehow that one little addition of color brought life to a woman's face . . .

I wrapped a colorful himation around my shoulders and stood as straight as the pain would allow. Then I stepped out of my bedchamber.

No one waited in the front room. Mystified, I moved to

the kitchen where I saw Matthew standing by the table, his back to me as he talked with Miriam.

My heart warmed. I had not seen him in several days, because Miriam insisted I take time to recuperate from my unexpected trip to Caesarea. Then a physician appeared at our door, sent by Matthew, and the man insisted on seeing me. With Miriam standing by, the physician examined me, studied my spittle and urine, and then sat back and crossed one leg over the other. His gentle eyes crinkled at the corners as he smiled. "I think you know what I am going to say."

"I know I am dying." I met his gaze without flinching. "And I am ready to see my Son again."

"Then, dear lady," he had said, "you are more prepared for death than most people."

I was ready to go, but I was in no hurry. More than anything, I wanted to see Dina and Matthew married.

He must have heard my shuffling steps, because he turned and greeted me with a radiant smile. "There she is." He stepped away from the table. "I have brought you a gift."

I shook my head. "I do not need gifts."

"You will appreciate this one." He swung his arm toward the table in an elegant gesture, and there, arranged in a row, lay three scrolls, a ribbon around each one. "What's this?" I had a feeling I knew, and yet I wanted to hear him say it.

"This is your book." Matthew stepped closer, his eyes glinting as he smiled. "'The collected words and deeds of Yeshua the Messiah' . . . along with two copies."

I took a deep, quivering breath to still my stuttering heart. I walked to the table and placed my hand on the center scroll, then lifted it. "It is heavy."

"I know." Matthew laughed. "We both knew we couldn't

record every story, but I think we included the most significant events." He stepped closer. "Here—let me help you."

He set the scroll on the table, then gently lifted the open side and spread it out. I ran my fingertips over the rough texture of the papyrus and smiled at the title above the first entry: *The Story of Yeshua Before His Birth*.

Matthew smiled. "I thought that one should be placed at the beginning."

I sank to the bench and unrolled the scroll, scanning the chapters. *The Story of Yeshua with Abraham, As Melchizedek, and Wrestling with Jacob*. A few pages further, *The Story of Gabriel Speaking to Mary and Her Visit with Elizabeth*.

"It is all here," I murmured, rolling the papyrus as I scanned the stories of Yeshua at the Temple, Yeshua's temptation, Yeshua with John the Immerser. Yeshua calling Peter and Andrew, James and John Zebedee . . . and Matthew.

My fingers caressed the name Matthew Levi, son of Alphaeus. I had been with Yeshua that day in Capernaum, but back then I would never have imagined this moment.

"I could spend all night reading this," I said, glancing up at Matthew and Miriam. "I'm sure you want to take it with you—"

"Those are your copies, so do with them what you will." Matthew crossed his arms. "I have the original—I was going to give it to you, but some pages are smudged because I could not decide what to write. I also have two copies, and one of them is already promised to a friend."

"Really?" I smiled, delighted to think of someone reading our book. "Who?"

"Luke, the physician who visited you."

Miriam stepped closer. "Mary, are you in pain?"

I blinked. "No—why would you ask?"

"You are crying."

I touched my cheek. "Oh." I laughed. "I am not weeping—I simply cannot contain my joy."

I pressed my palms to the scroll, then lowered my head to my hands. "Praise you, HaShem, for using me for one more task. Thank you for giving me the strength to finish. Thank you for sending Matthew. And thank you for giving us Miriam, who kept us fortified while we worked."

When I lifted my head, Miriam and Matthew were shedding tears as well.

Miriam had been baking for days, first the breads and cakes, then the dishes that could not be preserved: grilled fish, lamb stew, grape leaves stuffed with cheese. Our table groaned under the weight of pottery bowls filled with honeyed yogurt, Roman wafers, cheese dip, and mounds of globi. At one end of the table lay the sweets, which seemed especially suited for a wedding: nut cakes spiced with cinnamon and saffron, cinnamon pears, walnut-stuffed dates in honey, and semolina cake with almonds.

My James and James Zebedee had brought several casks of wine—no one wanted to run out, since Yeshua was no longer available to make more. Shimon promised to bring a barrel from his father's storehouse, and Peter promised to hold some in reserve in case all Jerusalem decided to come to the wedding.

The day before the wedding, Miriam and I decorated our courtyard with flowers, vines, and palm branches, banishing the chickens and the goat to a neighbor's house. I moved slowly, of course, and frequently had to sit and rest, but

I wanted to do this for Matthew. His parents, apparently, would not be attending the ceremony. Matthew had sent an invitation to Sepphoris but heard no response.

Peter would bless the couple with a prayer, and James the Just would pronounce them man and wife. Damaris and Shimon, Pheodora and Chiram, Tasmin and Jude, Simeon and Joses—all my children had promised to come and bring their families.

My children would not be the only out-of-town guests—all of the Twelve who were still in Judea had been invited. While we had not heard from everyone, Thomas was reportedly in the East, and no one was sure where Thaddaeus was preaching, yet many had promised to attend, HaShem willing.

The morning of the wedding, I stood in the courtyard, wrapped my arms around a decorated pillar, and breathed in the sweet scent of jasmine blossoms. For weeks, Miriam and I had looked forward to this wedding with great anticipation. It would be a family reunion, a foretaste of heaven. The seven days would pass all too quickly, and then . . .

I swallowed hard, realizing how much I would miss Matthew.

"Perhaps you should lie down for a while," Miriam said, lightly chiding me as she adjusted the angle of a bench. "You might want to save your strength for the dancing."

I winced at the thought of jostling my bones in a dance. "I am fine. Let me help."

"You need to rest."

"I will have eternity to rest—until HaShem gives me another task."

Miriam shook her head and hurried back to the kitchen.

The guests began to arrive. This would not be an expensive wedding—we had no attendants to wash our guests' feet, no one to carry food on trays or to refill the table as the food disappeared. We had what we had, and nearly every invited guest had been in our home before. We wanted them to feel comfortable, to behave like what they were—family.

"Ima." Pheodora, with the new baby on her hip, nudged me with her sharp elbow. "Who are those people?"

I turned toward the gate, then brought my hand to my throat as two couples, one older, one younger, approached the house. I recognized the women immediately—Matthew's mother and sister, accompanied by their husbands.

My weary heart began to pound in an erratic rhythm. "Where is Matthew?"

Pheodora glanced around, then gestured to Chiram and Shimon. "He's with them. Should I fetch him?"

I did not need to answer. In that instant Matthew turned and saw his family. For a moment he froze, his face filling with astonishment, then he broke free of his paralysis and ran toward them, his arms open wide. As tears streamed over his cheeks, he embraced his father, his mother, his sister, and his brother-in-law.

I held my breath as he turned again to his father. I feared the man would say something harsh or judgmental, but Matthew spoke first. "Welcome, Abba." His strong voice cut through the noise of the many who had gathered inside and outside our home. "Welcome to our wedding."

And then, while Miriam and I watched and swiped away tears of our own, Matthew led his father to a seat of honor near the bridal bower.

Shortly after his family's arrival, Matthew gathered his friends and went to Peter's house to claim his bride. Most of the younger people went with him, shouting and celebrating as they wended through the streets of Jerusalem.

Miriam and I stayed behind, content to make certain everything had been properly arranged. Matthew's parents remained with us, and I took a moment to greet them. "Shalom," I said, offering my best smile. "Welcome to our home."

Matthew's mother inclined her head. "It is good to see you again."

"And you." I shifted my gaze to the proud man next to her. "A pleasure to meet you, as well. You should be proud of your amazing son. HaShem has blessed him with so many talents and abilities."

The man tilted his head and blinked as if he did not know who I was talking about. "Levi?"

"We know him as Matthew," I reminded him. "Perhaps, after the wedding, you will be able to make up for the lost years. After all, did not the Lord tell Joel that He would restore what the locusts had eaten?"

I smiled at Jael, who had linked her arm through her father's. Unless I missed my guess, she had been the one to convince him to come. Perhaps her gentle example would also point him to Yeshua.

Miriam came up and took my arm. "Come," she said, gently leading me away. "You need to rest." She led me to a chair in the shade, where I waited, my heart overflowing, until the bridal party trooped through the courtyard gate—Matthew and his friends, Dina and her maids.

Matthew and Dina stood together under the flower-bedecked bower, and Peter took his place between them. He read the traditional vows, my head buzzing with the words. I stood to see them better, but as the ceremony progressed,

I swayed until James caught my arm and held me upright. "Do you need to sit?" he whispered. "I can lead you to a bench—"

"Just let me go inside," I whispered back. "Let me close my eyes a few moments."

James carried me inside and settled me on one of the dining couches. I lay back and closed my eyes, quietly rejoicing when I heard the crowd shout in celebration. A moment later, Matthew came in and squeezed my arm. "My parents have come!" His voice vibrated with repressed emotion. "Abba and Ima are here—did you see them?"

I opened my eyes and tried to smile. "I did see them, and I am so happy for you."

Matthew squeezed my arm again and went back outside. I heard the musicians begin to play and knew the party had moved into the street. The men would be dancing in a circle, Matthew at the center, while the women linked arms and danced around Dina. Peter and James and John would be among those clapping, and I was fairly certain Miriam was dancing with the women, her curls escaping her headscarf as she stepped and smiled and celebrated.

Adonai was merciful to me. I enjoyed all seven days of the wedding, perfectly content to rest inside the house or lie on a cot outside in the shade. Though I did not have the strength to dance, I clapped with the music and smiled until my jaws ached.

On the afternoon of the last day, as the guests blessed the bride and groom and then took their leave, I let James take me inside to my bed. Lying there, with the sound of happy voices in the distance, I drifted into a doze in which events of the past week mingled with fragments of dreams. I heard Joseph call my name, saw his beloved face hovering above me.

"Mary!" Matthew spoke my name as his hand shook my shoulder. I swam up, torn between sleeping and waking, knowing my soul was no longer tethered to my weakened body.

My eyelids fluttered and lifted, and there he was, his eyes wide, his forehead creased. Behind him, like a hovering angel, stood Dina, her eyes filled with compassion and love.

"Dear ones." I could barely summon the strength to caress Matthew's bearded cheek. "I will see you soon."

"Mary!" Matthew called again, but this time his voice seemed farther away. My grip on wakefulness slackened and surrendered, and when I opened my eyes, the blinders had fallen off. I woke in a world shimmering with color and vibrating with music. I could see my bedroom and the departing guests in the street, but oh, how *alive* the world had become.

Joseph stood by my side and gave me a smile that lit his eyes like the sun. "Come," he said, taking my hand. "Let them go their way. Someone is waiting to see you."

I sat up, pain-free and more alive than I had ever been. A great crowd had gathered outside a gate, where angels with gleaming swords lowered their blades as we approached. I recognized faces in the crowd—Simeon and Anna, my parents and grandparents, all of them applauding my arrival, lifting their voices in praise to Adonai, their faces shining as they watched me move into the most beautiful garden I had ever seen . . .

My breath caught in my throat when I saw who waited inside the gate—the Son of Man, Yeshua. My Son, my Savior, and my God.

I fell on my knees, bowing before Him with inexpressible joy, wonder, and peace.

"Ima," He said, and my heart constricted to hear Him call me *Mother*. "Welcome home, beloved."

I rose and took His hand. With Joseph and other friends following, we walked into the Garden of God, the place where Adam and Eve had walked and talked with HaShem. Gorgeous flowering vines twined up the branches of ancient trees, scenting the air with sweetness. From somewhere in the distance I heard the sound of running water and could see the crown of a towering tree.

Yeshua followed my gaze and smiled. "The Tree of Life," He said. "Come with me and eat from it. Then I would like to introduce you to some women who have been eagerly waiting to meet you."

"Who?"

Yeshua chuckled. "The mother of all living, of course—"

Eve.

"And Sarah, mother to another child of promise."

I tucked my hand into His and smiled. "Behold, the servant of Adonai. I will do whatever you want me to do."

Yeshua looked at me, His eyes shimmering with unspeakable love. "You always have."

EPILOGUE

Matthew

Though it was not customary, Dina and I moved into the house with Miriam. We miss Mary—sometimes I turn and seem to catch a glimpse of her from the corner of my eye, but I know my mind is longing for the days we worked together.

She has been gone an entire year, yet I miss her more than I ever imagined I would.

My family did come to our wedding. Jael and David enjoyed themselves and were thrilled to meet the remaining disciples. David fell into conversation with Andrew and James Zebedee, and they talked long into the night.

Jael remained near my mother, who had to be overwhelmed by the fierce joy my friends exuded. My father embraced me, then sat near the courtyard wall, watching much and saying little. I do not know if he will embrace the salvation Yeshua offers, but Abba cannot say he never saw the difference Yeshua makes in a man's life.

I am still keeping records for the Jerusalem communities,

and Dina has shown a remarkable aptitude for numbers. Often she helps with the record-keeping, which gives us more time to spend on rewarding, even more fruitful efforts . . . such as the child we expect in the spring.

The book Mary and I compiled has spread throughout the region. Many who never had a chance to meet Yeshua have read it and now believe in Him. I am almost envious of them because Yeshua said, "Blessed are the ones who have not seen and yet have believed!"

John Mark, the young man who lost his tunic in the Garden of Gethsemane, has a copy of the scroll, and also the physician Luke. John Zebedee has requested a copy, and when I asked why an eyewitness would need one, he smiled and said he might write a book of his own one day.

"Sure you will," I said, laughing. "You have no idea how much work goes into writing such a book."

When I reluctantly agreed to work with Mary, I certainly had no idea of what lay ahead for us. But now I know the Ruach HaKodesh used her to mold my future, and the work itself opened my eyes to things I had been too immature to understand when I traveled with Yeshua.

I might write another scroll about Yeshua, but next time I will write in Greek so Gentiles can read it. I will focus more on the teachings and less on the miracles. After all, Yeshua told us to go and make disciples, and not everyone is called to be a miracle-worker.

The more I think about my life with Yeshua, the more I have realized that the greatest miracle is this: because of Yeshua, a despised tax collector became a different and abundantly blessed man.

Author's Note

Thank you for joining me in this third book of the JERUSALEM ROAD series. Many readers are interested in how much of a historical novel is based on fact, and how much is a creation of my imagination. After reading *this* novel, I have a feeling most readers will want to know why I thought Mary would want to write a book.

Two facts led me to that assumption: first, Scripture tells us that "Mary kept all these things and pondered them in her heart" (Luke 2:51). As a writer, I am familiar with the notion of carrying certain events—and the emotions associated with those events—close to my heart, because I may one day want to write about them.

The second thing that led me to believe Mary could have written a book was an article I read at www.JerusalemPerspective.com. This website, operated by messianic Jewish scholars, featured a series of articles discussing the Synoptic Gospels: Matthew, Mark, and Luke. A group of Messianic scholars is attempting to re-create a document that must have existed in the first century—a work, written in Hebrew, they are calling *The Life of Yeshua*. Based on a careful study of the first three Gospels, these scholars believe those men wrote their books after reading one or two other works: a Hebrew biography of Jesus' life or a Greek translation of that manuscript, and possibly an anthology of stories about Jesus.

Let me assure you that this hypothesis in no way weakens the orthodox belief that "all Scripture is inspired by God and useful for teaching, for reproof, for restoration, and for training in righteousness" (2 Timothy 3:16), or that the Gospels are inspired Scripture. Can God not direct men who research as well as write? Can God not guide the writers who recorded those foundational works? Luke, who also wrote the book of Acts, never met Jesus. John and Matthew were disciples, yet they did not know the stories of Jesus' early life *unless someone told them or they read the stories in a book.*

After reading this research, I asked myself, *Who witnessed most of Jesus' life?* Who had firsthand knowledge of His birth, His youth, and the beginning, middle, and end of His ministry?

I could think of only one person: Mary. His siblings were with him a great deal, but they were not disciples and did not follow Him around Galilee. His adoptive father, Joseph, was most likely deceased by the time Jesus began His ministry. But Mary was present during His conception, birth, youth, and ministry. She traveled with Him. She was with Him at the cross and must have been close to the other women when they learned of His resurrection. More than any other living person, Mary was best equipped to tell the story of Jesus.

But could she write? Were women literate in the first century?

Salome Alexandra, queen of Judea until her death in 67 BCE, established schools for girls. The women may not have been as formally educated as most men (after all, they also had to learn how to run a home, cook, sew, and handle a host of other domestic duties), but they were literate.

I am sure Mary could write. She must have felt intimidated by so large a task (I know the feeling!), so I had her enlist Matthew, who would have spoken Hebrew, Greek, and Aramaic, the common language of the day. As a tax collector, Matthew would have been fluent in languages and skilled with pen and ink. He would have frequently written reports for his Roman overseers. He would have friends—or at least acquaintances—among the Romans, and he would have been shunned by his fellow Jews.

Matthew's involvement in the writing of an early biography of Jesus is substantiated by the words of Paipas, a leader in the early church who lived from AD 70 to 160. In an ancient document, he noted, "Matthew . . . arranged the sayings [of Jesus] in the Hebrew language." Since Papias could not be referring to the Gospel of Matthew, which was written in Greek, he may have been referring to a Hebrew biography of Jesus. If Mary did not have a hand in the writing, she must have been interviewed for the work.

Such was the genesis of the idea for *A Woman of Words*.

Now, a few miscellaneous questions and answers:

Q. Was Achiakos a real character?

A. Matthew's friend Achiakos is fictional, but the events related in his letters, even many of the quotes from Caesar and Petronius, are historical (though I did edit them to make the material more readable for a modern reader). The story about Gaius Caesar (more commonly known as Caligula) and his plan to erect his statue in the Temple is historical fact.

I did take some liberty with a historical document: the women at Mary's prayer meeting read the letter from James, Mary's son and Yeshua's brother. Though no one has dated that epistle with certainty, it is reported as being written in the mid-forties, and I had the women reading it in AD 40. A small liberty, to be sure, and James *was* the first epistle written. James the Just, Yeshua's brother, was martyred in AD 62.

Q. Is sweating blood actually possible?

A. Yes. Luke *could* have employed a simile when he wrote that Yeshua had sweat like "drops of blood falling down on the ground," but Luke was a physician, so he would have found that detail interesting enough to record. The actual medical condition of sweating blood is called hematidrosis, and though rare, it can occur under stressful life-or-death situations. This stress triggers a rupture of capillaries in the tissue of the forehead and face. Leonardo da Vinci observed the same phenomena among soldiers facing battle. If ever there was an occasion for any man to sweat blood, that night in Gethsemane was such a night, for Yeshua knew He would spend the next day enduring a cruel death.

Q. Did Matthew really marry Peter's daughter?

A. No one knows the names of the disciples' wives, but they did marry, as did Yeshua's brothers. First Corinthians 9:5 tells us so when Paul asks, "Do not we have the right to take along a believing wife, as do the other emissaries [disciples] and the Lord's brothers and Kefa [Peter]?"

Q. In this book, Matthew is called *Levi* before he follows Yeshua. Did Jesus change Levi's name in the same way He changed Simon to Peter?

A. I have no way of knowing if that happened but thought it an interesting possibility. I adopted it because Matthew 9:9 refers to "Matthew" as a tax collector, and Mark 2:14 refers to the tax collector as "Levi, son of Alphaeus." Both passages refer to Jesus calling a tax collector to follow Him, so the simplest explanation is that both Gospels are referring to one man, Levi/Matthew. Since Matthew means "gift of God," I thought it fitting that it should be his "after Jesus" name.

Incidentally, the disciple James is also referred to as "the son of Alphaeus," but since the disciple James and Matthew are never described as brothers, it's far more likely that Alphaeus was simply a common name—like James. Peter's father was named James, there are two Jameses among the disciples, and Yeshua's brother was also named James (*Yaakov* in Hebrew; the same name can be translated *Jacob*).

Q. Why do you often sprinkle Hebrew words like *Ruach HaKodesh* (for Spirit of God) and *cohen gadol* (for high priest) throughout the book? And why do you use *Yeshua* instead of Jesus?

A. I use Hebrew words for a couple of reasons. First, because like fine herbs, they "season" a story with authenticity. Second, because I think it's good to stretch my knowledge, and I think my readers enjoy learning new things. Third, because I often use Jewish Bibles, which use Hebrew terms along with English words.

As to why I use *Yeshua*, I use it because that is His name. If you had a friend from Mexico named Jesus (pronounced Hey-soos), would you call him Jee-zus? No, if you care for him, you'd call him by his correct name with the correct pronunciation. I don't use Yeshua all the time, especially with people who have no clue who that is, but in a book like this one, I think it's only right to call Him by the name HaShem gave Him.

Q. You refer to the groups of believers as *assemblies* or *ecclēsia*. Why didn't you use the words *church* or *Christians*?

A. The word *church* was not in use during the time of this novel's setting, and neither was the word *Christian*. Oh, you may say, "Didn't Jesus tell Peter 'upon this rock I will build my church'?" Well . . . yes and no. A more accurate translation of Matthew 16:18 is: "And I also tell you that you are Peter, and upon this rock I will build My community; and the gates of Sheol will not overpower it."

The Greek word *ekklēsia* means "called out" and was synonymous with *synagogue* at the time. An ekklēsia was an assembly of any social, political, or religious group. According to Joe Lunceford, "In late Judaism *sunagoge* depicted the actual Israelite people and *ekklēsia* the ideal elect of God called to salvation. Hence *ekklēsia* became the term for the Christian congregation, the church" (*Holman Illustrated Bible Dictionary*).

The word *Christian* was first used by Ignatius of Antioch, who lived from AD 35 to 107. So the people who lived at the time of this novel (AD 40–41) probably thought of themselves as *believers* or *followers of the Way*. Jesus referred to himself as "the way" (John 14:16), so it was one of the earliest names applied to what we today would call the *Christian community*.

Later, the term *Christian* was applied to the believers, and on three occasions it is used in the New Testament. In the beginning, it was more of a jibe than a compliment, so Paul wrote, "But it is no shame to suffer for being a Christian. Praise God for the privilege of being called by his name!" (1 Peter 4:16 NLT).

Q. When Mary is sharing her stories, you have Miriam of Magdala give us a bit of *her* story. Why didn't you give us more?

A. Because I wrote Miriam's story in my book *Magdalene*. Whenever a character I have written about pops up in another story, I try to keep the details—even the fictional details—consistent.

Q. Sometimes you use bits of Scripture, but your wording is different from my Bible. Why is that?

A. Whenever I use snippets of Scripture, especially with the words of God the Father or Jesus, I adhere closely to the Word of God, but at times I try to use a translation that is closest to the original Hebrew or Greek text. I believe the Word of God is inerrant *in the original texts*, but many of the translations take liberties that may not convey the intended meaning. Whenever possible, especially if I intend to stress a theological point, I will use a literal translation of the Greek or Hebrew.

This is especially important in the mention of Isaiah 53:3. The literal translation is this: "He is despised, and left of men, / A man of pains, and acquainted with sickness, / And as one hiding the face from us, / He is despised, and we esteemed him not" (*Young's Literal Translation*).

We did not hide our faces from Yeshua; *He hid His face* from the Jews while He lived on earth. Isaiah 53:3 is a prophecy of the "Hidden Messiah," a motif that runs throughout Scripture. For a more detailed look at this subject, read *As Though Hiding His Face* by Julia Blum. Fascinating!

Q. Speaking of words, is it a challenge to write dialogue for first-century characters?

A. Yes and no. First, it is impossible to write the same words my characters would have used because they spoke Aramaic, not modern English. What I try to do is create a language style that is not quite modern, but more easily understood than ancient Aramaic language forms. I want my readers to feel like they are reading the words and thoughts of ancient people, but I also want the meaning to be easily grasped. It *is* a challenge, but I want to make sure my readers aren't unduly distracted by expressions and words they don't understand. The result is modern English (with few contractions) mixed with medieval English and a sprinkling of Hebrew.

On the other hand, I do try to be accurate about small details. For instance, the word *rabbi* was not used until after the destruction of the Temple in AD 70, but some Bible versions use the word because those translators thought the modern reader would understand what a rabbi is. While I agree with their reasoning, since the word was not used during the time of Yeshua, I use *Torah teacher* instead. That is what Yeshua would have said, but in Aramaic.

Q. Your characters express many theological insights, yet no one mentions the Trinity. Why?

A. Good observation! Though the Scriptures, both the Old Testament and New, are filled with references to God the Father, God-in-flesh, and the Spirit of God, the doctrine of the Trinity was not formally verbalized until the First Council of Nicea in AD 325. Until that time, the apostles and other believers spoke often of the Father, Son, and Holy Spirit, but they had not codified the doctrine, so they would not have used the word *trinity*. Clarification and codification became necessary when false doctrines began to creep into the church (some false teachers cast doubt on the Son's divinity), but Jesus made the truth clear when He told us to make disciples of all nations, baptizing them in the name of the Father and of the Son and of the Holy Spirit. All three are God, *echad*, and the early believers understood this.

Q. Did tax collectors really have to go through military training?

A. I don't know. It made sense to me, though, and provided a good backstory for the friendship between Matthew and Achiakos.

Q. You mention that Matthew went to find a copy of the Scriptures and found "the five books of Torah, thirteen books of the prophets, four books of hymns and wisdom, as well as the books of the Maccabees and Enoch." Are you implying the books of Maccabees and Enoch should be part of the canon of Scripture?

A. I am not making a statement about the canon of Scripture—I am stating what the typical first-century Jewish family would have had in their home. Most Jews during this time were quite familiar with the books of the Maccabees and the book of Enoch. In fact, you may remember that Jude, in the New Testament book that bears his name, quotes from the book of Enoch. Though these books may not be considered inspired Scripture, they are historical. The Jews of the first century were very familiar with them.

Q. What do we really know about the death of Mary, mother of Jesus?

A. Though Scripture is silent on the subject, early church tradition is unanimous in its opinion that Mary died in Jerusalem.[1] In my novel, she suffers from a form of cancer.

Q. What's this about Paradise being the Garden of Eden? I've never heard that before.

A. I never had either, but then I looked up the Hebrew word for *Paradise*. To the Jews of Mary's day, Paradise referred to the "garden of God," i.e., Eden. Later, the word came to simply mean "a walled garden."

As I thought about it, I realized how logical it is for Paradise to be Eden. After all, Jesus did cleanse believers from sin, removing our guilt before God. Genesis 3:22–23 tells us that God expelled man from the Garden so that he wouldn't eat from the Tree of Life and live forever in his sinful condition.

1. Utley, Robert James. *The Beloved Disciple's Memoirs and Letters: The Gospel of John, I, II, and III John*. Vol. 4. Marshall, TX: Bible Lessons International, 1999.

But after death, those who believe in Jesus will have eternal life, so we can freely eat of that tree! Revelation 2:7 confirms the connection: "He who has an ear, let him hear what the Ruach is saying to Messiah's communities. To the one who overcomes, I will grant the right to eat from the Tree of Life, which is in the Paradise of God."

The Bible tells us that earthly Eden contained the headwaters of four rivers, but its earthly location has proven impossible to pin down. (And we cannot discount the possibility that the Deluge displaced rivers and other geographical landmarks). But Eden is also a spiritual place existing in a realm we cannot see. The elect of God are there, and so is the Tree of Life.

Though the Scripture does not explain this mystery, I believe God dwells in a realm we cannot see with earthly eyes. Because Adam walked with God in Eden, and because angels guard its entrance, perhaps it is part of that invisible realm, and we will be able to see and enter it when we cast off our earthly bodies and enter eternity with Christ.

Q. Please tell me Mary was never used as a pawn intended for Caesar.

A. If she was, history does not record it. A novelist must make up *some* things.

Q. Is this the last book in the JERUSALEM ROAD series?

A. Lord willing, I plan to begin another one soon. It will feature a New Testament woman who was the apostle Paul's sister. That's all I can tell you at the moment, because that's all I know. One book at a time . . .

One more note, which comes straight from my heart. I used to hear about Christian anti-Semitism and was baffled by the idea. I did not know anyone who hated Jews or who scrawled swastikas on synagogues, so I didn't understand how any Christian could be anti-Semitic. After all, Jesus was Jewish, and an observant Jew at that.

Then I ran across a theological notion known as "replacement theology," and it is more common than I realized. Those who hold to replacement theology believe that God has "rejected" the Jews because they rejected Christ. They believe the church is now Israel, and all the blessings promised to Israel now belong to the church.

Oh, my friend, nothing could be further from the truth, and it hurts my heart every time I hear this belief professed. We have been grafted onto *Israel's* spiritual tree. We have been adopted into *Israel's* spiritual family. As adopted children, we are heirs to Israel's blessings, but we will never usurp the Jews' position as God's chosen people.

God's covenants are eternal. Yeshua came as a hidden messiah so salvation could be offered to the Gentiles. But Israel has not been rejected.

One day their eyes will be opened (remember the prophecy of Zechariah?), and those who accept Yeshua will be saved. Those who do not will be lost . . . in the same way we Gentiles are saved or lost.

Paul explained it this way when he wrote to the Roman believers:

> For, brothers, I want you to understand this truth which God formerly concealed but has now revealed, so that you

won't imagine you know more than you actually do. It is that stoniness, to a degree, has come upon Isra'el, until the Gentile world enters in its fullness; and that it is in this way that all Isra'el will be saved. As the Tanakh says,

> "Out of Tziyon will come the Redeemer;
> he will turn away ungodliness from Ya'akov
> and this will be my covenant with them . . .
> when I take away their sins."

With respect to the Good News they are hated for your sake. But with respect to being chosen they are loved for the Patriarchs' sake, for God's free gifts and his calling are irrevocable. Just as you yourselves were disobedient to God before but have received mercy now because of Isra'el's disobedience; so also Isra'el has been disobedient now, so that by your showing them the same mercy that God has shown you, they too may now receive God's mercy. For God has shut up all mankind together in disobedience, in order that he might show mercy to all.

Romans 11:25–32, Jewish New Testament

Praise God for His mercy to the child of Abraham and the child of Gentiles. Praise Him for His divine plan, which we do not fully understand, but in which we fully trust.

God is good. He is just. And above all, He is faithful to keep His promises.

References

Barclay, William, ed. *The Acts of the Apostles*. Philadelphia, PA: The Westminster John Knox Press, 1976.

———. *The Gospel of Matthew*. Vol. 2. Philadelphia, PA: The Westminster John Knox Press, 1976.

Barton, Bruce B. "Matthew." *Life Application Bible Commentary*. Wheaton, IL: Tyndale House Publishers, 1996.

Beasley-Murray, George R. *Word Biblical Commentary*. "John." Vol. 36. Dallas: Word, Incorporated, 1999.

Beck, John A. *The Baker Book of Bible Charts, Maps, and Time Lines*. Grand Rapids, MI: Baker Book House, 2016.

Blum, Julia. *As Though Hiding His Face*. USA: My Zion LLC, 2017.

Bock, Darrell L. "Luke." *Holman Concise Bible Commentary*. Ed. David S. Dockery. Nashville, TN: Broadman & Holman Publishers, 1998.

Borchert, Gerald L. *The New American Commentary*. John 1–11. Vol. 25A. Nashville, TN: Broadman & Holman Publishers, 1996.

Brand, Chad, Charles Draper, Archie England, et al., eds. "Annas." *Holman Illustrated Bible Dictionary*. Nashville, TN: Broadman & Holman Publishers, 2003.

———. "Congregation, Mount of." *Holman Illustrated Bible Dictionary*. Nashville, TN: Broadman & Holman Publishers, 2003.

Brenton, Lancelot Charles Lee. *The Septuagint Version of the Old Testament: English Translation*. London, UK: Samuel Bagster and Sons, 1870.

Brown, Michael L. *The Real Kosher Jesus*. Lake Mary, FL: FrontLine/Charisma House, 2012.

Byfield, Ted, ed. *The Christians: Their First Two Thousand Years*. Canada: Christian Millennial History Project, 2002.

Chilton, Bruce. "Annas (Person)." Ed. David Noel Freedman. New Haven, CT: *The Anchor Yale Bible Dictionary*, 1992.

Craig, William Lane. *Reasonable Faith: Christian Truth and Apologetics*. Rev. ed. Wheaton, IL: Crossway Books, 1994.

De Villiers, J. L. "The Political Situation in the Graeco-Roman World in the Period 332 BC to AD." *The New Testament Milieu*. Ed. A. B. du Toit. Vol. 2. London, UK: Orion Publishers, 1998.

Dickie, John, and James Orr. "Christianity." Ed. James Orr et al. *The International Standard Bible Encyclopedia*. Grand Rapids, MI: William B. Eerdmans, 1915.

Duling, Dennis C. "Matthew (Disciple)." Ed. David Noel Freedman. New Haven, CT: *The Anchor Yale Bible Dictionary*, 1992.

Dunne, D. A. Neal, and John Anthony. "Eden, Garden of." Ed. John D. Barry et al. *The Lexham Bible Dictionary*. Bellingham, WA: Lexham Press, 2016.

Edersheim, Alfred. *The Life and Times of Jesus the Messiah*. Vol. 1. New York: Longmans, Green, and Co., 1896.

———. *The Temple: Its Ministry and Services as They Were at the Time of Jesus Christ*. Mt. Pleasant, SC: Arcadia Press, 2017.

———. *Sketches of Jewish Social Life in the Days of Christ, Revised and Illustrated*. Clearwater, FL: Hunt Haven Press, 2019.

Elwell, Walter A., and Barry J. Beitzel. *Baker Encyclopedia of the Bible*. Grand Rapids, MI: Baker Book House, 1988.

Elwell, Walter A., and Philip Wesley Comfort. *Tyndale Bible Dictionary*. Elgin, IL: Tyndale House Publishers, 2001.

Fruchtenbaum, Arnold G. *The Messianic Bible Study Collection*. Vol. 22–23. Tustin, CA: Ariel Ministries, 1983.

Higuera, Valencia. "Hematidrosis: Is Sweating Blood Real?" *Healthline*, March 14, 2017. https://www.healthline.com/health/hematidrosis. Accessed 4/21/2020.

Hinson, David Francis. *The Books of the Old Testament*. Vol. 10. London, UK: SPCK, 1992.

Ironside, Henry Allan. *Lectures on Daniel the Prophet*. 2d ed. New York: Loizeaux Bros., 1953.

Johnson, B. W. *John: The New Testament Commentary, Vol. III*. St. Louis, MO: Christian Board of Publication, 1886.

Josephus, Flavius, and William Whiston. *The Works of Josephus: Complete and Unabridged*. Peabody, MA: Hendrickson Publishers, 1987.

Kasdan, Barney. *Matthew Presents Yeshua, King Messiah: A Messianic Commentary*. Clarksville, MD: Messianic Jewish Publishers, 2011.

Levertoff, Paul. "Sanhedrin." Ed. James Orr et al. *The International Standard Bible Encyclopaedia*. Grand Rapids, MI: William B. Eerdmans, 1915.

Lumbroso, Patrick Gabriel. *Under the Vine: Messianic Thought through the Hebrew Calendar*. Clarksville, MD: Messianic Jewish Publishers, 2013.

Lunceford, Joe E. "Congregation." Ed. Chad Brand et al. *Holman Illustrated Bible Dictionary*. Nashville, TN: Holman Publishing, 2003.

Martin, D. Michael. "1, 2 Thessalonians." *The New American Commentary*. Vol. 33. Nashville, TN: Broadman & Holman Publishers, 1995.

Meldau, Fred John. *The Prophets Still Speak: Messiah in Both Testaments*. Bellmawr, NJ: Friends of Israel Gospel Ministry, 1988.

Miller, Jeffrey E. "Papyri, Early Christian." Ed. John D. Barry et al. *The Lexham Bible Dictionary*. Bellingham, WA: Lexham Press, 2016.

Myers, Allen C. *The Eerdmans Bible Dictionary*. Grand Rapids, MI: William B. Eerdmans, 1987.

Osborne, Grant R. "Biblical Theology." *Baker Encyclopedia of the Bible*. Grand Rapids, MI: Baker Book House, 1988.

Resnik, Russell. *Creation to Completion: A Guide to Life's Journey from the Five Books of Moses*. Clarksville, MD: Messianic Jewish Publishers, 2006.

"Ships of the Roman Fleet." https://h2g2.com/edited_entry/A86206188. Accessed 4/29/2020.

Singer, Isidore, ed. *The Jewish Encyclopedia: A Descriptive Record of the History, Religion, Literature, and Customs of the Jewish People from the Earliest Times to the Present Day*. 12 Volumes. Brooklyn, NY: KTAV Publishing, 1901–06.

Sri, Edward. *Rethinking Mary in the New Testament*. San Francisco, CA: Ignatius Press, 2018.

Stern, David H. *Jewish New Testament: A Translation of the New Testament that Expresses Its Jewishness*. 1st ed. Jerusalem, Israel; Clarksville, MD: Jewish New Testament Publications, 1989.

Strange, James F. "Sepphoris." Ed. David Noel Freedman. New Haven, CT: *The Anchor Yale Bible Dictionary*, 1992.

Tasker, R. V. G. "Matthew, Gospel of." Ed. D. R. W. Wood et al. *New Bible Dictionary*. Downers Grove, IL: InterVarsity Press, 1996.

Vamosh, Miriam Feinberg. *Food at the Time of the Bible: From Adam's Apple to the Last Supper*. Herzlia, Israel: Palphot Ltd., 2007.

Wilson, Jim L. *Fresh Start Devotionals*. Fresno, CA: Willow City Press, 2009.

Young, Robert. *Young's Literal Translation*. Bellingham, WA: Logos Bible Software, 1997.

Angela Hunt has published more than 150 books, with sales exceeding five million copies worldwide. She's the *New York Times* bestselling author of *The Tale of Three Trees*, *The Note*, and *The Nativity Story*. Angela's novels have won or been nominated for several prestigious industry awards, such as the RITA Award, the Christy Award, the ECPA Christian Book Award, and the HOLT Medallion Award. Romantic Times Book Club presented her with a Lifetime Achievement Award in 2006. She holds both a doctorate in Biblical Studies and a Th.D. degree. Angela and her husband live in Florida, along with their mastiffs and chickens. For a complete list of the author's books, visit www.angelahuntbooks.com.

Sign Up for Angela's Newsletter

Keep up to date with Angela's news on book releases and events by signing up for her email list at angelahuntbooks.com.

More from Angela Hunt

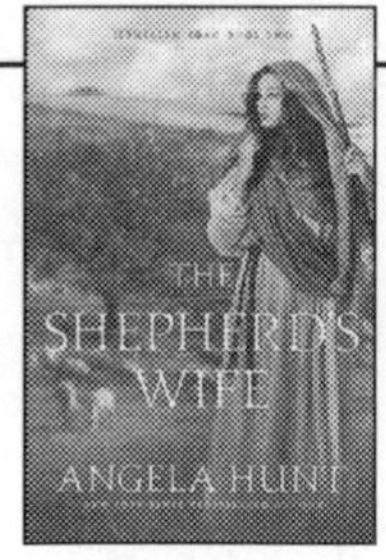

When her husband is thrown into debtor's prison, Pheodora—sister of Yeshua of Nazareth—pins her hopes on the birth of two spotless goats to sell for the upcoming Yom Kippur sacrifice so that she can provide for her daughters and survive. Calling on her wits, her family, and her God, can she trust that He will hear and help a lowly shepherd's wife?

The Shepherd's Wife
JERUSALEM ROAD #2

BETHANYHOUSE

Stay up to date on your favorite books and authors with our free e-newsletters. Sign up today at bethanyhouse.com.

facebook.com/bethanyhousepublishers

@bethanyhousefiction

Free exclusive resources for your book group at bethanyhouseopenbook.com

You May Also Like . . .

When a wedding guest tells Tasmin to have the servants fill the pitchers with water, she reluctantly obeys and is amazed when it turns into the finest wine ever tasted in Cana. But when her twin brother, Thomas, impulsively chooses to follow the Teacher from Nazareth, she decides to follow the group and do whatever she must to bring her brother home.

Daughter of Cana by Angela Hunt
Jerusalem Road #1
angelahuntbooks.com

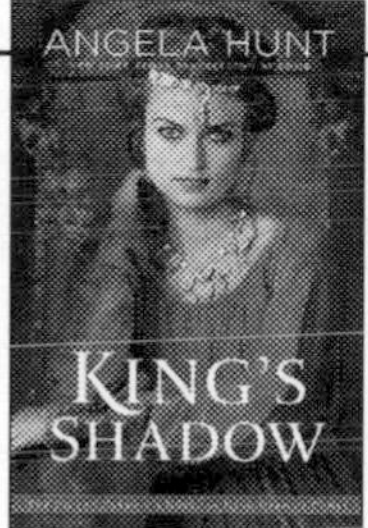

Two women occupy a place in Herod's court: the king's only sister, Salome, a resentful woman who has been told she is from an inferior race, and her lowly handmaid, Zara, who sees the hurt in those around her. Both women struggle to reach their goals and survive in Herod the Great's tumultuous court, where no one is trustworthy and no one is safe.

King's Shadow by Angela Hunt
The Silent Years
angelahuntbooks.com

After a heartbreaking end to her friendship with Lukio, Shoshana thought she'd never see him again. But when, years later, she is captured in a Philistine raid and enslaved, she is surprised to find Lukio is now a famous and brutal fighter. With deadly secrets and unbreakable vows standing between them, finding a way to freedom may cost them everything.

Between the Wild Branches by Connilyn Cossette
The Covenant House #2
connilyncossette.com

BethanyHouse